Where Two Rivers Meet

Where Two Rivers Meet

Londa Hayden

Disclaimer: This is a work of fiction. Names, characters and incidents either are the product of the author's imagination or are used fictitiously, and any resemblance to actual persons, living or dead, business establishments, events or locales is entirely coincidental.

Where Two Rivers Meet

Published by Tate Publishing & Enterprises, LLC
127 E. Trade Center Terrace | Mustang, Oklahoma 73064 USA
1.888.361.9473 | www.tatepublishing.com

Tate Publishing is committed to excellence in the publishing industry. The company reflects the philosophy established by the founders, based on Psalm 68:11,
"The Lord gave the word and great was the company of those who published it."

Published in the United States of America

ISBN: 978-1-68207-753-5
1. Fiction / Christian / Romance
2. Fiction / Christian / Historical
15.06.12

DEDICATION

In loving memory of my father

George Washington Proctor

Dear Patsy,

You're such a special person. I appreciate your support and friendship. You're a Blessing,

Linda Hayden

10-10-2015

Acknowledgements

Thank you to my husband, Steve Hayden. I couldn't have done all the needed research, much less written a novel, without his continued support throughout the years it took to finally get this novel on paper. Thank you to Carol Prothro, my online writing mentor, who endured through the painstaking process of earlier drafts.

Thank you to Elizabeth Garrett for all her help in editing this project, her constant encouragement and endearing friendship. Thank you to Nick Nixon and Geoff Nixon for helping with all the technical issues to create the book cover. Thank you to my writers' group for your listening ears, feedback and many prayers.

Thank you to all the great Christian authors and mentors I've had the privilege to be tutored under at one time or another. Marylane Koch, Tracy Crump, Dr. Dennis Hensley, Dr. Trisha Petty, Cecil Murphey, Susan Reichert, Bradley Harris, and Susan May Warren, I thank you from the bottom of my heart for always encouraging me to hone my skills and to always submit my very best work. I pray your efforts are honored here.

-1-

Blood Sisters

Washington's Woods, 1767

A search for my maidservant led me down a shadowy path. I stopped and listened. Sobs whispered in echoes above other night sounds, guiding me. I pushed the shed door. It didn't budge. Climbing to the top of a barrel, I slipped through an open window. A full moon illuminated the space. There she was—huddled in the corner, her dress bloodied and shredded. Her petite ten-year old frame bore the whelps of rage, glaring back at me.

"Jasmine, what happened?" I ran to her side.

"I spilled the foreman's drink at supper tonight," she said.

My heart sank as I studied her wounds. "I wish we didn't live in Virginia. I hate slavery."

Jasmine whispered, "Shh, Miss Constance, someone could hear."

I swallowed hard, choking back my emotions. "The people here are so mean." My voice quivered. "It makes me ashamed to be white." Tears moistened my cheeks as I knelt to tend her wounds. I tore a piece of fabric from my petticoat.

Jasmine flinched as I dabbed at her back. The smell of blood mingled with sweat, mold, and hay turned my stomach. I looked away. The nausea faded when my attention veered to a mouse, scampering down a wood stack, disappearing through a hole.

"The foreman shouldn't have done this to you. I'll tell my father tomorrow."

"No!" Jasmine pleaded. "Please don't. It will only make things worse."

"But I can't stand by and let him keep doing this to you." I sat back and sighed, realizing I couldn't do anymore for her. Pain surged when my finger hit against a sickle. "Ouch!" I raised my hand, a red stream trickled. On the boarded wall, my profile silhouetted in soft moonlight as dots fell, staining my dress. I turned to Jasmine. "You're my best friend. My only friend. We are like sisters, you and I. Don't you feel the same?"

"Yes. You know I do."

Taking hold of her finger, I pressed it to the sickle's edge.

"Ow!" she yelped. "Why did you do that?"

I held my finger to hers, allowing our blood to mingle. "Now we're blood sisters."

Staring back, she asked, "What are blood sisters?"

"Blood sisters are together forever. It means you

can never be sold or sent away from me. I vow to always be here for you and to never leave your side, Jasmine. Now you do the same."

Jasmine pushed herself to her knees, while keeping her finger pressed to mine. Looking into my eyes, she said, "I vow to always be here for you, Miss Constance, never to leave your side."

"By God's grace, let it be so." I nodded, indicating her to do the same.

"By God's grace, let it be..."

The latch rattled. We both winced and scooted together into the shadows as the door creaked open. It was the foreman.

"Well now, what have we here? Miss Constance is it?" he said, leaning in and squinting.

I held back, saying nothing.

"Come now," he said, snarling. "Does your father know you're here?"

I hesitated to answer, but my anger got the best of me. "Why do you hurt your own kind?"

"I'm not a slave," he snapped.

"But you're black."

"That don't matter," He scowled. "I'm still in charge here."

I stood to face him, fists clenched. "How dare you beat my servant girl. I'm going to tell my father what you did."

His eyes narrowed. "I don't think you'll be doing any such thing. In fact, my guess is Master William don't even know your whereabouts at all. Am I right?"

"That's none of your concern," I said. I took a deep breath and tightened my jaw.

He stepped toward me, pulling at his trousers.

I gasped, eyes shifting to Jasmine.

She pushed the sickle handle toward me. I grabbed hold and flung it at the foreman's calves.

He screamed, fell to his knees, lodging the blade deep into his flesh.

Jasmine and I scurried out the door. Clasping hands, we ran to the house. "You'll never be left alone again. I promise."

Fall 1773—Six Years Later

I was born a master's daughter at the farmstead, a haven for escaped slaves, but a prison for me.

Early morning came with Father's arrival. Horses snorted as the wagon wheels rumbled and skidded to a stop just beyond the front door. Excitement filled the house. The maidservants left their workstations and joined the family as we welcomed Master William Proctor home. We followed Mother like baby ducks to the two grand columns, gracing the porch. His smile and youthful trot up the front steps indicated a prosperous journey. First, he gave Mother an affectionate peck on the cheek, and then he took care to greet each child. This always made me feel like the most special one of all. Come my turn, I smelled the dust thick on his clothes, almost tasting it. He held my face, his touch so tender, my skin tingled. I lowered my chin and giggled.

"Constance, my firstborn, already sixteen," he said, eyes twinkling. Those loving, endearing, hazel-green eyes always seemed to favor me. "You'll make a fine wife to someone soon."

"Oh, Father," I said, heat blushing my cheeks. "Did you miss me?"

"Yes, of course. I missed all of you," he said, holding out his arms. "Now come inside. I have gifts for everyone."

Elizabeth, the youngest, leaped in front of me. "I missed you, Papa."

"I missed you too, Lizzy." He picked her up, carried her inside the house, and we all followed.

While the family finished opening gifts, Father whispered in Mother's ear. Her eyes narrowed, and she pressed her lips tight. I suspected it was news about the impending revolution. His political duties often pulled him away now, which burdened the family. Turning my attention to the dining hall window, I raised my chin to see the new slaves, awaiting instructions. This group was different, lighter in appearance, more chocolate. Unlike the dark coffee skins, who came broken down, beaten, and separated from their loved ones, this was a complete family.

I scanned past the lighter skinned children to a

tall figure, standing among them. That was the first time I saw Simon Miller. His supple muscles flexed, pressed against a tattered white shirt, contrasting his brown skin. Through the window, I could hear a muffled British accent. Simon's gaze met mine, penetrated my soul, as if he knew my every thought, every secret passion. My heart skipped as we stared what seemed an eternity. The instant connection between us ignited a flame, a deep desire. I knew he felt it too. *What was it about this young man? He captured me.*

The black foreman stepped between us; his distinct limp reminded me of a night six years earlier. I shuddered, pondering the memory, my chest rising, falling. A deep breath calmed me. I wondered what Simon's lingering gaze meant. Returning to the main room, I discovered my family already dispersed, my father in his study enjoying a cigar.

"Father, the foremen were cruel again while you were away."

With relaxed candor, he blew smoke into the air. "I'm afraid this is the way of the South, Constance. It is best to forgive them, and pray for their change of heart. In the meantime, I'll have a word with them."

"That never seems to help. They'll just wait until you leave again."

"I understand, but I need them to keep the farm productive in my absence. They are the best men available."

"But they're evil! They whipped Andrew the other day. He didn't deserve such harsh treatment. He works as hard as the other slaves."

"That is disconcerting news. I will most definitely speak to them," he said, brows flat.

"They won't listen!" I turned away. "Why do we have slaves anyway?"

Father rested the cigar on the edge of the desk. "What else would you have me do? This plantation takes a lot of work force. My political duties call me away more often now. "

"I hate living here," I said, blinking back tears.

"You know I don't have a choice. General Washington left me as his caretaker." He pulled a small book from his coat pocket. "However, my dear friend Ben Franklin gave me a book on the teachings of John Woolman. He was a Quaker minister, recently passed away. He preached about the civil treatment of slaves and the indentured. He's quite convincing and influences many with great conviction. You'd like him."

"Read some to me?" I asked, tempered now and leaning on the desk.

My father flipped the cover open and read. "Deep-rooted customs, though wrong, are not easily altered; but it is the duty of all to be firm in that which they certainly know is right for them. A charitable, benevolent man, well acquainted with a Negro, may, I believe, under some circumstances, keep him in his family as a servant, on no other motives than the Negro's good." He closed the book. "I feel we are meant to be here at this time in order to help the slaves. If I just let them go, they will face a greater evil. Many will die or be taken captive by others far less humane than I. But it is not my right or intent to hold them as prisoners either, only to offer them sanctuary in exchange for work."

I stood to face him. "Well, I am old enough now. I could go and live with our family in Philadelphia. They don't have slaves."

"But what about Jasmine, your beloved maidservant?"

"I can take her with me. As long as you provide her emancipation papers, she can go free."

"I don't want you to go, and your mother needs you here," he said. "Would you force such a decision on Jasmine? She may not want to leave her family."

My eyes pooled with tears.

Father rose and cupped my shoulders. "Oh, come now. I will give the foremen a stern tongue-lashing they will never forget."

"Promise?" I bargained, my eyes fixed on his intently.

"I promise." He kissed my forehead and held me close. "I appreciate your compassionate spirit."

Jasmine entered the room. "Miss Constance, your mother sent me to fetch you. She's in the quilting room."

"I'm coming." Taking a deep breath to calm myself, I wiped my eyes and hugged my father. "I'm glad you're home now, even if only for a while."

"I know living in a place filled with people who think contrary to you is difficult, but how else will change come without the persistent presence of those who determine otherwise?"

Frustrated, I said, "Persistence *is* a virtue."

Lifting my chin, my father peered into me, "Perseverance is a gift of the Holy Spirit."

Curious to know more about Simon, I sent Jasmine to assist his family with unpacking and settling in at the servants' quarters. I gave her clear instructions to find out more about them. It was after suppertime when she returned to my bedchamber and reported.

"I ain't never seen so many look-alikes in one place before."

"What do you mean, 'look-alikes'?" I asked, facing a round vanity mirror while Jasmine brushed my hair

"Look-alikes is twins, Miss Constance."

"So Simon is a twin?"

"No, ma'am. There's just one of him. He be the oldest, best I can tell. I didn't see no older boys, just all them young'uns running around." Jasmine's eyes widened as she remembered. "Oh, and they all speaks with a proper British accent."

"During supper, Father mentioned they came

from Uncle John's estate in England."

I guessed Simon to be about seventeen, but pretended not to care and changed the subject. "Oh, I wish Father would take me with him next time he goes away. I want to see more of the world than just this farm. I want to know the smell of salt air instead of tobacco, to broaden my horizons and meet men of culture who are educated and well-traveled."

"Come now, Miss Constance, you know there are plenty of good suitors for you here."

"And not one of them is capable of holding down a decent conversation."

"That Master McClain seems to have taken a liking to you."

In truth, he was an arrogant English nobleman who talked about himself incessantly.

"Ah, yes. Father would have me wed to him in no time, not for love, but for security and namesake only." I looked at the bed. "Are the sheets warmed yet?"

Jasmine walked to the bed and touched them. "Yes, ma'am." She removed the warming pan, and I climbed in.

"Hand me my needlepoint. I'm not tired yet."

"Yes, ma'am," Jasmine said. She looked through my knitting basket, found my sampler, and handed it to me.

She stoked the fire one last time, while I pulled the golden thread and paused. My voice lowered in contemplative tone. "In many ways I envy you, Jasmine. You can marry for love. In fact, the man you marry will love you unconditionally. He won't expect any more than what you already are."

"I'm just a simple slave girl, Miss Constance, no more. I'll learn to be happy with whoever the good Lord and Master William sees fit to give me."

"Yes, but that's just it. Don't you want to fall in love and know that the one you marry is in love with you?"

"My mama always says love will come in time, Miss Constance. Now, if that's all you'll be need of, ma'am, then I'll be retiring for the night."

"Yes. Sleep well."

Jasmine walked to the door and looked back, "Have blessed dreams, Miss Constance."

I looked up to acknowledge her and noticed something in her apron pocket. "What's that?" I pointed.

"Oh, I forgot to give this to you. It's a letter from a Miss Griscom."

Eager to see it, I wiggled my fingers. When Jasmine reached the foot of the bed, I snatched it from her. "Betsy?" I slipped my finger under the flap, breaking the seal. "This just made my day far richer. She's been away visiting her family in Philadelphia. That'll be all, Jaz."

Jasmine closed the door behind her, leaving me alone. I unfolded the paper and read.

Dear Constance,

The SSS will meet again soon. Upon my return, I will send word announcing the time and place. It is imperative you and your mother join us. Above all, know I miss you dearly.

Your close friend and confidant,

Betsy

The Society of Sister Seamstresses, or SSS, was a code name for something far more important than just a group of women who sewed. We helped transfer secret orders and strategies during wartime. I placed the letter on my nightstand and picked up my needlepoint.

Thoughts of Simon filled my head. I pricked my finger with the needle and raised it to my tongue. This was an evil, forbidden desire, but one I could not dismiss from my mind. Something I dared not confide to anyone, not Betsy, not even a priest. There was no justification for such sinfulness. I deserved to be stoned, or worse, whipped and hung. I chastised myself, but to no avail. The lust lingered as I slept. It invaded my dreams. I woke early and fell to my knees, praying earnestly for forgiveness.

"Have mercy on my soul."

-2-

Generations Later

Present Day

Students filled Riverview High School cafeteria, carrying lunch trays to their chosen tables. Kate turned her chair around to face me. Her eyes narrowed as she glanced over each shoulder

"You know his daddy's Judge Beck, the worst racist in town!" Her slight Southern drawl emphasized her point.

My jaw tightened. That dose of reality made me squeeze the sides of my chair. "Johnny's different!"

Her voice took a more serious tone. "What do you think is going to happen once he gets wind that his boy likes a girl with a black mama?"

I pushed back, widening the gap between us. Her sister-like advice kept coming. I looked away. Though I knew she was probably right, at that moment I hated her.

"Oh, Nikki. This isn't New York City or LA. This is West 'by God' Virginia. We're at least twenty, no—more like thirty—years behind the rest of the world.

Unfortunately, racism is still alive and kicking here in good old Hicksville, USA."

"You mean, Charleston," I said, correcting her.

"Whatever. You know what I mean."

I turned to face her. "No, I don't. And Johnny's nothing like his daddy. Besides, my daddy's white."

"His father's the leader of the freakin' KKK! How do you know Johnny isn't just like him?"

I straightened my shoulders. "He smiles at me all the time."

"Hello? He's class president and the football team quarterback. He smiles at everyone."

"Yeah, I guess you're right," I sunk into my chair. "He is kind of out of my league and a lot richer."

Kate tilted her head and said, "Hey, you're Nicole Durham, cheerleader extraordinaire, and one of the most popular girls on campus. That's nothing to scoff at."

I gave her a coy grin. "He did wink at me."

Kate threw her hands up in the air. "Whatever!" She popped her gum persistently.

"That's really annoying," I said, getting exasperated. "And don't call me Nikki."

She flipped through a magazine. "It's just a nickname."

"Only in private," I whispered.

"Okaaay."

Half a minute later, I heard *pop, pop, pop*—on purpose. I ate my lunch, turning my attention back to

Johnny. Noticing my *Fashion Today* magazine peeking out my backpack, I grabbed it with one hand and stuffed fries in my mouth with the other. I covered my face only to eye level and pretended to read, trying to remain inconspicuous as I studied his every move. The curve of his lips ... his broad shoulders ... the way he chewed his food. I even liked the way he wiped the ketchup from his mouth.

An article on how to create a clothing line caught my attention. During the busy season at my mother's alteration shop, I designed and modeled formal apparel for the wealthier clientele. I often sneaked off to a fitting room, put on a favorite gown, and danced like Cinderella with my pretend Prince Charming. A daydream captured my thoughts. Johnny Beck whirling me around the dance floor, pulling me close, his gaze intent, and his lips only inches from mine.

"Oh, Nicole," Kate said, waving her hand in my face, forcing me back into the present.

"What?" I said, miffed at the interruption of what was forming into a first-kiss moment.

"You want to come over after school?" she asked, now sitting upright.

"I have to meet with a librarian to go over the Durham family history." I told the truth, thinking there was no way she'd be interested.

Kate slapped her forehead. "Geez, that reminds me. I have to do the same assignment." She brushed away her bangs, and the black polish on her nails caught my eye.

I glanced down in disgust at my own ragged nail edges. Not really wanting to go to the library by myself, I decided to let our difference of opinion go. "You want to come with me?"

"Sounds exciting, but not if it involves hours of boring reading or rummaging through a bunch of old books." She foraged through her backpack and pulled out some lip balm.

"No, she's going to show me some stuff online. I think it'll be interesting."

"I don't know. My social agenda's pretty full for the day."

"Come on. I know you don't have to work."

"Okay. I'll be so glad when I finally get my own car." She rubbed balm over her lips. "What time?"

"Right after school, at the main library." I stood and adjusted my purse strap over my shoulder. "Dad's picking me up." I noticed her eyes crinkle. "What?"

"In the purple van?"

"No. Mom needed the van today."

"What about your little brother and sister?"

"Grammy is picking them up from school. What's with the third degree?"

"Nothing, just as long as the Durham bunch is on Grammy-watch. Don't forget the last time I rode in the car with them."

"How could I? It took me hours to get the gum out of your hair." I rolled my eyes. "That won't happen again."

On our way out, I made sure to walk a little slower while passing Johnny. The flash of those pearly whites sent tingles through my whole body. I turned my head and smiled, flipped my hair, and strutted toward the door like a runway model.

The entire lunchroom watched as Kate came alongside me.

"Work it, girlfriend," she said, a slight grin.

She pushed against the double doors leading to the main lobby. "See you in gym."

"Yeah, see ya," I said, still in a dream state.

Not bothering to look back, I gestured a goodbye over one shoulder. The honest flaw of a true friend with her in-your-face frankness was what I loved most about Kate. Such friends were hard to find and sometimes even harder to keep. Deep in my heart, I knew that was exactly the kind of friend I needed to keep my wide-eyed stumbling in check. I could hear Kate's slight raspy voice echo inside my head. "Pretty is as pretty does as long as stupid ain't in it."

While walking the hall to my locker, I caught glimpses of florescent greens and oranges beneath the primer paint, skinhead remnants. My thoughts were still on Johnny, when Ronald Ripley with his acne and black-framed glasses, rudely awakened my senses.

"Hi Nicole," he said, salivating in a nasally tone. "Do you remember that we got paired up for the science project?"

"Hi, Ronald." *I always knew that teacher had it out for me.* I quickened my pace, but Ronald managed to stay with me. He sucked air with a mild snort before speaking again.

"When do you want to start working on it?"

Still trying to lose him, I glanced over and saw him pick at a pimple. A nervous twitch? *Okay, that's really gross.* "Uh, I'll have to check my schedule and get back to you on that." As I continued to weave through the crowd, Ronald practically glued himself to my side.

"Wait! We should exchange numbers." He jotted down a number on a slip of notebook paper and handed it to me. "Here's mine."

My lips tightened because he used the same hand that had just picked at the pimple. I grabbed the paper, stuffed it in my pocket, and kept walking.

Ronald stayed by my side like a lost puppy. "I need *your* number."

Still facing away from him, I rolled my eyes. Ronald Ripley was the last guy on earth I wanted to give my phone number to, but I couldn't be rude to him since he was the principal's son. I bopped my forehead with my hand. "Oh, silly me. I don't have a pen." He did and held it out to me, same hand again. I hesitated to take it. "Where do I write?"

He pushed his notebook toward me.

I scribbled down the number, hoping it wasn't legible. "Okay. Talk later," I said, almost breathless, and relieved that the encounter was over. Why did I give him my real number? *Duh!* I turned to leave, but his words echoed like a throbbing, irritating ache.

"I'll call you later, Nicole," he said, loud enough for everyone to hear. My head ducked down between my shoulders, and my face grew hot. What little reputation I thought I had was so over now. I moved through the crowd as quickly as possible. Good thing I was heading for psyche class—I needed to chill out.

Finally, the bell rang to signal my last class. Still trying to shake off the embarrassment from Ronald, I pushed the door leading to the gym. I recognized a foreign exchange student everyone called Mo, short for Mohammad. He stooped, gathering his books now splayed on the ground as a small gang of skinheads circled him, taunting and cursing.

"We don't want no camel jockeys taking our jobs or our women!" One of them yelled and pushed his finger into Mo's shoulder.

Mo held his hands up in defense. "No trouble. Please."

Two of the boys pushed him down and then threw his backpack against the fence, laughing arrogantly.

I stood motionless, far enough away they didn't see me. My fair complexion, influential friendships, and popularity had always shielded me from such prejudice attacks. Still, I felt bad for anyone who suffered just because they were a different race. I thought how nerdy Ronald Ripley often fell victim to jokes and pranks. This made me feel guilty and sorry for him to a certain extent, but then I considered the facts. He was white and the principal's son. That in itself was enough to at least keep the skinheads at bay. So I figured, he was one of the lucky ones.

Speaking of Principal Ripley, his familiar prosthetic clunk—a leg lost while serving overseas—drew closer. I released the door, allowing it to slam. The small gang of rebels bolted. One of them bumped my shoulder. His eyes fixed on mine, and I felt the sting of seething hate piercing through me. Shaken, I took a deep breath and ran to Mo, still huddled in the corner.

"I'm going to report those guys."

"No, don't. Please." He stood and slapped the dirt away from his pants

"Why not?"

"No, no trouble. Don't say anything." He reached for his backpack as I held it out to him, and he turned to leave.

That was it? I couldn't believe it. He seriously didn't want help. Then I sensed someone watching me.

When I turned around, there was Johnny Beck dressed in his football gear. I figured he'd heard the commotion and came over to check things out. My heart skipped at the chance to talk with him.

"Stupid skinheads. They give everybody a hard

time," he said.

That's just what I needed to hear. Convincing evidence that Johnny was nothing like his father. "Yeah, but he didn't want me to report anything." I leaned over and pulled a swastika sticker off the fence, twisting it into my fist.

Memories flashed through my mind of Grammy telling stories about the KKK, which consisted mostly of prominent white businessmen who often employed skinheads. She said clergy, and even a few law enforcement officers supported them in secret. "You know what the funny thing is?" I said. "Some of these guys act like it's their religious duty or something."

"Well, he seems to be all right. Just a little shook up, is all." Johnny craned his neck, squinting his eyes to see around me.

"Yeah, he should be fine," I said, taking a quick peek over my shoulder. There was Principal Ripley standing behind the double doors, peering at us through the window. I flipped my hair, effectively recapturing Johnny's attention. "He just doesn't want any more trouble from them."

"Can't blame the guy. I wouldn't either." Johnny put on his helmet. "Well, better get back to practice. See ya." He turned and ran toward center field.

"See ya." I watched him, and a flutter tickled the pit of my stomach. A door slammed, interrupting my thoughts. The familiar clunky steps grew louder, closer. The last thing I needed was another tardy slip. Turning on my toes, I headed to the gym. I couldn't wait to tell Kate that Johnny wasn't like his racist dad at all. I made it to the door just in time.

-3-

Late Spring 1774

I looked out the bedchamber window, spying Jasmine. She sat firm in the saddle, slapping the reins back and forth. Her shadow raced through barren tobacco fields as the horse's breath billowed steamy wisps. Pounding hooves carried my maidservant to her lover, her husband, and my secret passion. My own breath grew rapid as I daydreamed, vicariously, of her seeing Simon Miller one last time—the man we both loved.

Snow often dusted the ground this time of year. I stepped away to sit near the fire and warm myself. My gaze fell upon the sampler laying across my knitting basket. I picked it up along with the list of symbols to memorize. As the needle moved gently through the fabric, my thoughts found their way to Jasmine once more.

In my mind, I saw the horse and rider brush against a pine branch, causing a clump of snow to fall onto the reins. Crisp white flakes contrasted against Jasmine's dark brown skin. I imagined the horse racing along the river path, keeping just ahead of the keelboat which resembled a rustic, miniature Noah's

Ark. She'd pull the reins to align the horse as it neared the bend, coaxing it uphill with a kick and a loud "Yaw!" Embedded hoof prints trailing behind them in the muddy snow until they reach the bluff overlooking the place where two rivers meet. How I wished *I* were the one leaving on that boat with Simon. Instead, Jasmine and I must wait for word of his safe arrival to wherever he finds work. I say a prayer for his protection and good fortune.

Jasmine lived my dream. She, a slave, free to marry the man she loved. I, born free, in bondage to the rules society imposed. I imagined Jasmine waving back at Simon amidst the horse's breaths, billowing into the crisp early morning air. I thought about her watching him, her passion burning deep like simmering embers waiting a stoke, the fog enshrouding him and sweeping him from her sight. Once Simon made enough money to settle in a new place, I knew she would join him. That did not ease the pain in either of our hearts with his departure now. I turned my attention back to the sampler and coded symbols my mother gave me to memorize. The fabric, now damp with my tears, needed to dry.

I used to beg Jasmine—almost command her—to tell me everything down to the last detail, all the while living my dream of finding true love through her. I even dared to pretend to be her, a secret shame I only shared with one other person in great discretion. It was at a quilting bee when I pulled Betsy aside, pretending to ask her advice.

"I still have feelings for him," I confessed in a whisper.

"Feelings come and go," Betsy said. "They mean nothing."

"But, mine do."

"No! You can't let them," she said.

"How can I *not* feel these things for Simon?"

"You remember what will happen to him if suspicions arise."

"They will kill him," I said, touching my hand to my lip.

"You remember what will happen to you and to your family," Betsy continued. "They'll kill all of you, Constance." Tears filled her eyes and her lips trembled. "And I couldn't bear that."

"I'm not going to do anything," I said, holding her arm.

"Of course not," she said. "The mere fact you're thinking about him so much worries me." Betsy lay her needlepoint in her lap as she leaned in to whisper. "You have to stop this now. Otherwise, it'll just get worse."

"I know." I said, blinking.

"Promise me, you'll try?" Betsy asked, eyes piercing mine.

"I will." I nodded. "I promise."

I wiped away that memory along with my tears and stood to stretch. Gazing out the window, I searched for Jasmine. The snow was melting, which prompted the slaves, both indentured and African, to work the fields. They built small hills in preparation for transplanting seedlings that matured during the summer months, for harvesting in the fall. A lone horse and rider came into view, heading toward the stables. My pulse quickened when I recognized the hooded cape fluttering in the wind. I wanted to hear all about their sweet farewell. *Did he speak to her? What did he say? And, did he kiss her goodbye?* I reveled in that forbidden thought for just a moment until my gaze returned to Jasmine on the horse. Even from that distance, I could see tears glistening on her face. My own heart sank into despair for our loss, and tears dripped off my chin. I feared Etta, another house servant, might see Jasmine riding to the barn. The other kitchen maid, Willow, may also question the matter. Nevertheless, I trusted their loyalty to cover for her absence.

After washing my face to cool the sting in my eyes, I sat near the fire again. A knock alerted me to my rousing family. "Come in."

The door cracked open and a bonnet-covered head appeared. "You're not dressed? Aren't you feeling well?" Mother shut the door, hurried to my side, and pressed her hand to my forehead.

"I'm feeling a little tired. My time for the bleed might be coming soon."

"Oh. I'll tell Jasmine to bring the rags."

"No. I'm not bleeding yet. I told her to come later this morning, because I wanted to rest. She should be along soon."

"All right then. I'll tell your father not to expect you at breakfast." Her hands cupped my face. "I can't believe how much of a woman you are now. You've blossomed like a beautiful butterfly coming out of its cocoon." She glanced down and saw the sampler. "How are the symbols coming?"

"I've only done a few so far, but I'm working on them diligently."

"No rush. Just be sure you memorize them properly. It's very important."

"Yes, Mother."

She reached for a doll on the shelf and looked at it fondly. "It seems like just yesterday when you and Jasmine were having tea parties in the rose garden. It won't be long before we'll be planning your wedding." She set the doll back in place.

"Mother, please. I haven't any suitors."

"Not to worry, dear. They'll be here before you know it."

Something crashed against the wall, and I heard Elizabeth cry out.

Mother dashed to the hallway to survey the damage. "Thomas, you pick up every single piece." The door closed behind her and muffled voices faded down the hallway.

I set the sampler down. Searching my garment

cabinet, I dressed myself as best I could. My fingers fumbled to tie the loose ribbons behind my back, but my hair remained a disheveled mess. I heard panting at the door, and Jasmine entered the room. My hand flew to my heart as I breathed out a sigh, relieved that the two foremen missed seeing her. "Finally, you're back. I was beginning to worry," I fussed. "I need help with these ribbons, and my hair is a mess."

Jasmine came to my assistance and tied the back ribbons quickly. "I'm sorry. It took longer than expected. Thank you, Miss Constance, it means a lot to me that you helped me to see Simon off."

I watched in the mirror as she burst into tears while braiding my hair. Compassion rose within me. As children, Jasmine was my only playmate and friend. Opposite stations in life eventually forced us to detach from one another, or at least we had to make it seem that way. Since the farmstead was isolated from other settlers in the area, I remained close to Jasmine, which was no secret to the immediate family. I felt inside my dress pocket, pulled out a handkerchief, and turned to face her.

"Try not to cry." I dabbed away her tears and blinked to hold back my own. "If Father sees you, he might regret he allowed Simon to leave. Worse yet, he'd send you away on the next boat to keep you from running away on your own, and I'd never see you again."

Jasmine wiped her cheek. "I'll try, but I have no

idea when I'll get word from him."

Throwing aside all etiquette, I stood up and hugged my lifelong friend and confidante. "I'm sure you won't have to wait long until he sends word for you to join him." I released my embrace and saw a hopeful grin come to her face. "That's better." I smiled back. "I'd better go before Father misses me." I turned to leave and made my way down the hall, thankful for the sisterly bond we still shared in secret. The thought of her leaving overwhelmed me at times, which was evident in my tear soaked pillow and gown. *How would I manage without her? How would I endure without Simon?*

Before reaching the stairs, I stopped, did an about face, and walked back to my bedchamber. I hesitated at the door, not sure what to say. The bed, which stood out from the wall, sat in a jumbled array of rose patterned quilt and shams. Jasmine fluffed the pillows, ever mindful of my comfort, a good and faithful servant. But what was I to her? Did she value my friendship as much as I valued hers? Or did she just tolerate it, waiting for the day she could finally leave this place for good? It really wasn't *that* bad here, was it? Father never raised a whip to any slave. The foremen did on occasion, but never to the house servants, save only once when Jasmine was a child. Master William taught math to the slaves he trusted—Captain James, Andrew, and Simon—to send them to market. Elizabeth and I taught them how to read at

Father's insistence. In many ways I felt as close to them as any of my family. Caught up in my thoughts, I did not realize how long I stood at the doorway. My gaze moved upward to see Jasmine's curious face looking back at me.

"Uh," I searched for words. "I just wanted to say, thank you for staying."

After a long pause, Jasmine nodded with a wry smile. Her eyes started to tear again.

I swallowed hard, trying to hold back my own emotions, simmering just beneath the surface. We stood there staring at each other. "I know you wanted to leave with Simon, and I would not have stopped you or held ill-will toward you for doing so. It was, in fact, your loyalty to our family which dissuaded you from such a luxury. I wish to thank you for remaining my good and faithful servant, if but only for a season."

Jasmine nodded, using her apron to wipe her face. She studied her finger, the one I had cut on the sickle years earlier. Her eyes fixed on mine as she turned her hand toward me. "Blood sisters," she said softly.

"Yes." I nodded, holding my palm to hers. My chin quivered. "I wish we could stay this way forever."

Jasmine held out a handkerchief. "You best get on to breakfast now, Miss Constance."

I dabbed my cheeks, then giggled when I saw it was the same one I had given to her earlier. Stuffing it into my pocket, I headed toward the stairs at a brisk pace.

Father always sat at the head of the table with my mother, Susanna, by his side. My two brothers, Thomas, fifteen, and twelve-year old George W, punched each other under the table. Elizabeth, ten, my only sister, tightened a ribbon on her dress, then held her hands up in prayer-like position again. I walked quickly to my seat. All heads bowed as Father continued.

"... In the name of our blessed Lord and Savior, Amen." He looked up: "Ah, nice to see you could join us, Constance. I trust you are feeling better."

"Yes, Sir."

I knew Mother had already made him aware of the feminine circumstances, and there was no further explanation expected.

Thank God none of the foremen saw Jasmine leaving the plantation with one of our best horses. Stealing a horse was a crime punishable by death, but a risk well worth taking for her. In such instances, most slave owners held to the unwritten law, which gave them full liberty to kill, rape, or maim a slave as they saw fit. Father held true to his abolitionist convictions and never went that far. He taught us to treat all people with dignity no matter what their station in life.

The smell of fresh coffee, ham, eggs, and biscuits lingered in the air. My mouth watered in anticipation as Willow held out a basket. I grabbed a warm biscuit and savored the first bite. Through the window, I could see Andrew, a trusted slave, driving a large wagon filled with cured tobacco leaves. Dust clouds billowed as the wagon rumbled toward the sorting barn, a place I often visited to roll cigars for Father while secrets lay in the dark.

"I see Andrew has a full load today," Father said in serious tone, craning his neck.

Willow finished serving the biscuits, and I noticed a familiar glance between her and Etta. I looked out the window to study Andrew again, and there it was—the signal—the red bandanna hanging on the back of the wagon.

Etta continued to pour coffee. "Yes, Suh, Masser William. The Lord has sure blessed your crops."

Father turned to Mother, who nodded in unspoken understanding. His compassionate stare lingered on her doe-like beauty. Tension infused the moment, and as always, he squeezed her hand in a comforting gesture. I stopped chewing. My heart pounded. Even *I* knew what a full load meant. All of us in that room—and only a few others—knew.

-4-

Central Library

An African-American woman, wearing a red bandanna and cowboy hat, greeted me at the service desk.

"I have an appointment with Ms. Williams."

"Are you Nicole?"

"Yes."

The upbeat librarian held out her hand and smiled. "I'm Anna May Williams. Feel free to call me Anna May. It's a pleasure meeting you. Welcome to Pioneer Day at the library."

Taking her hand, I noticed her cheery manner, the confidence in her grip. I smiled back. "It's nice to meet you, too. This is my friend, Kate. She's doing the same assignment. "Can she come along?"

"Of course," she said. Her warmth exuded the love for her job. "If you'll both follow me, we can get started."

We climbed the stairs to the reference area and sat in front of a computer monitor. I sat next to Anna May, while Kate pulled up a chair. Anna May pushed her beaded hair back and started typing. "The computer system's been running real slow all day so this might take a while. Just bear with me."

A poster of Abraham Lincoln signing the Emancipation Proclamation hung on the wall. Along the bottom read, "I do order and declare that all persons held as slaves within said designated States, and parts of States, are, and henceforward shall be free." I couldn't help but think of the stories Grammy constantly shared with me and all her grandchildren. She always stressed we should never forget all the hard work and dedication it took to get us to this place of freedom we have today. "And never take it for granted, children," I could hear her words echo in my mind.

Anna May turned to me, and said, "Here we go, finally. We usually begin a search with the mother's maiden name."

I fumbled through my backpack and pulled out a piece of paper with a picture of a big tree. Lines next to each branch held the names of family members, only a few lines were blank.

"This is fairly extensive. You have a lot more than most folks," Anna May said.

"Thanks, my mother and grandmother are big on family history," I said, and pointed to a line on the tree. "My mom's maiden name is Luella Miller."

Anna May's fingers flew across the keyboard, typing the name and date of birth. She moved the mouse to click the search button. Several matches showed on the screen.

"All right, now we need to narrow this list down some. "Are you Caucasian, African-American, native-American, Asian, Hispanic, biracial, or multiracial?"

"My father is white, and my mother is African-American. So, biracial," I said.

"Do you know of any slaves in your background?"

"Oh, definitely. My grandmother tells me stories all the time."

"Good for her," she said. "Those stories are going to mean a lot to you later in life." She continued to ask questions until we were able to pinpoint an exact branch in which my direct ancestors were represented. After helping me, she turned her attention toward Kate.

"Do you need to do a search for your family?"

"Yes, but I don't have a list like Nicole does."

"That's all right," Anna May said. "Just tell me your mother's maiden name, and we can work from that point."

"Okay, my mom's name is Marilou Walker. Her maiden name was Proctor."

I watched and listened intently while Anna May typed.

"And you are Caucasian?"

"Yes," Kate said.

Anna May did a quick search and found several matches. She showed both of us several different ways to continue our research at home. After an hour of her undivided attention, she said, "Well, girls, it's been fun working with both of you today. Feel free to call me any time." Anna May escorted us to the entrance and held out her hand. "Here's my card."

I took it and smiled. "Thank you, Anna May."

"It was nice meeting you," Kate said.

"Any time. Hope to see you again soon. Bye now." Anna May waved as we walked out the door.

Mother waited curbside in the rattling purple van. A loud backfire made me jump as I slid the side door open, allowing Kate to climb in amid the trash and toys. I took the passenger seat in front. We dropped Kate off and went straight home. In my room, I surfed the web for more ancestral clues and found some unexpected family connections. I jotted down a few references to check later.

Something hit the window, jarring my attention. I raised my head to see Daddy, Shelby, and Jackson playing catch in the front yard. Old feelings nagged at my heart. I narrowed my eyes, tapping my pencil rapidly on the desk.

Childhood experiences still haunted my dreams. I remembered my daddy, stumbling down the hall, and my mother, begging him to get help. The pencil fell. Reaching for a Teddy bear, I squeezed it hard to my chest. Feelings of rejection surfaced. Tears welled. Me as a child, hidden in the closet with stuffed animals piled high to cover me. My parents screaming—bad, angry words. Slapping. Hitting. Hearing the thunk ... seeing my mother's bruises the next morning. My lower lip trembled. Jaws tightened. Eyes shut tight. *Breathe.*

I was just starting to understand my daddy a little better when Mama had Shelby. And then came Jackson, the little worm, which prompted the need for a bigger house and longer work hours. I hardly ever saw Daddy then. A grateful thought—at least I got my own room. An old photo came into view. Seeing Grammy and Pappy together on the old porch swing conjured loving memories and tears. I missed my grandpa. After he died, I was glad Grammy came to live here. I needed her sympathetic ear and comforting wisdom. A photo of me and Kate caught my attention, both ten years old. A smile crossed my face. I recalled our instant friendship when Marilou, Kate's mom and our realtor, sold us the house. How we've managed to remain besties through middle school and now high school, I don't know. Kate tends to speak her mind a little too candidly. Even after I joined the cheerleader squad—not Kate's thing at all—we stayed friends. *At least some people care about me ... everyone but Daddy anyway.*

My cell phone rang. I didn't bother checking the caller ID first. "Hello," I said, flatly.

"What's wrong?" Kate asked.

How is it she always seems to know when something's wrong? "Nothing!" I snapped. "Sorry, bad mood. I'm fine. Just doing homework."

"Oh. You want to take a break and meet me at

Grandma Winnie's?"

"What for?" I wanted to take a break, but not necessarily for that.

"We bought her a universal remote for her TV, and I could use your help explaining it to her."

I needed the break to refresh my mind. "I guess so."

"Okay. I'm riding my bike. You want to meet me there?"

"Yeah. Let me tell my mom. I'll leave in a minute."

"Okay. Bye."

I set the phone down, closed my notebook, and changed into jeans.

Standing in her grandmother's living room, Kate and I struggled to remove the packaging.

Grandma Winnie walked out of the bathroom, rubbing lotion on her hands. "I just don't understand why you need so many gadgets for one TV."

I finally managed to jerk the remote control free from the all-encompassing packaging and handed it to Kate.

"Look Grandma, I brought you a universal remote. You only have to use *one* now. There's a button to push for each thing." She pointed. "TV, Cable, DVD, and VCR."

"Okay, so what should I do with all the rest of these gadgets?" Grandma Winnie said. "I know, I'll put them in my knitting basket so they won't get lost."

When she stooped to do so, a piece of embroidery fell onto the floor. Kate, preoccupied, didn't notice. I bent down, retrieved the fabric, and handed it to her grandmother.

"You dropped something."

"Thank you." She looked at the stitching. "Oh, this reminds me. I have to get something from the bedroom. I'll be right back."

Kate chewed her gum like a cow. I held out my hand. She tossed me a half torn piece of gum, still wrapped in foil.

"Thanks." I figured if I couldn't stop her, then I'd join in the fun. We started a gum popping competition while waiting.

Grandma Winnie entered the room, carrying a framed picture. "This is a very special family heirloom. Now, I know you don't like sewing or knitting, but you *are* the only granddaughter." She placed the item in Kate's hands.

Kate pulled back her chin. "What is this?"

"It's your great aunt's star sampler. Remember when I told you about Great Aunt Constance and her friendship with Betsy Ross? This is one of the samplers used as a model for some of the very first flags representing the colonies."

Kate looked at the framed piece of fabric, now yellowed. I interpreted the expression on her face to say ... *Sure, it's pretty cool, but who cares anyway?*

"Thanks, Grandma." She tucked the frame under

one arm and fingered the new controller.

"Can I see it?" I pulled it from under her arm.

Kate turned her back to Grandma Winnie and whispered. "This will definitely be decorating the closet."

I studied the framed sampler, ran my finger down the glass, and understood the importance of such a family treasure. Kate continued to instruct her grandmother, who seemed a bit miffed.

She grabbed Kate's arm. "Promise me you will take care of the sampler. This is important Kate. It's all I have left to give you and your mother besides the farmstead."

"Okay, I'll take care of it. I promise." Kate reexamined the sampler, more intently this time. "It is pretty cool!"

"If you ever have children, you must promise to pass it along to one of them."

"Okay, but there's no guarantee of that happening any time soon." She snickered.

"Well, if you never have children, then I have stipulated in my will for your mother to give it to the Smithsonian Institute."

"Or I could sell it online to a collector. You never know what this old stuff's gonna bring in."

"What?" Grandma Winnie gasped. "This is a priceless heirloom, young lady. Don't you dare go selling it to some stranger!"

Kate held up one hand in surrender. "I'm just

kidding, Grandma. Relax. Don't get all discombobulated."

"Don't worry, Ms. Winnie," I said. "I won't let her do that."

Grandma Winnie put her hand to her chest. "Oh, dear God in heaven. Don't scare me like that."

"Sorry," Kate said.

I picked up the remote control and started going over the instructions to help get Grandma Winnie's mind off the sampler. Nearly half an hour later, she understood the basics, but remained unsure about the other functions.

"Well, if you still have trouble, call me and I'll come help you," I said.

"I still don't think I can remember how to do this recording thing."

Kate slid the framed sampler into her backpack. "Grandma, it's not like you're so busy you're going to miss every show. I mean, you're here practically all day."

Grandma Winnie raised her chin and straightened her shoulders. "I may be close to eighty, but I'll have you know I'm a very active senior."

"Okay, well just call me or Nicole like the day before you want to record something, and one of us will come set it up for you."

"Oh, I don't want to be a bother."

"It's no big deal, Ms. Winnie. Honest, I don't mind a bit," I said.

"Grandma, it's no bother. I just have to go home and do my homework now."

"Okay, Sweetie. I'm sorry to keep you and Nicole. Do you want me to drive you home?"

As we exited, Kate said, "No, thanks. We rode our bikes."

Grandma Winnie waved. "Bye."

We took off down the tree-lined street. My cell phone rang. I pulled it out of my pocket.

"Hi, Mom."

"Are you on your way home?"

"Yes. Hold on a sec." I pressed the receiver to my chest and whispered, "Can you come over for dinner?"

"I guess so. Mom's working late tonight," Kate said.

I lifted the phone to my ear again. "Since Marilou's working tonight, can Kate come over for dinner?"

My mother answered, "Sure, as long as she clears it with Marilou first."

"Okay," I said. "She will. Love you." I disconnected. "You have to call your—"

"I'm on it." Kate held her phone to her ear. A few uh-huh's and nods later, "Yes, it's okay with Luella. Love you too." She pumped her bike pedals hard and fast. "Race ya."

I caught up while turning the corner to my street. We entered the back door, washed our hands, and set the table.

After dinner, we hurried to my bedroom. I flipped through a notebook and pointed out some things I'd discovered during my online genealogical research. Like a confluence of rivers, I saw two bloodlines converging into one. Every piece of the puzzle was set in place, all except for one. I explained to Kate that at a certain point around the time of the Revolutionary War, a link remained missing.

"You mean, we could actually be like related to each other?" Kate said.

I leaned forward and said, "Yes. That's exactly what I'm saying." I grabbed her hands. "We could actually be cousins."

"Well, that's pretty freakin' awesome."

We both bounced on the bed, screaming and hollering, like little girls.

Suddenly, I slipped off the edge, with a thunk, still laughing.

I heard Grammy yell out, "Y'all turn down the joy juice in there."

"Sorry!" I yelled back. The goofiness wore off as I regained my sensibility. "The question is—exactly how are we related?"

As I flipped through the pages again, the truth about my heritage surfaced. My jaw tightened with this sobering realization. I set down the notebook and stared. A disturbing thought came to mind. The truth about my ancestry was kept hidden for generations, and I wanted to know why. *What happened? Who was responsible for this?* After a moment of deafening silence, Kate punched my shoulder.

"Hey, you all right?"

"Uh, yeah." I glanced away, avoiding eye contact. "We both need to do a little more research."

"Okay, I'll see what I can come up with from my end." Kate grabbed her backpack, headed for the door. "I've got to get going before Mom gets home."

"Sure. See you later." My voice trailed off. Kate left the room. Looking down at the notebook again, I wondered what other secrets might be there.

My fingers parted the blinds. It was after sunset, and the streetlights glowed in a halo of mist. I saw Kate pumping on her bike and guessed she'd take those well-known shortcuts, making it home before her mother. Fearing the star sampler might very well be placed in her closet, I shook my head. *Does she really have no idea?*

My cell phone rang, startling me. The caller ID showed it was Ronald Ripley. I rolled my eyes and shook my head, then allowed it to go to voice mail. Before disconnecting, the phone line cut out, signaling another caller.

Thinking it might be Kate, I answered, "Hello?"

"Hi, Nicole. This is Johnny."

Heart throbbing in throat, I struggled to find words.

"Hello?" he said.

"Ha, hi ..." I said, breathless.

We talked for a few minutes, and then hung up. I called Kate right away.

"What's up?" Kate said.

I plopped across the bed on my tummy. "Oh, my gosh. You are so not going to believe this!"

"What?"

"Johnny Beck just asked me out. Ahhhhh!" I screamed into the phone.

"No way. Where's he taking you?"

"For pizza or something—who cares? It's Johnny Beck! Oh, no!" I gasped. "What if I say something stupid and he doesn't like me anymore?"

"Okay, okay, calm down, breathe. You're going to be alright," she said, sounding more like a big sister.

I nodded my head several times, as if she were sitting right next to me. "Okay." I exhaled into the phone.

"That's good. Keep breathing. Now, when is this big date supposed to happen?"

"Friday, right after the big game. Oh, no, what am I going wear?" I pulled my feet around to sit up. "Oh, I know—those new jeans you got the last time we went to the mall."

"The skinny jeans?"

"Yeah, those would look great with my new jacket. Can I borrow them, please?" When I heard the familiar sound of hangers squeaking on the rod, I knew Kate was in the closet. I heard a crash and glass shattering.

"Oh, no!" she said.

"Kate? Are you all right?"

"Yeah," she said, her voice weak.

"What's wrong?"

"It's my Aunt's star."

"Oh no!" I ran my fingers through my hair. "Please tell me you did *not* put that in the closet."

"Well, yeah, but the sampler's okay,"

Kate said. "I just have to get a new frame for it."

"Oh good." I was relieved. "What about the jeans?"

"I've got them right here."

"Good, I'll pick them up later." I heard glass shards being swept across the floor, and then silence. "Kate, you still there?"

"Uh, yeah. Looks like something's in the frame."

"What?"

"I don't know," Kate said. "There's a bulge in the backing. Probably just old framing."

The clanking sound of shards being tossed into the trashcan came across the phone. I heard another plunk, thinking she must be throwing more stuff away.

"Hey, it's not every day you go out with Johnny Beck, right?" Kate said.

Just then a 'beep' interrupted our call. "Wait that could be Johnny calling me back." I checked the caller ID. "Again?" A name I was tired of seeing that day. "It's that nerdy guy from science class, Ronald Ripley."

"Ronald Ripley? Why would he be calling you?"

"We got paired up for a project, and now he calls me about every little thing. I have to be nice to him, because he's Principal Ripley's son. I'd better call him back. Later. Bye." I set my phone on the nightstand. Instead of calling Ronald, I hugged and kissed my pillow, pretending it was Johnny. Clicking the mouse on my favorite song, I cranked up my computer volume and danced.

-5-

The Sorting Barn

Two foremen sat at a barrel playing checkers near the sorting barn entrance. They tipped their hats as Jasmine and I passed. The one who had threatened me in the shed a few years earlier glared at us. Jasmine hesitated, her shoulders tensed. I raised my chin and stared. He lowered his eyes, pushing a black checker forward a square.

Jasmine sidled next to her mother, Tessa, who separated tobacco leaves into stacks according to texture, color, and size, while others packed leaves inside hogshead barrels for shipping. My small preparation table near the back stall beckoned me. I picked up several leathery leaves, tore strips from the stems, and placed them in a short stack. After flattening each strip into a wide wrapper, I proceeded to cut, stuff, and roll, then tapered and capped off the ends. A homemade humidor protected the newly formed cigars and kept them fresh. The aroma reminded me how much I loved the smell of tobacco. It helped to cover up the stench of body odor which often accompanied hardworking slaves.

I busied myself like a fly on the wall and could

overhear Tessa talking with Maggie, Simon Miller's widowed mother, while they worked.

"Most our men folk are leaving. That worries me," Tessa said.

Maggie replied, "My Simon is doing the right thing. He'll bring us all to freedom." She continued stacking leaves.

"Yes, I know, but we're left here in the meantime—alone," Tessa said.

From where I sat, I could see her wipe the sweat from her brow. I looked up from rolling a leaf and our eyes met.

"Master William has been kind," Tessa added, her gaze still locked onto mine.

For a brief moment, I acknowledged her with a slight grin. Maggie glanced over at me as she tucked her hair under her bandanna.

"The Proctors are a right and kindly lot. Miss Constance gave us some blankets she made herself. She sewed them good and proper, she did. The stitching is so fine, they almost look good enough to market."

She spoke loud enough, I presumed for my benefit. Although, the comment made me feel she appreciated my efforts, it came across like a staged response in order to keep my favor. I wished slaves—ours in particular—wouldn't do that. It put me in an awkward position of authority over them, one I did not want, especially where Simon was concerned.

With all the abolitionist talk going on in the house, surely they knew me better than that by now, or so I thought. They could be saying these things as a cover for the foremen, but then again, they might be acting for me. Perhaps they felt they had no choice, lest they face punishment.

My hands and apron stained with brown streaks. I continued my task of rolling tobacco leaves, looking up every now and then while listening in on their conversation. I watched as Maggie bunched leaves to one side and handed a couple to Tessa, who started a new stack.

"We needed them. Even if they are practice quilts, it sounds like she made them very well," Tessa said.

"I saw Pearlie playing with the cornhusk doll I made her," Maggie said with a little grin.

Tessa smiled. "Yes, she loves it, but I think Miss Elizabeth might want one too."

"Oh," Maggie said, her eyes wide. "She has such beautiful dolls in her room. Have you seen them?"

"No, but I've heard all about them. Sometimes Pearlie plays with her inside the house."

My ears alerted me to the sound of rolling wood and the clink of chains nearing the barn door. I motioned for Maggie to come toward me. Andrew hopped down, dust clouded his legs as he tipped his hat toward me.

"Good day, gentlemen," he said. The two

foremen nodded and went right back to playing their game. I placed my hand on my stomach and took a deep breath. Andrew stepped inside the barn and looked around with caution. He whispered, "Is it clear?"

I nodded. Maggie and I moved into a vacant stall, removed hay, and uncovered a secret hatch, while Andrew guided the horses and wagon into the barn. Tessa started to sing a spiritual hymn, and the other slave women joined in to help camouflage any suspicious noises. From the stall, I watched as they took arm loads of tobacco leaves and lay them aside. First a leg appeared, then an arm. As the small group of escapees came into view, they moved like cats with stealth-like precision into the stall.

Through the opened hatch, I saw the ladder supported against the dirt wall, the glow of a lantern just a few feet lower. As I started to descend, I hesitated when I heard the voice of an unexpected suitor calling my name.

"Oh, no!" I said.

Jasmine ran to the barn door, craning her neck for a quick peek. She ran back to the stall and whispered in exasperation. "It's Master McClain come a calling."

"I can't believe Father arranged this without consulting me first. Tell him I'm at the house preparing for his visit. Go quickly now. "

"Yes, Miss Constance." She ran out of the barn, and I heard her timid voice greet him. Everyone froze as if in a still-life painting and waited with baited breath. I motioned for Tessa to keep humming. She started up again and the others followed in harmonic tones. I heard the husky voice of my father call out. He must have seen Master McClain riding toward the barn, while he was out inspecting the fields.

Breathe, I reminded myself. Then continued my descent down the ladder. The escaped slaves followed me. Willow met me at the bottom with two lanterns. She handed me one. The other, she kept for herself. I led the way through the secret tunnel and heard the vacuum from the hatch closing behind us. We stood in the dark, our faces shadowed in dim lantern light. I turned to face the darkness and the others followed me with Willow at the end. When we reached the basement wall beneath the farmhouse, I bent down to feel for the lever. A hidden passage opened up in the wall, and we ushered the escaped slaves into a small room, where an inviting aroma greeted them.

Lanterns and candles provided comfortable lighting. An oblong table with benches stood in the center of the room. Next to the wall, clean linens and quilts wrapped feather-filled mattresses. A wash tub and lye soap sat on the floor, partitioned off by another quilt hung over a rope.

The traveling slaves had not eaten hot food in several days and needed a hearty meal. Since it was customary for the cook to prepare several meals at a time before the heat of the day, a pot of hot stew, fresh-baked bread, churned butter, and a pie, along with bowls, plates, and utensils graced the table.

One of the slave women looked around the room. Tears welled up in her eyes. She clasped her hands together and said, "He hath gone forth and prepared a place for thee. Oh thank you, Lord."

In that moment, I forgot about the guest who waited for me in the parlor. The escaped slaves ran to the table and started gulping down the food.

Mother stood next to the basement stairs, and I met her there. She spoke with a gentle voice. "Welcome to our home. Enjoy your meal. There is plenty more. We brought some clean clothes for you to change into. You are safe here, but you must remain hidden and quiet. Etta and Willow will bring hot water down and take care of whatever you need. We'll bring down more food later tonight." Susanna pointed to the rope next to the stairs. "If you need anything just pull this rope, and it will ring a bell upstairs. You'll be leaving very early tomorrow morning, so try and get some rest. Master William and Andrew will show you to the boat when the time comes."

I remembered the visitor waiting for me as we ascended the stairs to the kitchen, where Etta covered the latch hidden in the floorboard with a rug. To avoid an unpleasant encounter with my unwanted suitor, I bounded up the servants' stairs to my bedchamber. Jasmine filled the washbowl as I entered the room. I undressed down to my petticoats, splashed cool water on my face, and wiped my underarms. Jasmine held up a clean dress for me to slip over my head. She arranged my hair, while I sat at the vanity and saw my flushed cheeks. I opened a drawer and pulled out a fan. The cool whisked my bangs, drying sweat beads. My chest rose as I took deep breaths to regain my composure. Jasmine pinned a sprig of lavender on my shoulder. I took in the soothing aroma of the petite bouquet and descended the stairs to greet my guest.

Master McClain sat across from me in the parlor. "Well, I must say, it was certainly worth the wait. You look lovely."

"Thank you," I said, smiling. After serving him, I poured myself a cup of tea with a slight shake in my hands, still tense with fear he may suspect something. I tried my best to remain poised and hoped the lavender covered any lingering body odor.

An awkward silence fell between us. All I could remember was Father telling me Master McClain ran cattle or some sort of livestock. Church services offered little time for mingling. The gossip at the weekly quilting bees I attended rendered little information. Not even Mrs. Busby, the town know-it-all, had much to say during our brief encounters at the general store. Still, I attempted to converse.

"So, how are the cattle?"

"I wouldn't know. I manage horses," he said with a cocked brow, then burst out a shocking hyena laugh.

"Oh," I cringed, embarrassed. "We have those. I ride them sometimes." Realizing the absurdity of what I'd just said, I started laughing, too. It was obvious my attempts at small talk were in vain. Finally, I gave up all together. The only thing I really knew of him was that he accepted the whole idea of slavery, but I felt it best to avoid that subject. Father forced this unwanted suitor upon me, and I didn't have a choice in the matter. "Master McClain, I really don't know much about you at all."

"Well then, allow me to fill you in."

"Do, please."

"First of all, please call me Matthew. My given name is Matthew James Garrison McClain the third." He proceeded to tell me about his family, his scholarly achievements, and his many accomplishments, all very impressive at the ripe old age of twenty-seven, eleven years my senior. I felt inferior to say the least, and certainly not his type. However, there wasn't much else to choose from—out in the middle of nowhere—with limited suitable acquaintances. What was I to do? I was doomed to fulfill the wishes of my father. As Master McClain continued talking about himself, I was relieved to see Etta enter the room.

"Shall I bring a fresh pot of tea?"

Another awkward pause. "Come to think of it, I have a history test to study for," I said in earnest.

Master McClain sat up. "I love history. Ask me anything. I'll help you pass that test with flying colors."

Wrong subject. Now what? "Oh, I mean ... quilting ... yes ... now I remember. Mother is teaching me a very special technique in quilting, and I have to practice. I've entered a contest in the town fair."

"Oh, yes, the town fair. How lovely. I'll have to be sure and look for your quilt."

"Thank you," I said with a smile and stood. Before he rose, I glanced toward the door as a signal. Etta took the cue and retrieved his hat.

"I should be going as well. Business as usual." He reached for his cane, resting against the wall.

"Thank you for coming all the way out here." I hesitated, but then politely held out my hand to him. He kissed it longer than I would have liked.

As his head lifted, our eyes met. "I should like to call upon you again." A deep gaze searched for my approval.

The real Constance inside wanted to say, *absolutely not, you selfish, egotistical pig*. Yet, for my father's sake and good name, I could not refuse him. "Of course," I said, and accompanied him to the door. I stood next to the wide column on the porch, going through the motions as was expected of me.

He climbed into the saddle, and the eye of the stallion widened with fear. Its head jerked back as Andrew held the bit tight before handing over the reins. Master McClain nodded toward me and tipped his hat. I forced a smile to my face and watched an arrogant sneer come to his. He pulled the reins taunt in an attempt to control the jittery steed. Its hooves stomped in rapid motion beneath him, when suddenly, the steed reared up with a loud neigh. His foot slipped from the stirrup, and the English gentleman tumbled to the ground. I cupped my hands over my mouth to hide my laughter.

He stumbled to his feet, brushed his pants, and leered. His lips tightened, and then the most horrific offense to man I'd ever witnessed took place. He grabbed the whip from the saddle and struck Andrew several times, relentlessly. "Heathen!" he screamed. The horse neighed and backed away. "You're frightening my horse." He lashed at Andrew again, who fell to his knees, covering his face.

"I'm sorry, sir," he cried out, blood flying from his arms.

"On your face, boy! I'll give you a lashing you'll never forget." Master McClain kicked him in the ribs several times.

Andrew curled up in agony on the ground as the whip thrashed his back.

"Etta, run and get Father!" I shouted.

"Yes, Miss Constance!"

I stood motionless in shock. Everything within me wanted to shout out at him to stop, but this time I honored my father's wishes. It jarred every nerve within me to keep from saying anything. I covered my mouth, remembering the words of my mother. A woman dared not speak her mind in dispute of a man's authority. My lips trembled and eyes pooled as I watched in horror. Master McClain, without conscience, continued to thrash Andrew—our devoted, sweet-tempered, and kind Andrew. How could he?

"That's enough, Master McClain!" The deep, angry voice of my father boomed forth, a side I did not see often.

Master McClain stopped mid-way to casting the whip again.

Through a tearful haze, I saw a blurry figure and focused on Jasmine as she drew closer. She covered her lips while passing Andrew, bent over, bloodied and huddled on the ground. Running up the porch steps, she cupped my shoulders to turn me away.

"Come, Miss Constance, you should not bear witness to this."

My face streamed tears. I dared not let Master McClain see me this way. I ran into the house, sobbing, heaving rage.

"Andrew will be all right. He comes from strong stock," Jasmine said, sadness in her voice.

I sensed she was reassuring herself more than anything. Distraught, I confessed, "I'm so sorry, Jasmine. I never meant for any of this to happen." I knelt and hugged her knees. "Please forgive me."

"Miss Constance, come now. You get up off the floor. You ain't got nothing to be sorry about. Master McClain was just being the only way he knows to be.

I'm thankful to Master William for stopping him."

I must have looked as much a fool as I felt. Tears flowed no matter how hard I tried to stop them. Watching Andrew whipped, shocked me back into a harsh reality. My lust for Simon had caught me off guard. An epiphany tore off the veil of deception over my heart. "This was all my fault." I still held tight to her knees. "I'm so sorry. This should never have happened, not to Andrew." I felt Jasmine pry me away from her legs. She held my trembling shoulders, guiding me to my bedchamber, where I fell on the bed, inconsolable.

"There now, Miss Constance. You just rest." She covered me with a shawl, and then sat in a rocker to watch over me.

After a while, the tears dried as I lay in bed thinking of the evil I had brought upon Andrew. Even though I tried to hide my amusement at Master McClain's falling off the horse, Andrew might not have suffered as much if I hadn't laughed.

How naive I was to think all men—especially Southern Gentlemen—were anything like my father. Perhaps I deserved to live elsewhere, outside the comforts of home, with Grandmother or another relative in Pennsylvania. Either way, it was clear to me that I did not belong in Washington's Woods any longer.

"Jasmine," I said, downcast.

"Yes, Miss Constance?"

"I want you to go and look after Andrew."

"Much as I want to, Miss, my duty calls for me to stay here."

"I know, but he's been like a brother to you. Go now. Clean and dress his wounds."

"Are you sure you'll be all right without me?"

"Yes, I'm sure."

"I'll be going then. Thank you, Miss Constance."

Somehow, her departure made me feel better. Though a small thing, I felt I had done something to right the wrong. The book of John Woolman's teachings lay on my dressing table. I'd borrowed it from Father's study. An essay regarding the slave trade peeked my interest. Considering the horrifying incident I had just witnessed, I thanked God for this man's noble efforts as I read.

"If we bring this matter home, and as Job proposed to his friends, *Put our Soul in their Soul's stead.* If we consider our children and ourselves as exposed to the hardships, which these people live, how would our cries ascend to God, who in his own time is a refuge for the oppressed? If they who thus afflicted us, continued to lay claim to religion, and were assisted in their business by esteemed pious people, who strengthened their hands in tyranny. In such a state, when we were hunger-bitten, and could not have sufficient nourishment, but saw them in fullness pleasing their taste with things fetched from afar! When we wearied with labour, denied the liberty to rest, and saw them spending their time at ease. When garments answerable to our necessities were denied us, while we saw them clothed in that which was costly and delicate. Under such affliction, how would such painful feelings rise up as witness against their pretended devotion? And if the name of their religion was mentioned in our hearing, how would it sound in our ears like a word which signified self-exaltation, and hardness of heart! Where a trade is carried on, productive of much misery, and they who suffer by it are some thousand miles off, the danger is the greater of not laying their sufferings to heart."

I could not have agreed more to that same sentiment.

A few weeks later, I stood once again in the secret tunnel at the basement wall. I handed the lantern to the slave behind me and knelt down to feel for the lever that opened the door. My fingers touched the cold metal, and I gripped the latch to pull it.

Light streaked into the darkness. I stood up and felt a tiny hand slip into mine. The warmth of the room invited us in, and I bent down to pick up the little girl who shook from the cold and fear. I covered her with my shawl as she hugged me tightly around my neck. I stroked her back and swayed with her in my arms for a long time. This was my penitence—to give comfort and remedy the wrong done to Andrew and to all who suffered the bondage of slavery.

-6-

Portal to the Past

Kate handed me the star sampler. "What do you think these symbols mean?"

I studied them until my natural curiosity took over. "I can only think of one person who might know the answer to that question. Are you thinking what I'm thinking?"

Kate nodded. "Let's go." We grabbed our bikes and took off.

Grandma Winnie opened the door with a big smile stretched across her face. "Hey, you two. What a nice surprise to see you back so soon!"

She poured us a glass of iced tea while we sat at the kitchen table. Kate explained how the frame broke into pieces when it fell to the floor, careful to leave out the part about setting it on a shelf in the closet. She pulled the sampler out of her backpack.

"We'll have to get it professionally framed so that doesn't happen again," Grandma Winnie said.

"That's a good idea," I said and pointed to the sampler. "Ms. Winnie, we found these markings around the edges. You know anything about them?"

She picked up her reading glasses and pulled the sampler close. “Oh, those were symbols used by only a select few seamstresses who knew the meanings.”

“Well, do you know how we can find out?” Kate asked.

“Hmm, I remember my grandmother saying something about when the symbols were given to her. I never found the paper with the meanings. I suppose we could look in the journal entries. Maybe Aunt Constance wrote about them.”

My eyes widened. “You have journals?”

“Why, yes, dear.”

“From the 18th century?”

“Oh, yes. I’ve kept them hidden to protect the family from being exploited. I think Aunt Constance would've wanted it that way. And even though she was close friends with Betsy Ross, I didn't want her ancestors holding us libel for anything either. So I thought it best not to chance anything,” Grandma Winnie said.

“How so?” I asked.

“She and Betsy shared a close friendship before either of them married from what I understand.”

“Can we see the journals?” Kate asked.

“Of course.” Grandma Winnie rose and walked to the bedroom. We followed and helped her kneel next to the bed. She stretched her arms and pulled out a storage box. “Here they are.”

Kate and I filtered through several books, all

dated from the late 1700s until the time of Aunt Constance's death. The journals opened to handwritten calligraphy on aged parchment, bound with leather and floral fabric covers.

I picked up a journal and flipped through it, sitting cross-legged on the floor.

"Can I take them?" Kate asked. "I'll bring them back. I just want to read them."

"Certainly. In fact, you can keep them now. I was planning on giving them to you anyway."

"Thanks, Grandma."

"You're welcome, Honey. I'm so glad you're finally taking an interest in the family history." Her eyes passed back and forth between us. "You know, girls, it's in the weaving of your heritage that you find out who you really are."

As I listened to Grandma Winnie talk to Kate, I felt flushed with envy, and a tinge of jealousy made my nerves bristle. *I'm* the one who was interested in this stuff in the first place, I thought. Kate could have cared less. I browsed through one of the journals and wondered if there was anything that might prove my suspicions.

"You come from a pretty special line of ladies, and I think once you read those journals, you're going to find out just how special," Grandma Winnie said.

"I love you, Grandma." Kate leaned in to hug her.

"I love you too." Grandma Winnie hugged Kate back. Then she handed her a stack of journals. "Now get to reading. And let me know if you find out anything juicy."

"I will," Kate said, smiling.

Grandma Winnie pushed against the bed to pull herself up from the floor, and we walked back to the kitchen.

Kate stuffed some of the journals, along with the star sampler, inside her backpack. I helped carry the rest in mine. We rode our bikes along the tree-lined streets, and I relished the crisp early autumn air. Red, orange, and yellow hues flecked the leaves. I took a deep breath, filling my lungs with fresh, clean air. At a certain spot on our route home, Kate and I went our separate ways. I could hardly wait to get home and study the journals.

I scoured each one for clues. The first entry from May 1774 read, "My maidservant, friend and confidant, Jasmine, has married. Her husband, Simon Miller, an indentured slave, has paid his debt to my father. He has gone to find his fortune in the North and to prepare for Jasmine to join him later. My heart feared the thought of Jasmine leaving me. She has been my maidservant from childhood, and I would surely be lost without her. Come the day of Simon's departure, in an attempt to keep Jasmine loyal, I offered my help to bid her husband a secret farewell as a token for her faithful service until the day he called for her."

A piece of paper fell from the journal. It was an

old newspaper clipping about how the farmstead came into the Proctor Family's possession.

Ravenswood Times, October 8, 1954, *Proctor Estate Bears Nobility:* A real Southern plantation still sits atop Turkey Run Hill. Once known as Washington's Woods, it boasted a two-thousand acre spread. Initially intended to be the original Mount Vernon estate, military duties required a change in plans. Prior to General Washington taking Presidential office, he turned over all caretaking duties to his trusted friend, Master Planter, William Proctor. Martha Washington sold the stately yet modest farmstead to William Proctor following the death of her husband.

So that's how it came to Kate's family. I checked my watch and set the journals aside to start getting ready for my big date with Johnny.

I stood posing in front of the mirror, when the cell phone rang. I glanced over to check the caller ID and grabbed it off the nightstand. "Hey there—the jeans look great with my black shirt."

"Well, I'm sure my butt looks better in them than yours does," Kate teased.

"It's not your butt Johnny's going to be looking at," I shot back.

"He better not be," she giggled. "Maybe you should wear your cowboy hat and boots."

"Oh, boots! I forgot about those." I opened the closet, rummaged through piles of shoes scattered on the floor.

"I just now remembered you have the other journals."

"Yeah, I do. I can bring them over tomorrow. I'll call you after I get home from my date tonight."

"Okay. Have fun. Don't do anything I wouldn't do," she said.

I shoved the boots into my duffel bag. "Then that won't be much," I said, giggled, and hung up.

My cheerleader uniform lay across my bed, crisp, straight from the cleaners. I slipped out of the jeans, folded and placed them along with the black shirt inside the duffel bag to change into after the game.

As I primped in front of the mirror, I applied a little more makeup. My helpless romantic side took over, and I imagined myself as a damsel in distress waiting for my handsome prince to fight the horrid troll at the drawbridge. My knight in shining armor, Johnny Beck, stood with drawn blade, dodging the poison that spewed forth from the busted pimples on the face of troll, Ronald Ripley. After conquering the foe of my discontent, Sir Johnny lifted me to the saddle of his trusted steed, a jet black Corvette, and carried me away to yonder castle, his favorite pizza joint and in-home theater.

On Saturday, my parents allowed me to drive the

family car over to Kate's house. I arrived just before noon and attempted to turn into the driveway. The car bounced over the curb and hit the trashcan. Over my shoulder, I saw a nosy neighbor from across the street peek out of her living room window and shake her head at me.

Kate yelled out instructions to me from her bedroom window, "Back up and cut the wheels to the right."

With my foot tapping on the brake pedal, I backed out of the driveway, but hit the curb again.

"Your other right," Kate scoffed.

I looked up at Kate and threw both hands up in surrender. Driving forward, I managed to align the car parallel to the curb and got out to view the trash strewn across the street.

Kate retrieved a broom and dustpan from the garage and met me in the driveway. "I thought you were going to call me last night."

The car door slammed behind me. "I would have, but I got home really late." I pointed to the dented trashcan. "Sorry about that."

She met me in the street and handed me the dustpan. "Oh, don't worry about it." She started sweeping up the mess. "So how was your date?"

"It was nice," I said with a shrug. I held the dustpan, while she swept debris into it, and then dumped the contents into the trashcan.

"Just nice?" she said, pushing down on the bent

lid.

"Well, I don't know," I said, tilting my head.

"What happened? You seem disappointed." Kate pushed the trashcan to the curb.

I remained silent all the way to the house. The expression on Kate's face didn't help either. I tried to ignore her until we reached her room, where my bottled emotions finally uncorked. "It's just ..." I pressed my thumbnail to my front teeth. My eyes blinked with tears and my chin quivered. "I don't understand why my being biracial is such a problem."

Kate sat next to me and placed her hand on my shoulder. "It isn't," she said, and reached for a box of tissues and handed it to me. "Did he say something to you?"

"No, he didn't." I wiped my eyes and sniffed.

"Does Johnny have a problem with it?"

"No, I think it's his parents. I mean, we were having a great time. After the football game, he took me out for pizza, and he gave me his letter jacket to wear. Then we went back to his house, and I met his parents." I sniffed again.

"I hear they live in a really nice part of town," Kate said.

"Yeah, they do. His mom kept looking at me kind of funny. It creeped me out. She asked about my parents, where they worked. I told her my dad is Sam Durham, and he works for the *Charleston Gazette*. Then I told her about Mama, that she makes quilts and runs the alterations shop downtown. Mrs. Beck said she had one of Mama's quilts in the guest bedroom upstairs. She gave me a tour of the house and then it was as if she went cold all of a sudden. She was still nice, but I felt uncomfortable around her after that. Judge Beck just said hello and went upstairs to his office. I hardly saw him."

"Well, we know his daddy's a racist, that's no secret," Kate said. "But, Johnny sounds like he's cool with it. I wouldn't worry too much."

"His mom finally left us alone, and we watched a movie. Johnny was nice to me. We talked a long time and then...he kissed me."

Kate bumped against my shoulder, "Oooh, a kiss."

"Yeah, it was sweet. I hope we go out again." I relaxed some. We went to the kitchen for lunch, and then back to Kate's room to start skimming through the journals.

"The language back then was so different. They wrote kind of funny," Kate said.

"I know. Makes you wonder how the human language got this far—or not."

"It would be hard to write using quill pens and ink, but it's so pretty," Kate said, chewing on a pretzel.

I turned another page. "It's not really that hard—just takes a steady hand."

"Wow, could you imagine living back then? No electricity, no indoor plumbing, and cooking in a fireplace." Kate slurped her soda through a straw. "No junk food or sodas either. I could never survive."

"The Amish still live that way." I sat up and read with sudden intensity.

"Yeah, but I think there's a difference when it's by choice," Kate said.

My eyebrows lifted. "Bingo!" I held up the journal and began reading aloud. "I could never tell anyone of my time alone with Simon Miller ..."

"Who's Simon Miller?" Kate raised up from her relaxed position on the bed and scooted closer, while I continued to read.

"I had suffered the loss of my beloved Henry, and he the loss of his precious wife, Jasmine. Upon moving to Philadelphia, Jasmine remained my closest friend. I am glad we finally resided where slaves lived respectably as free people. Simon Miller was as true and noble a man as any Christian gentleman I ever knew. It was by neither plan nor spite that we found ourselves together in that moment of despair. Fate stepped in and allowed us the time to comfort one another. Although only once, yea but a precious few hours, we shared a blissful tenderness which endears itself to my heart with great happiness to this day. I likened it to a beautifully orchestrated piece of music. Ebony and ivory keys played in perfect harmony. I shall always remember it that way. Such a gift of love I will never forget nor look back on with disdain. Though shame shadows me now, it will not steal my memory, the secret of which I have stitched within the symbols on the star sampler. Few know their meaning. Yet I dare not write another word, lest the product of the secret not remain hidden."

Kate swallowed the last bite of pretzel with eyes open wide. "Whoa! If she's saying what I think she's saying—who knew Aunt Constance had it in her?"

"Come on." I jumped up and gathered the journals. A sudden rush of adrenaline surged through my body.

"Where are we going?" Kate asked.

"We have to get to the library before it closes. Anna May's the only one who can help us find out the meaning of the symbols."

"Oh, right." Kate reached for her backpack.

"Don't forget the sampler." I turned back around to make sure Kate retrieved it from her dresser drawer.

I slid into the driver's seat, buckled up, and turned the key. Shifting into reverse, I backed out of the driveway, missing the trashcan this time. My foot pressed deep on the accelerator, forcing my shoulders back. Moving into forward drive, the wheels squealed, and I glanced at Kate. "Buckle up!"

Kate fumbled for her seat belt and clicked it shut. "Hey, Dale Earnhardt, what's the rush?"

"I'll tell you later."

"I expect to pass through this world but once. Any good therefore that I can do, or any kindness or abilities that I can show to any fellow creature, let me do it now. Let me not defer it or neglect it, for I shall not pass this way again." —William Penn

-7-

At the Dock

Early next morning, Jasmine held the light to my face, forcing my eyes to squint.

"Master William is asking for you, Miss Constance. I laid out your work dress for you."

I was not surprised at my father's untimely request. When children were transported, he depended on my special way to help calm their fears and keep them quiet.

Father and Andrew led the slaves down the hill by lantern to the docked keelboat. Jasmine and I followed behind. The trembling hands of two young children clung to mine as they walked on either side. Several hogshead barrels, weighing at least a ton each, filled the main cargo hold. To prevent crushing an unaware victim to death, a hidden space toward the aft provided little room for escaped slaves.

Captain James Parker directed them around the barrels to the secret area behind the false wall, keeping them hidden and safe. “Don’t move them barrels around so much,” he said. “The leaves are still tender. We don't want to cost Master William his profits.”

I pinned a small embroidered angel to each child’s sleeve as he or she left my side to join their mother. “Go now,” I said. “The angels will watch over you.” The little girl with swollen eyes, endearing and helpless, did not take her gaze from me. Even when her mother beckoned, the child backed into the storage opening, watching me until the darkness consumed her. I glanced over at Jasmine, who wore a blank stare. “What’s wrong?”

“My Simon’s been gone for two weeks now,” she said.

My thoughts went back to when Mother and I had fitted Simon in proper gentleman’s attire, head to toe, as a parting gift from the Proctor family. I did the measuring, while Mother prepared the fabric. I remembered my fingertips touching his skin and the passion rising at the sensual feel of his muscular shoulders and strong legs. I shivered, not from cold, but from the warmth of his breath as it whisked through my hair. My arms encircled his waist and chest, and his manly smell sent my senses to places I dared not go. As I raised my arms above my head to measure for hat size, our eyes met, faces only inches apart. Warm tingles on my thighs and up my spine caused pulsating sensation. I tried not to pant or be so obvious. Once again, I saw that same penetrating stare that had made my stomach flutter, my spirit weak, and my legs go limp. I released the measuring string and turned to the table, forcing my thoughts back with a scolding reprimand in my mind.

"You're a free man now, and you should dress like one. People in the Northern colonies will take you more seriously and treat you with respect," I said.

My father entered the room carrying a parchment bearing his insignia seal, Simon's passage to freedom assuring him safe travel. Father held out the scroll. "Simon, you leave me just before planting season. It's a good thing you have so many brothers and sisters. Nonetheless, I feel compelled to care for you, at the pressing of Constance, for Jasmine's sake." He reached into his pocket, pulled out a small leather pouch, and handed it to Simon. "Should things not work out, you can always come back. I'll not turn away a hard worker. Send word to me when you find work. I'll see to it that Constance keeps Jasmine informed as well."

Simon bowed. "Yes, sir. Thank you, sir," he said in his proper British accent. After Father left the room, Simon cocked his head and strutted about in gentleman-like fashion that made me laugh.

The memory brought a smile to my face. My father's voice jarred me back into the moment.

"Take the helm Captain James. Fetch me a good price."

With skill, Captain James pushed the boat away from the dock.

"They should reach Pittsburgh in a fair amount of time if the weather holds," Father said.

I reached for Jasmine's hand and gave it a gentle squeeze. "He'll send word soon."

As we walked to the house, we passed the river's edge, the place where I was baptized though not in the customary way. Jasmine and I were still children then, and I wanted to be baptized with my friend. I tried to keep it secret from my family, but one of my brothers saw me, dripping wet among the slaves.

"You can't get baptized like a negra. It won't count," he said.

"I can to."

"I'm telling."

"God doesn't care how we get baptized or who we get baptized with, just that we do. You keep your mouth shut." I pushed him aside and kept walking.

"I'm telling," he yelled.

"Go ahead," I scowled. Our sisterly bond grew even stronger that day. My understanding of how God sees the human race—not separated by skin color but as a whole—compounded my passion for social justice.

Father never scolded me, but he later insisted I redo the ceremony in the acceptable manner. "For your namesake, it must be documented in the church records."

"All right," I said afterwards. "I believe I've been thoroughly dunked now."

Jasmine and I parted ways at the back porch. Before entering, I heard retching and looked back to see her dark figure, silhouetted in the moonlight, leaning forward.

I stepped off the porch. "Jasmine?"

Holding her stomach, she raised up one hand to stop me. "Don't you worry none about me, Miss Constance."

"Are you sure?"

"Yes, ma'am. I'm feeling better already. I'll be at your service in the morning."

I hesitated, but felt it best to respect her wishes. "All right then." I turned back and entered the house.

-8-

Miss Fanny

Anna May was quite busy when we arrived at the library, but she looked over the journal, albeit briefly, and made a suggestion.

"Well, this is an interesting development." She looked at the sampler. "Exquisitely crafted. I have a friend with the historical society who may be able to help you."

"Who?" I asked.

"We all call her Miss Fanny." Anna May smiled. "In fact, Fanny from Savanny is a running joke around here. She's a lovely, ninety-year old woman who moved from Georgia after her husband passed away, to live with her daughter. Unfortunately, she doesn't like wearing her false teeth—so it's hard to understand her all the time. You have to listen real close. Oh, and just be aware, she tends to spit. But her memory is sharp as a tack, and she was born and raised right here in Charleston. She still gets around and comes to our meeting every Sunday afternoon at two-thirty."

"Tomorrow is Sunday," Kate said.

"Yes, do you think you can make it?" Anna May glanced between us.

"Sure." I nodded.

Anna May lifted her finger. "We meet upstairs."

"Sounds good," Kate said.

"We'll be there." I pushed against the door to leave.

"Great, I'll see you two then." Anna May turned back to the checkout counter.

Sunday afternoon at two-thirty on the dot, Miss Fanny appeared at the library door. We met her at the counter. She wore a flowery dress under a sweater jacket. Her hat, a big flower pinned to the side of it, hung down over her forehead. She carried a cane in one hand, a purse in the other.

"Hi, doll baby."

"Hi, Miss Fanny," Anna May said and gave her a hug.

"I'd like you to meet Nicole, and this is Kate."

"It's very nice to meet you," Miss Fanny said.

"My, we got some young'uns here today. That's a nice change." She chuckled through a toothless grin.

Anna May escorted us to the meeting room. "They have come across something intriguing about their family history. Some old journals show evidence that supports a possible coded message in the symbols on an heirloom sampler."

The old woman's face lit up. "Can I see it?" Some spit flew toward Kate, and she barely dodged it.

"Sure," Kate said, as she fumbled with her

backpack and pulled out the sampler. Fanny sat down, pulled out her reading glasses, and adjusted them on her nose. She held the sampler up to the light.

"Fine workmanship. I haven't seen this kind of detail since I was a little girl. Very few know about such symbols. The heart behind a tree means a secret or forbidden love. Here's a cradle—means a baby was born. Oh, and another cradle—could mean twins. Black and white threads weaving around each other indicate agreement or unity. One cradle is stitched with white thread and the other, with black thread—that's showing different races." Fanny looked at Kate with flattened brows. "Are you going to write this down? Surely you don't expect to just remember everything."

"Oh, yeah." Kate grabbed a pen and paper from the table.

I watched as Fanny adjusted her glasses and began interpreting more of the symbols.

"A carriage means they traveled a long ways. Half a woman and half a man in silhouette ... hmm ... that could mean a widow and a widower. The two rings between them show a break in the stitching, which means they weren't married to each other. That makes sense. Many people lost their spouses in the Revolutionary War. But what was so important about including this on the sampler? The fact one was a slave makes no sense either. Nobody cared about slaves back then, but obviously there was something important about this particular slave and widower."

"How can you tell it was sewn during the Revolutionary War?" I asked.

"It's dated right here—1776 next to the letters SSS." Miss Fanny turned her eyes up to peer over her trifocals at Kate. "Am I right?"

"Yes. That's amazing, how you knew all that," Kate said.

Fanny chuckled. "My mother was a seamstress and did very fine work just like this—she learned from studying the stitching of antique samplers. She taught me everything she knew, and I passed the meanings along to my daughters."

I turned my head just in time to miss some flying spit, but tried to look casual about it, hoping Miss Fanny didn't notice.

"How do you know the meaning of the symbols?" I continued.

"My grandmother taught them to me. Your grandmother might have them written somewhere, but over the years they may have gotten lost." Fanny tapped her crooked finger on the table. "My grandmother made my sisters and I memorize every one of them till we knew each one by heart and could recite them in our sleep."

I sat up, interested. "Are you saying there was some sort of secret society of seamstresses back then?"

"Yes, that's right. There were only a select few of

the finest seamstresses who really cared about maintaining the quality of work they designed. During wartime, using secret symbols was the best way to pass secret messages and skirt the enemy."

Miss Fanny explained how the military worked with the SSS, the Secret Society of Seamstresses, to sew the symbols on nurses' aprons and doctors' coat sleeves to pass along secret orders. The symbols sewn along the edges of blankets, the lining of a soldier's jacket or under the lapel of a uniform blazer, carried war strategies from one commander to another in the field.

"How clever," I said.

Anna May politely interrupted, "Ladies, this is a fascinating discovery, but we really need to get started with our meeting now. You can talk about this later if you like."

"Wow! This class project is a lot more interesting than I first thought," I said.

"Yeah," Kate said. "Who would have thought a bunch of dead people could be so exciting?"

After the meeting, curiosity consumed me as we walked to the car. "We need to talk with your grandmother again about these symbols. Maybe she'll remember something."

"Okay. She should be home now," Kate said. While she drove, I checked in with Mom. Grandma Winnie answered the door with excitement in her voice. "How nice to see you two again."

I stepped through the door and jumped right into the reason for our visit. "We were wondering if you remember any time when your mother or grandmother talked about the symbols on the sampler."

We sat at the kitchen table. Her eyes grew more focused and contemplative. "I remember my grandmother mentioned an old story, but we never knew if it was really true or not."

"Did it have anything to do with the symbols?" I asked.

"I suppose so."

"What was it about?" Kate asked.

"The story makes reference to a possible biracial baby born about the time of the Revolutionary War," Grandma Winnie said.

Kate looked at me. "This could be the missing link you were talking about."

"Maybe," I said.

She turned her attention back to Grandma Winnie. "Sorry. Go on please."

"Of course, a biracial baby was never talked about in those days, even though they did exist. Sometimes a Master took a slave girl for his mistress or worse." Grandma Winnie cleared her throat. "Well, this is a rather long story, and the only way I know to tell it is start at the beginning."

I listened, intent on finding the truth as Grandma Winnie told the story in detail.

"It was at the old farmstead near Ravenswood, when they still called it Washington's Wood. There was a young slave girl named Jasmine, born there. She married Simon Miller, who was an indentured slave. He paid off his debt to Master William Proctor and decided to move north. Once he found work, he planned to send for his wife and to make a better life for his family. Shortly after he left, Jasmine discovered she was pregnant.

I interrupted, "Wasn't there a drought that summer?" I remember reading about it in one of the journals."

"Oh, yes. That's right," Grandma Winnie confirmed. "Most of the crops died, and since they hid the slaves in the tobacco leaves, they only managed to smuggle a few to freedom. Captain James had sent several messages to Simon, which Constance helped to write for Jasmine. They only heard from Simon once. I think it might be in one of the journals. Can't you just imagine the excitement once that letter finally arrived?"

-9-

Letter from Simon

Andrew stopped the carriage at the front of the house to let me out. I clutched the letter from Simon in my hand. Instead of waiting for assistance, I jumped down from the carriage on my own and ran inside the house, looking for Jasmine. I found her tending the garden out back near the servants' quarters and ran toward her, waving the letter above my head. "Jaz! Jaz! It's a letter from Simon."

Jasmine dropped the hoe, grabbed the letter and tore it open. She inspected the handwriting and raised the paper to her nose, inhaling slowly. I assumed she did this to capture the scent of her husband, but then she handed the letter back to me. "Here, Miss Constance. You read it. I'm too excited, and I can't read that well yet."

My panting calmed as I reached for the letter and started to read it aloud. "My Dearest Love, Jasmine ... I made it to Philadelphia. I've become an apprentice at a print shop, and I now work for Mr. Benjamin Franklin." My eyes widened, and excitement filled my soul. "Oh, Jaz, Benjamin Franklin is a great inventor. Father knows him, too."

"Yes, go on, please!" She bounced like a little girl and clasped a hand to her mouth.

"All right, where was I?" I continued, "I am being paid well and will send for you soon. With much desire to see our baby, I love you with all my heart. Yours forever, Simon."

Her bottom lip quivered. "Oh, I can't wait to see him again, but it sounds like he won't send for me until after the baby is born now." Her voice squealed with emotion. "I was hoping to be together when the baby comes." She gasped for breath and shut her eyes tight.

I swallowed to keep my own emotions at bay. Simon's absence was both a blessing and a curse to me. The blessing of his absence left me without the constant lure of temptation, the self-condemnation, penitent prayers, and confessions. However, the curse of his memory did not diminish my longing to see him again. I folded the letter to return it to the envelope and slid it into my pocket. "Traveling is difficult in your condition. I know it's hard to be patient, but best for you and the baby. We will be here for you, Jaz."

"I know, Miss Constance, and I *am* grateful to you. I just miss my husband so much."

I encouraged our relationship to grow closer over the summer months. We were more like childhood friends again rather than a master's daughter and maidservant. However, Jasmine and I made a concerted effort to keep our friendship private. Only my family and a few slaves knew of the favor I bestowed upon her. I longed to see Simon as much, if not more, in ways I dared not share. Even so, my attempts to console her seemed futile.

"At least you still have your family with you." The grass crunched behind me, and I looked back to see Jasmine's mother walking toward us.

"What's wrong?" Tessa said.

"Nothing's wrong," I said. "Jaz just got a letter from Simon, says he's working for Benjamin Franklin."

Tessa wrapped her arm around her daughter's waist. "You miss him, I know, but he's fine. You have to be strong. Come back to work. It'll keep your mind off it."

Jasmine pulled back. "But the baby is coming soon, and I want to be with Simon."

"Jaz, you can't expect more than what he can do right now. He is doing all he can do. Be thankful."

My eyes shifted between them as Tessa tried to reason with her daughter.

Jasmine shook her head in distress. "But I need my husband with me." She walked toward the servants' quarters, and I followed. "The Captain can take me tonight with the other slaves. I can get to Philadelphia on my own."

"Jaz, please listen. You should wait, at least until after the baby is born."

She reached the porch and stopped. "It would be better to get there before the baby is born."

Tessa raised her voice. "But what if you don't make it in time?"

"She's right, Jaz," I said. "What if you go into labor on the way, especially if you were all alone?"

Jasmine stopped, rubbed her belly gently, and thought for a moment. Supporting herself with one arm, she eased down onto the steps of the servants' quarters. Tears wet her apron. Tessa and I sat on either side of her. She wiped her eyes and sniffed.

"Benjamin Franklin—an inventor—what sort of things has he invented?"

"Come inside the house with me, and I'll show you," I said.

On the way, I saw Elizabeth and Pearlie playing tea party in the garden, a sweet reminder of my own childhood days. I led Jasmine to the parlor.

"Here they are." I picked up Father's spectacles. "These are bifocals. Here, look through them." I turned them around to slide over Jasmine's nose. "You can see near and far away at the same time."

She pushed them up to her eyes, "I can't see a thing. It's all blurry."

"That's because you have good eyes. Mr. Franklin doesn't see well, so he created these special lenses."

"Well, he certainly must be a smart man to have invented them," Jasmine said.

"Yes, he is, Jaz—and your husband is very fortunate to be working for him now. He is a fair and generous man. I'm sure Simon will learn a lot from him." I set the spectacles down and spied a book on the shelf. "Remember me telling you about John Woolman?"

"He's the minister who teaches against slavery, right?"

"This should help you feel better." I opened the book to a favorite passage and read it aloud. "Many lives have been shortened through extreme oppression, while they labored to support luxury and worldly greatness; and though many people in outward prosperity may think little of those things, yet the gracious Creator hath regard to the cries of the innocent, however unnoticed by men. The Lord in the riches of his goodness is leading some unto the feeling of the condition of this people, who cannot rest without laboring as their advocates; of which in some measure I have had experience: for, in the moving of his love in my heart, these poor sufferers have been brought near me."

"Oh!" She held her belly and grabbed hold of a wing back chair to steady herself.

"What is it?" I took hold of her arm to offer support.

"The baby just kicked."

"Did it hurt?"

"No," she giggled and laid my hand on her belly. I bent to listen. The baby moved, and I smiled, amazed.

"Maybe you should name him Benjamin."

"Assuming it's a boy." She chuckled and waddled

back toward the servants' quarters.

I stood at the backdoor and called out, "Do you still want to leave?"

She turned back. "No, this is the best place for me and my baby. I'll just have to wait for Simon to be ready." She turned to walk away, but then looked back at me. "Thank you, Miss Constance."

I ran to her and hugged her tight. "We've known each other since birth, Jaz. I will miss you terribly. I don't know how I'm going to get along without you."

She pressed her palm to mine, and said, "Blood sisters, remember? You're just going to have to marry a man from the North and come live near me."

Suddenly, a wonderful thought came to mind. "Now that's a plan that might work. We do have family there."

"Uh-oh, don't you be getting any funny ideas now, Miss Constance."

"No, listen Jaz, my Aunt Harriet lives in Philadelphia..." I curled my arm around hers as we walked the path together.

-10-

Chips and Salsa

Kate pulled down chips and salsa from the cabinet, setting them on the table. I grabbed one. The salty taste satisfied my craving, but also made me thirsty. I sipped on iced tea, while Grandma Winnie continued the story.

"Unfortunately, back then they just didn't have the medical knowledge we have today. Women died in childbirth all the time and it wasn't uncommon for babies to be stillborn."

"How sad," I said. "Did Jasmine die?"

"No, but it was too dangerous for Simon to go back to the farmstead alone. Even though he was free at the time, many in the Southern colonies refused to recognize the rights of freed slaves. If memory serves me right, that's when Benjamin Franklin stepped in and offered to arrange for Simon to go as his personal valet. He and Master William served as delegates around the same time, which gave him good reason for a visit."

"Are you serious?" I asked. "Ben Franklin?"

"Yes, and that's when Aunt Constance convinced her parents to let her move to Philadelphia with

Simon and Jasmine. Mr. Franklin was more than happy to act as chaperon. She lived with her Aunt Harriet, her mother's sister. I'm sure Harriet really needed the extra help, with a dozen kids running around. After a few months, Constance started working in the family upholstery business. That's when she met her first husband, Henry Leverton. They actually eloped, which was quite a scandal in those days."

The phone rang and Grandma Winnie got up to answer it.

"Hello?" A moment later, "Oh, my goodness," she said, glancing at the clock. "My granddaughter's visiting, and I lost all track of time. I'll be right there." She hung up and said, "Would you girls like to take a field trip to see the old farmstead later this week?"

"That'd be great," Kate said.

"I'd love to go, but can you finish telling us about the scandal part first?" I leaned forward on my elbows and fluttered my eyelashes. "Please?"

Grandma Winnie smiled and said, "I'm sorry, Honey. Time got away from me. I have to get to the church. It's my turn to call out bingo numbers. Will Saturday work?"

"Okay, I'll call you to find out what time," Kate said, while putting away the chips and salsa.

Did I really have a choice? Trying not to show my frustration, I pulled out my cheerleader schedule, relieved to see no game on Saturday. "That'll work for me too," I said.

Grandma Winnie retrieved her purse and keys. "Good. I'll tell you the rest on Saturday then."

We followed her out the door.

-11-

Birth Pangs

My family sat on the front pew whenever Father preached. “Master McClain will be joining us today,” he said, while leaning forward.

“No!” I whispered. “I won’t have anything to do with him.”

“Come now, Constance, Darling.”

“Father, I won’t have that man near me. He is the epitome of evil as far as I’m concerned.”

“Yes, I understand your viewpoint. Nevertheless, we are commanded to forgive. And what better way to show it?”

“Father, please!” I said, careful to maintain a hushed tone.

He gestured, waving a finger to silence me. “Now, now, I’ve spoken with Master McClain at length in regards to our more forward-thinking on abolitionism, and he seems to be very agreeable. He's even consented to read the teachings of John Woolman.”

“I don’t care! I won’t be near him!”

“Constance.” His stern look made denying him almost impossible.

I crossed my arms. “Father!”

Moments later, I found myself sitting next to a man I detested. I tried to maintain interest in the sermon, but the heat and humidity made it difficult to stay alert. My head started to nod, and Mother, who sat on the other side of me, nudged me. A faint breeze drifted across my face and brought a moment of clarity and relief. I fluttered my lashes and waved a lace fan in front of my face.

"Let us pray," Father said. I bowed my head and tried not to fall asleep again. The time came for singing, which always helped to perk up things.

During the hymns, Master McClain's deep baritone bellowed next to me, which threw my own voice completely off key. His unpleasant nasal clearance into a handkerchief roused me out of a drowsy stupor during the sermon. It sickened me to think that I once considered him a potential suitor. I turned my head to the window. A storm hovered over the horizon and reflected my mood toward Master McClain.

Rain pounded on the carriage roof all the way back to the farmstead. When we arrived home, everyone retreated inside the house. Andrew held an umbrella and assisted the women one at a time to the covered porch. Drenched, he climbed to the bench and flicked the reins, a quick slap. The horses, wary in the storm's fury, neighed as the wheels splashed along the muddy path.

Etta stood at the door wringing her hands. "Miss

Jasmine is having her baby."

"But it's too soon, Mother. We have to go to her," I said.

Elizabeth stood on the other side of me. "I don't mind helping, but I don't want to see the bad parts."

"All right, girls, go change out of your Sunday clothes first," Mother said, and looked at Etta. "Tell Tessa and Maggie we'll be right there."

We entered the servants' quarters, and Jasmine's sudden outcry startled me. "Ah!" She panted for breath while Tessa wiped her forehead.

"This baby's in a hurry," Tessa said.

"It's all right, Jaz. We're here to help. Just breathe," I said, holding back my own panic.

Mother and I set fresh linens on a table, Elizabeth carried in a clean bowl, and Pearlie toted a kettle of hot water. Elizabeth glanced at the bloodied sheets, and Mother seized the moment to affirm her coming of age.

"Elizabeth, you're too young to understand these things now, but soon it'll be as natural as churning butter."

"I think I'm going be sick," Elizabeth said, and ran out the door.

Pearlie followed her, but then she poked her head back inside the door. "I ain't never seen a baby being born. Can I watch?"

"Ah! Get out!" Jasmine screamed.

Tessa motioned for Pearlie to leave. "Go on, child!

See after Miss Elizabeth."

Pearlie pouted. She stomped off the porch and sloshed through the mud after Elizabeth.

Maggie, acting as midwife, leaned in to check the baby's position. "Hold up, Miss. It isn't time to push. Got a wee bit more yet." She felt of Jasmine's belly again and then tightened her brows. She motioned for Mother and me to come outside to the covered porch.

"What's wrong?" I asked. The pouring rain almost drowned our voices.

"Begging your pardon, Miss Susanna, but I fear the baby needs a turning," Maggie said.

"Oh dear," Mother said. "Constance, go tell your father we need Doc Shaw out here right away."

"But mother, I don't think he'll come in this storm. You know how he feels about slaves."

"He'll come. If we pay him well enough."

Tessa appeared at the door and grasped Mother's hand.

"Thank you, Miss Susanna," she said with trembling lips. "I don't want my baby girl to die." She burst into tears.

Mother embraced her. "Now Tessa, you can't let Jaz see you like this. You'll frighten her. You're family has meant so much to us. I won't let anything bad happen if I can help it."

Maggie went back inside to tend to Jasmine, who was now between labor pains and resting. Willow carried soiled linens in a large bowl and stopped short of running into me at the door. Her tears spoke for her.

I stood at the door.

Jasmine said weakly, "Where's Simon? I need my Simon."

"Eh now, Miss. Best save your strength," Maggie said. "Word will reach Simon soon enough."

The rain, like the sudden flood of the falls from a winter thaw, drenched the ground. Thunder growled. My heart sank, for without the aid of a skilled physician, I feared death might take her and her unborn. In desperation, I sprinted all the way from the servants' quarters to the house to find help. Mud stained the hem of my dress and petticoats. My hair flat, dripping wet as I entered the study, where Father sat reading, smoking a cigar.

"Father, we need Doc Shaw to come right away."

He rose to his feet, shocked to see me in such condition. "Whatever for?"

"Jasmine's baby is breech!"

"Oh my!" He set down his cigar, reached for my shoulders. "Constance, sometimes these things happen. There's nothing we can do."

"No!" My chin trembled. "We can't just let her die!" I cried. "Father, please! Please, get Doc Shaw." I fell to my knees, held onto his legs and wailed with despair. "Don't let her die! Please!"

"All right! Come now, that's quite enough, my dear Constance." He pulled me up from the floor. "I'll send Andrew to fetch him."

"Thank you, Father." I hugged him and kissed his hand, holding it to my cheek. "Thank you."

"Yes, yes. Now you get some dry clothes on before Doc Shaw has to attend to *you*."

I climbed the stairs to my bedchamber and heard Father instructing Andrew to tell Doc Shaw that there was an emergency and nothing more. Mother returned to await the doctor's arrival, and helped me change my dress. I paced the front porch until I heard the horse and carriage making its way up the dirt road to the house.

"Mother!" I yelled from the front door. "He's here!"

In the foyer, a disgruntled Doc Shaw handed me his hat and Etta his coat and umbrella. His half-bald head uncovered, damp gray strands lined the nape. Usually, on visitations such as this, he wore a white wig, but with the late hour, I surmised he'd declined the effort. He turned to my father, who stood near to greet him.

"Thank you for coming at such short notice," Father said.

"Yes, well, what is this emergency?"

"Our beloved maidservant is having trouble birthing her firstborn."

Doc Shaw ignored all cordiality. "I do not appreciate being called out here, especially in such weather as this, and most certainly not for a slave. This is a highly inappropriate expectation of my practice as a physician."

"I do beg your pardon for the inconvenience. But, you see, this is not an ordinary slave. This is my daughter's maidservant from childhood. If anything happens to her, my dear Constance would fall into great despair."

Doc Shaw shook his crooked finger and scolded, "All the more reason why you should never have allowed such a relationship between slave and kin. Children do not have the capability to discern such things for themselves. Now, it's too late. Dear me, I hate to think of what sort of household this child will run in the future." He glanced my way.

I shrank back into the shadows.

Mother appeared in the foyer, a bit overdressed, I thought. The rain stopped, offering a momentary pause, like a rest in a music. She carried a small leather pouch. "We are ever so grateful for your benevolent understanding, Doc Shaw." Her smile and gentile manner helped to transform the room's ambiance.

"Susanna." Doc Shaw nodded. The corners of his mouth turned up, and his pinched forehead softened.

A realization came to light as I saw how he fancied my mother.

Like the peaceful coo of a dove or the purr of a kitten, Mother's instinctive qualities tempered Doc Shaw's mood, as she held her hand out and curtseyed. She received the customary kiss on the hand and held out the other containing a small bag of coins.

His hand bounced, judging the weight. "This should do quite nicely. Very well then, where is the patient?"

She looked past his shoulder and nodded at Etta, who handed Doc Shaw his umbrella and coat. I gave him the hat. Mother picked up a lantern and an umbrella, and then led Doc Shaw out to the servants' quarters behind the main house. I followed the bobbing canopies as our feet sloshed down the path.

Doc Shaw complained. "Must we go trampling about in the mud to get there?"

"Only a short distance further." Mother walked with quickened steps as Doc Shaw tried to keep up.

I went around him and ran past Mother in order to alert the others. Jasmine's screams pierced my heart. It was frightening to think what she must be going through. I was scared that she and her baby might die, and she may never see Simon again.

Captain James sat in a rocker on the covered porch. When I arrived, he stood and was careful not to make eye contact with Doc Shaw as he came up behind Mother.

Maggie lay a towel on the table and put her hands in the air. "Oh, thank the Lord you're here."

"Mind you, speak only when spoken to," Doc Shaw said with indignation.

Maggie looked down in submission and stepped aside to get out of his way. He handed his umbrella and hat to her, set his bag on a stool.

Tessa sat on the bed behind Jasmine, who whimpered and panted from exhaustion. She wiped the sweat from Jasmine's chest and forehead using a fresh rag that Willow handed her.

When Doc Shaw leaned in to examine her, Jasmine started to scream again.

"Don't push, Jasmine," he said. "You mustn't push at this time."

"But I don't know if I can keep from it," she said.

"Hold on, Jaz. Just take deep breaths," Tessa said.

Jasmine inhaled slowly and deeply, which seemed to calm her for the moment.

Doc Shaw stood, wiping his hands with a rag. He motioned for Mother, Maggie, and me to meet him in the corner and spoke in hushed tones.

I glanced over at Tessa, who leaned in to hear.

Jasmine screamed again, which pulled her mother's attention back.

Doc Shaw muttered, "Susanna, she's lost a lot of blood. I have limited resources. Any other slave, and I would leave her be."

Mother held his arm and spoke with earnest. "Oh, please, Doc Shaw."

I pleaded, "Please ... do whatever you can to save her and the baby."

Doc Shaw stepped away and dabbed his forehead, then rubbed his neck. After a long pause, he said, "Maggie, I will need your assistance."

"Yes, sir."

He set his bag on the bed. "You will need to hand me certain items when I ask for them," he said. "I will point to what I need."

Maggie nodded. "Yes, sir."

The doctor unbuttoned his sleeves and started to roll them up each arm. "I will need more hot water."

Willow left to fetch another kettle.

"Constance, I need you to hold Jasmine," Doc Shaw said, then looked at Susanna. "You may need to help her."

"All right," she said, while tying an apron around her waist.

He sat at the foot of the bed. "Jasmine, your baby is in a breech position. I'm going to try and turn it around. This is going to be extremely painful, but I will do my best to save your life and the life of your child."

"Please, Doc. Save my baby," Jasmine cried.

"At this point, we'll be lucky if either of you survive," Shaw said.

"There, baby girl. You're going to be fine," Tessa said. She wiped Jasmine's forehead and motioned for me to take her place.

I slipped in behind Jasmine to give Tessa a much-needed break. This placed me in a better position to hold Jasmine down once Doc Shaw started to work.

"I'll be on the porch if you need me," Tessa said, and closed the door behind her.

Throughout the night, amid the crackling thunder

and lightning flashes, Jasmine screamed. After a couple of grueling hours, I called for Tessa to relieve me and went to sit on the porch alone. I rocked and clung to my knees, my eyes squeezed tight. Tears misted my face as I sniffed and prayed silently through trembling lips.

Lightning struck a tree not far away. I jumped as thunder rumbled in the distance. I shuddered, fearing it might happen again. Through a watery daze, my eyes focused on a red bandanna tied to the handle of a water bucket, which sat near the step. I remembered the one Andrew tied to the tobacco-filled wagon as a signal to let us know about the escaped slaves, and a symbol of freedom. My fingers folded one end of the bandanna and pulled out the corner. I dabbed my cheeks and dried my tears. The door creaked open, and I glanced back over my shoulder.

"Miss Constance, she's asking for you," Tessa said, standing at the door, panting.

"Has the baby turned yet?"

"No, ma'am." She wiped her forehead.

"I'll take it from here, Tessa." I said, and entered the room.

Doc Shaw stood drying his hands. "Ready for another go at it, old girl?"

Jasmine whimpered. "No more, please."

"Now, now, Lassie," Maggie said. "Such a prize doesn't come without cost. Rest assured, it'll be worth it once you see the babe for the first time."

Sidling next to her sweaty, limp body, I said, "Only a little while longer, Jaz." I folded the bandanna into her hand, holding it taut. "Look, remember what this means? Simon wants this for you and the baby." I glanced at the bandanna and back to her. "Maggie's right. This prize is worth it."

Jasmine focused on the bandanna "The prize."

"Yes." I nodded, and whispered in her ear. "Think about Simon and where you will live with your new baby soon."

"The prize." Jasmine took a deep breath. She repositioned herself on the bed. "I'm ready."

-12-

Skinhead Encounter

I stayed after school to make signs for the upcoming pep rally, having asked Kate to pick me up when I was finished. She was supposed to borrow her grandmother's car and wait for me in front of the school.

I made my way down the hallway alone. The feeling someone was watching my every move only compounded my paranoia. Knowing Johnny's father was a judge, who most likely had the eyes and ears of all the community on his side, didn't help matters either. I had never felt so singled-out. No one ever mistreated me because of race before. Then again, very few people knew I was biracial. Or so I thought.

Something dropped on the floor and startled me. I swirled around and leaned over to peer into a vacant room. Nothing there. Maybe someone left a window open, and the wind knocked something down. My heart pounded as I kept a keen watch ahead. A shadowy figure ran across the hall. What was that? Oh, man, I must have drank too much Gatorade at practice today. That always makes me jittery.

Suddenly, doors slamming followed by the

roaring of a mob startled me. What was going on? I looked back at a gang of skinheads headed right for me. Their eyes held the glare of evil. They carried baseball bats and crowbars. My heartbeat raced as loud banging echoed through the halls, a deafening noise.

I looked for an escape, but the skinheads caught up to me. I looked around for anyone, a teacher, or the principal, even a janitor. All the rooms were empty. The door to the outside world was just ahead, but it was too late. The hot breath of hatred surrounded me. Just as I reached the exit, one of them jumped in front of me.

"Hey, where do you think you're going?" he said as he looked me up and down.

I panted, too frightened to speak. Through the window, I saw Kate parked just outside at the curb. Her head stopped bobbing, and she removed her headphones to check the batteries. The skinhead hit the bat against the door. I screamed, jumped back. His jeering continued, and I backed away only to find myself surrounded.

When my gaze reached the window, I saw Kate running toward me and an adrenaline rush hit.

The skinhead continued to harass. He touched my chin, stroking my neck with his fingers. "You hear me, beautiful?" I stared at him, saying nothing. He jerked his hand away and screamed into my face, "What's the matter? Are you too black to talk now?"

"Ju...Just let me go, please," I replied, stuttering.

The other skinheads circled me again—as if I was freshly caught prey—and started to heckle.

Kate banged on the door, startling them. "Leave her alone. The police are on their way," she screamed. I was so glad to see her, but feared they might hurt her, too.

"Oh, yeah?" He sneered and pushed the handle, allowing an opening to face his opponent. "You really think they're going to do anything?"

Kate stared him down, unrelenting. He reached out to grab her, but she held out a can of mace, spraying directly into his face.

"Ahhh!" he screamed and covered his eyes, stumbling backwards.

I ran past him through the open entrance, made it outside, and stood behind Kate, still holding up the mace, defiantly.

"Anyone else want a piece of me?" she yelled. She stood her ground, but I was worried about how far this standoff might go.

Just then, sirens blared and police cars rounded the corner. The gang scattered, leaving behind the guy temporarily blinded by mace.

A janitor appeared. "I called the police," he said, and walked past the agonizing skinhead. "So much for gang brotherhood."

Still shaken, I looked at Kate. "Oh, God, I thought we were goners for sure. Are you all right?"

"I'm fine. Come on, let's get out of here."

I buckled my seatbelt. "I have a feeling Judge Beck was behind this somehow."

Kate nodded. "You're probably right. Pressing charges is a waste of time. We'd better steer clear of any police interrogation."

Later that day, a news story about the guy blinded from mace said he was charged with vandalism. Juvenile Hall released him. Judge Beck dismissed the case, confirming my suspicions. He did conspire to hurt me. Even though the KKK and Skinheads weren't known to work together, I knew Judge Beck had great influence over all types of people. He could easily set things up without a soul knowing he had anything to do with it.

Kate drove straight to her house, where we reported everything to her mother. Marilou was furious. But, based on all she knew about Judge Beck, she reasoned it was best to leave things alone.

"Thank God you had the mace and the presence of mind to use it," Marilou said. We sat down on the sofa on either side of her. She put her arms around both of us and pulled us close. I rested my head on her shoulder. All three of us held onto each other for a long time.

"It was pretty freaking scary," Kate said between sniffs.

"I'm just glad Kate was there," I said through my own tears.

Marilou stroked our heads. "It's going to be okay, but you will have to tell your parents."

"I know. I'll tell them when I get home tonight."

At the dinner table, I picked at my food, waiting for the right moment to say something. Dad beat me to it.

"It looks like I'll be hanging around the house a bit more. The newspaper let me go today."

"What?" Mom said.

"Don't worry, Luella. I've already applied for unemployment. I will still have some salary coming in for a while, and that should give me plenty of time to secure another job."

"What happened?"

"Bob said sponsorship is low, and budget cuts forced him to let go of staff."

"That's odd. Bob's always said you're the best reporter on staff," Mom said. "It doesn't make sense for him to let *you* go."

"I know, but Bob wouldn't tell me anything else."

Seizing the moment, I decided to speak up. "Um, Mom, Dad, I have something to tell you." Their attention turned to me. "Remember that gang at school I've been telling you about? Well, today they cornered me in the hall."

Almost in sync, Mom and Dad glanced at each other, and then back at me. Dad swallowed quickly.

"Did they hurt you?"

Mom dropped her fork. "What happened?"

"No! I'm fine. Kate came to my rescue. It was really kind of cool. I sprayed this one guy with mace, and we got away. No problem."

"Thank God Kate was there. Did you report them?" Mom asked.

"The janitor saw everything and called the police. They arrested one of them."

It didn't take much for my dad to put two and two together. He squeezed my arm. "I want you to be very careful from here on out, Nicole. I mean it. Don't go anywhere alone. Judge Beck is behind all this. I just know it. I don't know how, but I'm going to find out. In the meantime, you can't see Johnny anymore."

"No way! It's not Johnny's fault his dad's a jerk!"

"Nicole, it's the only way you're going to stay safe," he said firmly.

"I agree with your father on this one," Mom said. "You need to stay away from him."

"But Mom, we really like each other, and he's asked me to the Moonlight Dance. Johnny's not like his stupid dad."

"It doesn't matter what Johnny thinks," Dad added. "His father is Judge Beck."

"And his father has the power to ruin your life," Grammy said.

"Mommy, is Judge Beck a bad man?" Jackson asked.

"Is he going to kill us?" Shelby blurted.

"No, no, children," Mom said, looking at Grammy with eye signals. "He's not going to do any such thing. Now you two get ready for bed and stop this."

Grammy herded them down the hallway. "Come on, you two."

After pleading unsuccessfully, I stormed to my room and slammed the door.

-13-

Jasmine and Child

I placed the lantern near the bed, where Jasmine lay sleeping. She stirred slightly, moaned, and tried to look around.

"You're all right, Jaz," I said. "We moved you into my bedchamber until you get your strength back. Etta and Willow can tend to both you and the family this way."

"I can't see," she said with a weak voice. "Where's my baby?"

Tessa walked out of the shadows holding the small bundle in her arms. "You have a baby boy, Jaz," she said, smiling.

Jasmine tried to sit up. "Ah!"

Maggie bent over her and gently pushed her shoulder. "No, Miss. You must stay in bed. You lost a lot of blood."

"I want to see my baby."

Tessa lay the infant beside her.

Jasmine touched the tiny feet and hands with her fingers. She rubbed her cheek on the baby's head, but then started to panic.

"How come I can't see?"

I placed my hand on her shoulder. "Doc said you might have blurred vision for a while, but it should go away soon."

"I can't believe he's still alive," she said. "I wish I could see him. Oh, Mama, is he beautiful?" She pulled the baby closer to smell his sweet breath and rubbed his soft face. His tiny fingers wrapped around hers, his sweet gurgles brought a smile to her face.

Tessa drew closer. "Yes, he is a little miracle baby. And so are you. God is so good and he answered our prayers to save both of you. You're both a Christmas miracle."

The baby wheezed and coughed. He had trouble catching his breath.

"What's wrong? He's not breathing right," Jasmine said with alarm.

Maggie gently patted her arm. "Doc Shaw said the babe is a bit small, but he will grow in time."

Tessa took the baby and handed him to the nursemaid, sitting near the fireplace. "You don't worry, now. We'll take care of the baby, Jaz. You just rest. We have a nursemaid. Etta's sister just gave birth again and has plenty of milk. She's going to nurse your baby too. Isn't it wonderful how God provides?"

Jasmine turned when she heard the babe suckling at the breast. "I wish I could nurse him myself, but I thank you for seeing to my child's needs." She touched my hand. "Miss Constance?"

"Yes, Jaz, I'm right here."

"I want to name him Benjamin."

I smiled. "After Benjamin Franklin?"

"Yes, Benjamin Franklin, Simon, James, William Miller," she said faintly.

Etta walked in with an extra blanket just in time to hear all the names. Her eyes widened. "Think she got 'em all in there?"

Tessa crossed her arms and said, "Hmm-hum!"

I chuckled, and then said, "Well, that's a mighty fine name for a baby boy, Jaz. I'm sure he'll be a mighty fine fellow someday."

Jasmine started to laugh, but then flinched. "Ow!"

"You rest now," I said. "You need to get your strength back." I watched over her for a while until everyone left and all was quiet except for the sound of the crackling fire. After adjusting the blanket one last time, I blew out the lamp and closed the door behind me.

Elizabeth was already sound asleep when I crawled into bed beside her. Before dosing off, I folded my hands and whispered a prayer of thanks.

Two weeks after Jasmine delivered, gossip about the slave baby soared around town. At the general store, Andrew helped Elizabeth and me out of the covered buggy. I instructed him to meet us in front once he finished loading the supplies. The bell jingled as we entered the store. I could hear Mrs. Busby shush the others. Mrs. Willis stood at the counter, where I greeted her.

"Good afternoon, Mrs. Willis."

"Good afternoon, Constance ... Elizabeth," Mrs. Willis gave each of us a polite nod. "Your order will be ready in just a moment."

"Thank you," I said.

The Proctor family had a standing order to pick up once a week at the store, and Mrs. Willis always knew to have it ready. Elizabeth looked at the candy, while I noticed the two women glancing at us. I smiled politely, but Mrs. Busby turned her nose up and looked away. She stood at the fabric table in the far corner, whispering to the others, who sneaked peeks at me over their shoulders. None of them participated in the SSS, few knew of its existence. The women continued to whisper among themselves. Finally, Mrs. Willis finished bundling the items. I reached for the package with one arm, herding Elizabeth with the other.

"Let's go."

"I want a sugar plum," Elizabeth pouted.

"But I've already got everything," I said.

"You said I could get something if I was good, and I was good," she insisted.

"All right then." I looked at Mrs. Willis, and said, "Please?"

"Sure, what color would you like?" Mrs. Willis said.

Elizabeth took her time, and finally said, "Blue, please."

"Shall I put this on account?" Mrs. Willis asked.

"That'll be fine." As soon as Elizabeth got her sugarplum, I yanked at her arm.

"Stop pulling me," she whined.

"Hurry up," I said.

Andrew assisted us into the buggy and placed the bundled items beside him on the front seat. I glanced over my shoulder and saw Mrs. Busby—the town's biggest gossip—watching from the window. I should make sure to tell Mother about this when we arrived home.

On the way home, we passed the church near the center of town.

Elizabeth pointed. "Look Constance, it's the new cemetery and flower garden."

"Oh, they planted roses and jasmine just like in our garden at home."

This brought to mind the day Father arrived home with a box of essential oils from the Apothecary shop after a trip to Philadelphia. I remembered holding up the glass vials and taking in each bouquet.

"What do you do with them?" Jasmine asked.

"Make hot teas or healing potions. This one's a perfumed fragrance," I dabbed a small amount on Jasmine's wrist.

She sniffed. "Hmm! That's nice."

"It's jasmine oil. Here." I handed her the small

corked bottle. "My gift to you for your wedding night," I said, wishing it were I instead of her marrying Simon.

A jerk of the buggy jarred my thoughts back to the present. I chastised myself and whispered a prayer of repentance. Jasmine had given Simon a son, and here I was imagining myself in her place. How disgraceful of me to think such things or dare entertain such thoughts.

I arrived home and immediately checked on Jasmine and the baby. The babe coughed and gasped, desperate for breath. Jasmine, stressed, not having slept, paced the floor. She picked him up, patted him on the back, and bounced him on her shoulder. Nothing seemed to work.

"Miss Constance, I don't know what else to do."

Susanna entered the bedchamber. "How's the baby?"

"He can't breathe, Mother. What should we do?"

"Where's the box of oils your father brought from Philadelphia?"

"It's in your room," I said.

"Willow, run and fetch it for me, and tell Etta to bring a kettle of hot water, a bowl, and some towels."

"Yes, ma'am," Willow said. The nursemaid attempted to feed the baby again.

"What can I do, Miss Susanna?" Jasmine asked.

"Just rest for now. Save your strength."

Willow and Etta arrived, items in hand. Susanna opened the box, ran her finger along each bottle label, stopping at eucalyptus.

"Here it is." She opened the bottle and poured a few drops onto a dampened towel. When it had cooled to the touch, she lay it across the baby's chest, then another towel with more drops across the baby's neck. She instructed Willow to re-soak and reapply the towels every few minutes, and told Etta to keep the hot water coming. After several times, soaking and reapplying warm towels, the baby's cough subsided, his breathing calmed. He suckled for a full feeding and fell asleep.

"Thank you Miss Susanna. If you hadn't been here, I don't know what I would have done," Jasmine said. She crawled back into bed to get some sleep.

The baby struggled for several days. Hungry. Unsatisfied. The gasping and coughing faded to silence, and finally, sweet death, God's way of a mercy killing. I watched helplessly as Jasmine fell to the floor, wailing, rocking the small, lifeless body.

She cleared her things from my room later that day and returned to the servants' quarters, never speaking of her child's death again.

The following day as we both tended to chores, a horse drawn wagon came into view. Rather than the usual load, Andrew carried a small box and headed to the servants' quarters. Strain lines formed on Jasmine's face, and my heart sank. She left the house and followed as if in a funeral march, her arms limp. The box, a bitter reminder of the child she could never hold again.

Grabbing our cloaks, I caught up to her and covered her shoulders. Jasmine stopped near the steps of the servants' quarters, staring blankly at the intended coffin. Tessa came to her daughter's side and gently took her hand. "Come on, Baby. There's work to be done inside the house."

Christmas in the colonies incited controversy for some and celebration for others. The Proctor family honored the season without a lot of fanfare. Father kept the focus on the Christian faith. He allowed simple homemade gifts, but only one per person.

A tree stood in the parlor, modestly decorated with simple ornaments. Pine wreaths and garlands hung over the doors and fireplaces. The whole house smelled of cinnamon, gingerbread, and pine. Instead of the usual goose, Mother presented a baked ham from Martha Washington and fig pudding for dessert. Elizabeth and I started a new tradition. We made small bags, filled them with sweet surprises, and laid one at each plate. The joy of the season graced the farmstead with a peaceful, serene ambiance as a fresh snow greeted us on the yuletide morning.

Jasmine tied the bows on my dress. I could see in the vanity mirror, her drawn face and tight stare. Through the dining hall window, I watched snowflakes fall in the bitter cold, and I imagined her despair deepening in sorrow. It saddened me to think of

Simon’s pain when he received the letter, telling him the tragic news.

-14-

Field Trip

I could hardly wait for Saturday to get here. I looked forward to getting away from the city, leaving Johnny, the skinheads, and my father behind. Till then, I kept busy helping Kate with homework assignments. The science fair was the following week, and she still had work to do on her project. Even though the near-constant phone calls from Ronald Ripley were annoying, he came in handy on the forensic side of things.

Kate lay on the ground in the driveway as Ronald drew with chalk to outline her body, while I recorded the evidence.

"Am I dead enough yet?" Kate said, flatly.

"One more second." Ronald twisted around on his knees to finish off the line at the top of her head. "Done." He stood up and gave Kate a hand to help her to her feet. "Okay, we've created the crime scene," he said, while adjusting his glasses. "Now we have to dust for fingerprints." Ronald pulled out a vial of powder he had concocted and started the dusting process.

Kate took pictures of the crime scene, while I

completed my notes.

Ronald finished all the dusting and then tried to talk us into helping him analyze everything on the computer.

"I have to be at work in a half-hour," Kate said. "And I still have to put on my uniform."

"Yeah, I've got stuff to do too," I said.

"Oh, okay, don't worry about it, then," Ronald said. "I can take care of the analysis."

"Great! So I guess this means we're almost done?" Kate said.

"Uh, almost. We still need to type up a report, then make the display."

"I can do the typing," I said.

"Great! I'll email the results from the analysis to you, and we can meet later to create the display." Ronald put on his helmet. "By the way, Ladies, I've made special arrangements for the Moonlight Dance," he said with a juicy, goofy grin on his face.

"Okay," Kate said. "Thanks, Ronald. I really have to go now."

He hopped on his moped scooter and revved the engine before taking off.

I walked with Kate back to the house. "Woo-hoo, a real hot rod, there!"

"I hope he doesn't think of us as a couple," Kate said. "I mean, he's already said he considers me to be one of his best friends."

"He does come across a bit needy," I said.

"I feel guilty for agreeing to participate in this plan of yours, Nicole. Don't you think we might be taking advantage of Ronald?"

"Look, I don't think we're hurting his image at all. If anything, we're helping him."

"While *I* could end up being the laughing stock of the entire school and destroy my reputation forever. Is this really worth it?" She put a finger to her chin. "Gee, let me think—not!"

"You're not going to be humiliated. I guarantee the dress I've made for you will make you look drop dead gorgeous."

"It better!"

Kate worked the birthday party shift at Build-a-Bear in the mall. We made plans to meet after work. Kids ran and screamed throughout the store. It was pandemonium as I made my way through the mass of small bodies hurling themselves toward me in all different directions like a fireworks display gone badly.

Suddenly, I backed into someone. "Oops! Excuse me." I turned and saw a familiar face.

"Hey," Mike Coolsby said with a handsome grin.

"It's kind of hard *not* to run into somebody in this place."

"Yeah! What brings you here?" I said.

"It's my niece's birthday. Oh, there she is ... gotta go. See ya," he said, reaching for a little girl's hand.

I spotted Kate with stuffing nested in her hair, dressing a bear in bloomers and a petticoat to create

Scarlett O'Beara, complete with lace bonnet and camisole. Mike appeared next to her. I got within earshot and decided to hang back, giving Kate her moment with him.

When she saw him, the surprised look on her face said it all. There he was—Mike Coolsby—the cute guy from drama class in the last place she expected to see him.

"I thought I recognized you," he said.

Kate just stared, dumbfounded.

Come on, girl, say something.

"Uh, what brings you here?" Kate said.

"It's my niece's birthday," Mike said with a shrug and a crooked grin.

"Uncle Mike!" an ecstatic voice said, as a little girl about seven years old tackled him with a big hug.

"Hey!" Mike said as he scooped her into his arms. "Happy birthday, sweet thing!"

The little girl grabbed his hand. "Come on. I want to show you my bear." He had no choice but to follow. She pulled his arm, practically out of its socket.

"Oh, bye," he said, looking back. "I'll try to catch you later."

"Sure," Kate squeaked, her voice shaky and crackling slightly.

"Okay, just keep your cool," I said, coming up behind her.

She turned and looked at me. "How long have you been there?"

"Long enough to see you working it, girlfriend."

Kate rolled her eyes and smirked. "Oh, please. I hardly said anything before his niece pulled him away."

"Yeah, but he's really into you."

"You think?"

"Trust me. He keeps looking back over his shoulder to see you."

Kate took a quick glance. "Sure it's not you he's looking at?"

"No. You know the only guy for me is Johnny. Stop looking at him. You're way too obvious."

"No, I'm not. Am I?"

"Okay, let me help you out. Guys like a challenge. It's time to focus, Daniel San." I continued to coach Kate. However, her eyes did catch his at one point, and the blush on her cheeks gave her away. I shoved a bear in her arms for a quick recovery. "Hey, just smile and keep working," I said, "Okay, he's looking over his shoulder again. Pretend you don't notice."

Kate did just that, while I kept a lookout.

When Mike turned his gaze back to the party, I said, "Nice save!" High-fives.

Kate clocked out, and we walked to the food court. "How are things with you and Johnny?"

"It's okay. At first, I was mad, but Johnny started talking to me again at school."

"Yeah? Are you dating again?"

"Only in secret. It's a challenge, but something

about the secrecy keeps things exciting."

"That's got to be hard."

"Yeah, but we can't risk any of his Dad's people seeing us or suspecting anything. It really sucks."

"Have you told your parents?"

"No! And please don't say a word."

"Okay, but promise me you'll be careful. I'm worried."

"I'll be fine."

On Saturday morning, Grandma Winnie picked us up in her two-door marine blue compact car. I used our trip to the farmstead as an excuse to sleep over at Kate's the night before, and planned to meet with Johnny in secret. I didn't get back to Kate's house until sometime in the middle of the night, which left little time to sleep.

I slept in the car on the way, until we arrived at the old farmstead in Ravenswood, an hour-and-a-half later. Grandma Winnie parked the car next to the old deteriorated farmhouse. When we got to the front porch, she took a deep breath and closed her eyes, savoring the fresh country air.

"I haven't been here for years." She walked to the side porch and looked toward the back yard. "You can still see the river from here," she said. Her eyes gleamed as she pointed toward a clearing in the woods.

The front door opened, and a tall, elderly man

walked out to greet us. "Hello there," he said.

Grandma Winnie looked back over her shoulder and smiled. "Hi, Uncle Eyrie." She walked over to give him a gentle hug. "How are you, sweetheart? It's been so long since I've seen you."

"Well, it's good to see you. Where have you been?" he asked.

"At home, just busy with life," she said. "Oh, let me introduce you to my granddaughter, Kate, and her friend, Nicole."

"Hello." He held out a gnarly, arthritic hand.

Grandma Winnie said, "Kate, this is your Great Uncle Eyrie. He's your Great Aunt Linda's husband. You probably don't remember him, it's been so long." She leaned over and whispered. "He's eighty-eight years old and doesn't hear too well, so you might have to speak up a little."

"Nice to meet you," Kate said in a louder voice than usual. She attempted to shake his hand, taking care to clasp only one finger.

I did the same thing. "Hi," I said, feeling a bit awkward.

"Uncle Eyrie, do you mind if we take a look around?" Grandma Winnie asked. "The girls have been doing a history project at school."

"Sure, that's fine. Come on inside," Uncle Eyrie said. Grandma Winnie followed him and we filed in behind.

Kate whispered in my ear, "He looks like he's at

least a hundred and ten years old."

"Shh!" I whispered, afraid he might hear.

Winnie looked back over her shoulder. "Don't worry, he can't hear you."

Kate and I looked at each other and snickered.

The television blared from the living room. "If you don't mind looking around by yourselves, I'd like to get back to my program," Uncle Eyrie said, shoulders stooped, while walking to his chair.

Grandma Winnie patted his back. "That's fine. You go on, and I'll show the girls around."

Uncle Eyrie took slow, deliberate steps back to his chair and sat.

"Come on girls. There's something I want to show you in the kitchen." She went to the mudroom at the back door and started up a staircase.

"These are the servants' stairs. You can go all the way to the attic from here." We followed her up to the second floor and then down the hall to another set of stairs leading to the attic. "Remember how I told you this was a safehouse during the Civil War? Well, look here." She bent to pull a hidden lever behind an old chest. An opening appeared in the adjacent wall, revealing a small room.

"Is that where they hid the slaves?" Kate asked.

"Yes and there's another room downstairs in the cellar," Grandma Winnie said.

"But I thought you said they helped escaped slaves during the Revolutionary War too," I asked.

"Yes, that's when the hidden tunnel and the cellar were used. We added the secret room in the attic during the Civil War. Once the slaves made it across the Ohio River to free territory, many of them found work or started their own businesses. They purchased their own land and built their own houses. In fact, some very prominent black people lived during that time."

"Does Uncle Eyrie own this farm now?" Kate asked.

"Well, technically the historical society will own it upon his death. They want to make it into a museum and preserve it. Sue Proctor Miller actually has the deed to the property. She lives closer to town, though. She and Uncle Eyrie have an arrangement for him to live here. The historical society arranged for maintenance on the place until Uncle Eyrie dies or can no longer stay here alone. However, so far, he seems to be doing pretty well. So that could be a while yet."

"Who is Sue Proctor Miller?" I asked,

"She's one of the last living heirs, by marriage, to the Proctor estate."

"*One* of the last?" Kate asked.

"Your mother and I are heirs, and you are too, but we didn't want to take on the responsibility and expense of maintaining this place. Especially since, we live in Charleston. Come on, I want to show you the secret tunnel to the barn." She motioned for us to look out the window. "Can you see the barn?"

“Yes,” I said, teetering on my tiptoes.

Kate craned her neck. “I see it.”

“The tunnel starts there and goes all the way to the basement,” Winnie continued. “Come downstairs and I’ll show you.” The steps creaked as we followed her. She stomped to find a loose floorboard in the mudroom and bent over to pull it. A hidden hatch opened, revealing another set of stairs.

“Whoa,” I said.

“This is getting creepy,” Kate said.

Winnie pointed to a shelf on the wall. “Nicole, can you hold up that flashlight for me, please?”

I pushed some cobwebs aside and picked up the flashlight. Flipped the switch, but nothing happened, so I shook it. The light flickered, and then a stream of light pierced the cellar’s darkness.

Grandma Winnie found a broom and used it to clear cobwebs as we each made our way down the stairs. “Look around for a light switch.”

Two old oil lanterns rested at the bottom of the stairs. Kate found some matches and lit them. That helped to light the room until Grandma Winnie knocked the broom against a florescent ceiling lamp. She pulled the chain, and a dim light flickered. She pulled it again, and the entire room lit up so brightly we covered our faces.

“Well, this place obviously hasn’t been lived in for quite some time,” Grandma Winnie said, as she waved the dust away from her face and coughed.

"Personally, I can't wait for the historical society to get it and start renovating. It's been upgraded to add indoor plumbing and electricity, but not really renovated. It's over two hundred years old now." She started pushing on some of the stones in the wall. "Let's see, which one is it?" Suddenly the wall moved back and revealed a doorway, "Ah ha, here it is girls, the secret tunnel."

"Whoa!" I pointed the flashlight into the tunnel, leading the way through the door. Kate followed behind me, carrying one of the lanterns.

Grandma Winnie turned down the wick on the other lantern and watched the flame die. Then she followed us into the tunnel. "Careful now, those beams don't look very steady."

"This is so cool! But it's cold down here," I said, rubbing my arm.

"And creepy." Kate jumped back a little. "I see something in the corner." The shadowy figure of a rodent ran across the tunnel wall. "Eeww!"

"I hope there aren't bats in here," I said.

Grandma Winnie reassured us. "Oh, a little mouse isn't going to hurt us."

"That's a big so-called mouse, Grandma," Kate said.

"I don't think bats can get down here. Just follow the tunnel all the way. It comes out at the barn. You should see a ladder. Just climb to the top and push on the hatch." We walked steadily for what seemed a long way as Grandma Winnie shared a childhood memory. "I remember one year, we decided to make this tunnel into a haunted house. None of the kids wanted to walk through it, because it was so spooky and scary. Can you see the ladder yet?"

"No," I said. "It's just dark ahead."

"Anyway," she continued, "All the church people in town got upset, because they thought we were doing devil worship. Mama and Papa made us close it up."

"Grandma you're not helping the creepiness," Kate said.

"Wait, I think I see it," I said.

"Finally," Kate said.

"Oh good, I'm not used to walking this far, and my feet are starting to swell," Grandma Winnie said.

"Okay, almost there," I said.

Kate hung the lantern on a hook while I climbed the ladder. When I reached the top, I pushed against the hatch. "It won't open."

"Here, I'll come up to help you," Kate said. She pulled herself up to the top rung alongside me.

Grandma Winnie stood at the bottom and held the ladder steady while Kate and I pushed with all our might. The hatch stuck a little, but then flew open and dropped backwards with a thunk. Kate climbed out first, and I followed. Her grandmother made it to the top of the ladder, handed me the lantern, and climbed out onto the barn floor.

"Oh, my." Winnie coughed, panting heavily.

"Are you all right?" I asked as I set the lantern on a crate, turned the wick down, and watched the flame die.

"I'll be fine. I just have to rest a little."

I pushed open the stall door and walked into the middle of the barn, eyes darting from one dark corner to another. A loft shadowed the large open area.

After a few minutes, Kate asked, "Do you want me to bring the car over here, so you don't have to walk back to the house?"

"Oh, that would be good." Winnie retrieved her keys from her pocket and tossed them to her. A few minutes later, fully recovered, she sat up and wiped off her clothes.

"Feeling better?" I asked.

"Oh, yes. I'm fine now."

"This has been really fun and interesting. I really appreciate you taking the time to bring us all the way out here." I sat beside her.

"Don't mention it. I love this place. I grew up here. I have so many fond memories." She took a deep breath. "Hmm! You can still smell the tobacco, even now." I helped her stand, and we walked around. "We used to have barn dances in here when I was your age. It's amazing how some things stay long after people have gone." She took another deep breath, "You never know how significant your life is while you're still alive. I suppose that's why knowing where you come from helps make you who you are in life."

"I know what you mean," I said. "My mother and grandmother have always talked to me about my heritage. I think it's helped me feel a sense of belonging."

"Yes, it does. It gives us a sense of purpose for being here too."

Kate arrived. She drove to the house, and we said goodbye to Uncle Eyrie.

On the way home, Kate sat in the backseat. I sat in the front with Grandma Winnie.

"Okay, girls, what do you say we go to the Burger Hut?" she asked.

"I'm all for that. I'm hungry," Kate said.

"I'm thirsty," I said.

"Great, we're on our way. There's just one more stop before we head home."

After lunch, we found ourselves standing on the front porch of Sue Proctor Miller's home. I sipped on my drink, while Grandma Winnie pushed the doorbell. Chimed music played *"There's no place like home,"* and she sang along with it.

The door opened and a petite, elderly woman stood before us. With a sweet smile, she said, "Hello, what brings you here today?"

"Hi, Sue, remember me? I'm Winnie. Eyrie's niece from Charleston," Grandma said.

The woman paused and squinted her eyes to focus her gaze. "Oh, yes. How are you?"

"I'm doing great. I was just out at the farmstead to show it to my granddaughter, Kate, and her friend, Nicole." She pointed to each of us. "I was wondering if we could talk with you a bit."

"Sure." Sue opened the door wider. "Come on in. I have some fresh tea brewing. Would you like some?"

"We just ate, but iced tea sounds refreshing." Grandma Winnie sat her purse in a chair near the door. "Be back in a moment girls." Her voice trailed as she walked toward the kitchen. "I'd be glad to help."

I sat on an antique floral sofa, while Kate sat in a chair across from me.

"It smells like old people in here," Kate said, wrinkling her nose.

I rolled my eyes. "Duh ... that's because an old person lives here."

Winnie and Sue returned with refreshments.

"Here we go," Sue said, setting a plate of cookies on the coffee table in front of us."

"You don't have to go to all this trouble for us." Grandma Winnie set a glass pitcher filled with iced tea on a doily.

"Oh, it's no trouble, I enjoy having company. How's Eyrie doing?" Sue asked, while taking a seat on the sofa next to me.

Kate grabbed a snickerdoodle.

Grandma Winnie sat in the chair next to her. "Eyrie seems to be doing fine. He was watching TV when we left."

"How'd the house look?" Sue inquired.

"Well, it looks as good as it could, considering it's over two hundred years old now." She drank her tea and chatted while Kate and I sipped our sodas. Finally, Grandma Winnie got to the real reason for our visit. "Sue, would you mind showing the girls that map you have of the original Virginia colony? They're doing a school project for history."

Sue said, "Oh, sure, it's right over here on the dining room table."

Winnie pushed the dimmer switch. There on the table lay a large piece of parchment with distinct lines and legends—an old-world kind of map.

"The king of England gave this land to George Washington," Sue explained. He surveyed it initially. William Proctor purchased the land from Martha Washington a few years after her husband's death. The table and chairs came with the estate. Been in the family ever since."

"Wow," Kate said. "Mind if I take a few pictures?" She pulled out her cell phone.

"Go right ahead," Sue said.

"What are you planning on doing with the map?" I asked as the camera clicked and flashed around me.

"I have contacted the Smithsonian Institute in Washington, D.C. and they are very interested in acquiring it."

"That sounds like the right place for it." I moved around to the other side of the table so Kate could take more pictures.

"The furniture will go back to the farmstead, once the historical society renovates it for public viewing. But that's going to be a while yet."

"Just one more." The flash of the camera blinded me. "There, that should do it," Kate said.

On the way home, I ached with anticipation to know the rest of the story Grandma Winnie had promised to tell. Kate fell asleep in the backseat, while I sat in the front and finally mustered up the courage to ask.

"Um! Remember when we were talking about the symbols on the sampler, and you started to tell us about Aunt Constance and the twin babies?"

"I'm surprised it took you this long to ask." She looked in the rearview mirror. "Kate's asleep in the backseat. Be sure and tell her later for me."

"I will."

"Well, there's a reason why I never gave those journals to Kate before now. We've been very careful to keep this a family secret. I think you'll know why, once you hear it." She sipped her drink, and then continued, "After her first husband died in the war, Constance discovered she was pregnant during a visit back home at the farmstead. Her mother insisted she stay until after the birth. Of course, in those days they didn't know they were having twins before they gave birth. The first baby came out all right, but the second baby ..."

"The doorstep to the temple of wisdom is a knowledge of our own ignorance." — Benjamin Franklin

-15-

Mr. Franklin's Hat

At the settlement's general store, Andrew waited while I went inside to pick up our weekly order of supplies. I bounced on my feet as I waited in eager anticipation. Suddenly, the stagecoach barreled into town, snow billowing. The arrival was always a highlighted event. Parents with children and shopkeepers made their way to the covered walkways. I stepped onto the boardwalk just as the coach came to a stop. A stout gentleman wearing spectacles peered through a snow dust-covered window. I recognized him immediately in his fashionable travel attire.

My heart skipped a beat when Simon appeared carrying bags. He wore an overcoat with a white wig and a tricorn hat. Careful to keep his composure, he opened the door and stood back regally, holding out an arm to support the special passenger as he stepped down.

"Mr. Franklin, sir?" I said.

"Yes?"

"I'm Constance, daughter of Master William Proctor. I'll be accompanying you to the plantation from here."

"Ah, lovely to meet you, my dear. I'm looking forward to seeing your father again," he said, tipping his hat. "This is my personal assistant, Simon Miller."

Simon bowed.

I curtseyed.

At that same moment, Mrs. Busby walked the steps to the general store, ogling our every move. I sensed the wonderment and envy of the whole town surrounding us.

Andrew grinned, I presumed humored at Simon's appearance. He cleared his throat and wiped the smirk from his face as I and Mr. Franklin walked past him. Simon assisted first Mr. Franklin and then me into the carriage. He took a seat next to Andrew on the front bench.

A short distance away, I noticed Mrs. Busby peering out the general store window. No doubt, the entire town would be buzzing about the special arrival in a matter of minutes.

Andrew slapped the reins and the carriage jerked to a start. I sat across from Mr. Franklin and tried my best to carry the conversation until we reached the farmstead.

Upon entering the foyer, my father greeted him. "Ben, my old friend," he said, and then smiled, reaching to shake his hand. "How wonderful to see you again. Please come in. Maggie, tell Etta to bring some tea."

"Yes, sir," Maggie replied.

He led the way into the parlor.

Mr. Franklin removed his hat. "I do apologize for such late notice."

"Nonsense, you are welcome here anytime. I was quite pleased to hear of your visit. Did you wish to preside over the ceremony?"

"It will be my pleasure," he replied. "When Simon told me Jasmine named the child after me, it touched me deeply. However, I do realize a slave's funeral is not usually recognized. I hope this doesn't place you and your family in a bad light with the settlement."

Father continued, "On the contrary. I am not concerned in the least. There is a movement toward the abolitionist view here about. In fact, your being here has only helped to further enlighten the settlers' understanding. Besides, I'm sure it will help promote healing for the loss as well."

Mr. Franklin dabbed at the snow melting on his wig, and I handed him a handkerchief. "Father, Mr. Franklin may be in need of rest now."

"Oh, do forgive me," Father said. "You must be

tired after such a long journey. Would you like to take leave before dinner is served?"

"No, no, I'm fine," he said.

While the two men continued to talk, I slipped out to find Mother in the kitchen. She grew nervous when she heard Benjamin Franklin had arrived.

"Oh, my goodness! Etta, check the guest chamber. Make sure everything is perfect. Let's see, I think we may need a few more things for supper tonight."

"But, Miss Susanna, I have to serve the tea," Etta said.

"I'll take care of that. I need to visit with Mr. Franklin anyway. Constance, I need you to go back to the general store and take Elizabeth with you. She needs to get out of the house. Willow, run and fetch Andrew before he gets to the barn. Tell him I need him to take the girls into town, and then come help Etta finish preparing supper."

"Yes, ma'am," Willow said. She rushed out the back door.

"What can I do to help, Mother?" I said.

"Hand me that tray and fill the sugar bowl," she said, as she continued listing things she wanted to get.

We arrived at the general store and Mr. Willis, the owner, greeted us in his usual grumpy manner. I preferred going in the mornings when Mrs. Willis worked, but with Mother so rattled, I had no choice but to comply.

"Well, what do you want?" he said.

"Good afternoon, Mr. Willis. My mother has a few more things to purchase." I handed him a list. "And we will need some apple cider for dinner tonight."

"Just sold my last gallon this morning," He said. "Are you celebrating something?"

"We have a special guest."

"Who is it?"

I hesitated, but Elizabeth blurted it out. "It's Benjamin Franklin!"

"Benjamin Franklin? Is that the older gentlemen I saw walking around outside when the stagecoach arrived?" Willis said.

"Yes, sir! We picked him up earlier," I said. "He decided to come at the last minute."

Mr. Willis leaned on the counter and narrowed his eyes. "Is he here for that slave baby funeral?"

"Yes, sir, the baby was named after him," I said, rather shocked at his candor.

Mr. Willis pounded his fist on the counter. "What's a slave doing naming her baby after such a great man as Benjamin Franklin? That's just going too far. Who does she think she is? I'm not selling anything to help a slave benefit herself by taking a good man's name like that. Now get on out of here."

I pushed Elizabeth out the door. Mrs. Busby stood nearby and watched as the scene unfolded. Soon the whole town heard about what happened.

Back at the Farmstead, Elizabeth and I entered the parlor in tears.

"Girls, what's wrong?" Mother asked.

"Mr. Willis won't sell us anything," Elizabeth said. "Because the slave baby was named after Mr. Franklin."

"What?" Father said.

"It's true. He was awful to us," I cried. "He thinks Jasmine is trying to use Mr. Franklin's good name for her own benefit."

Mother stood up. "How dare he accuse Jasmine of such a thing." She looked at Mr. Franklin, and then regained her cordiality. "Oh, Mr. Franklin, please excuse me. Girls, we're forgetting our manners." With appropriate gestures, she proceeded. "You've already met our eldest daughter, Constance, and this is our youngest, Elizabeth."

We both curtseyed to him.

Mr. Franklin looked back and forth at both of us. "What lovely girls. I'm so sorry to hear of this unfortunate occurrence."

Mother sat again. "Mr. Franklin, I assure you, Jasmine would never have done such a thing. I'm afraid Southern colonists are still very much caught in their old stubborn ways of thinking."

"Yes, Mr. Franklin," I said in all earnest. "Jasmine is innocent. She only wanted to honor you for all you've done for her husband. She didn't even know who you were until she got the letter from Simon, and I told her about you."

Franklin wiped his spectacles with a handkerchief. "Well, no doubt the townspeople have a misunderstanding of sorts. Simon has been a bright and loyal worker. He should be at master printer level in the not too distant future."

"That's quite good of you, Ben," Father said.

Etta entered the parlor. "Dinner is served."

The day of the ceremony, the entire settlement showed up at the farmstead. I suspected much speculation and gossip circulated about Mr. Franklin's arrival, which no doubt prompted Mrs. Busby to influence wise propitiousness in honor of such an esteemed visitor. Even Mr. Willis showed up with a jug of cider. Mrs. Willis said he found it in the cellar. There was not enough space to accommodate all the horses, carriages and wagons. Thomas and George directed everyone to move near the barn. Simon and Jasmine stood together, looking around, confounded at the turnout.

"Who are all these people?" Jasmine asked.

"They're all from the settlement," I said.

Mr. Franklin stood at the gravesite surveying the townspeople mingling about him. My father stood next to him, and I lingered near. Mr. Franklin leaned over my father's shoulder and said, "I'm afraid it will take little ritual, but more clever speech to lead these new found friends to righteousness."

Father nodded as Franklin cleared his throat to speak.

"Welcome, friends. We gather here today to remember a precious one given to us but for a short time. It is for God alone to know His purpose in giving and in taking away. Here lies Benjamin Franklin Simon James William Miller, whom some of you have said was not worthy of such an honorable name. Yet, who are we to judge for the Almighty and just God as to who is worthy and who is not worthy?" He paused. "This family grieves a great loss for one whom they will never see to maturity. All flesh is the same inside no matter what color the skin. It matters not how well we speak, how noble our heritage, or how much our deeds may prove our character. We all bleed the same color. We all feel the same pain when life delivers the bitter with the sweet." He paused again while turning the pages of his Bible.

"To Simon and Jasmine Miller, the word of our Lord says, His grace is sufficient for thee." He looked out over the crowd. "And to you, my dear brethren, the word of the Lord says, for to whom much is given, much is required. Let us pray. Dear Lord God, forgive us our trespasses as we forgive those who trespass against us. Lest all our longsuffering benefit us not, and those who remain ignorant of the gospel of peace should find us in contempt toward one another. For thine is the kingdom, and the power, and the glory forever. Amen!"

Franklin raised his head. His eyes scanned faces. He placed his hat upside down on top of the small coffin. "If there be any repentance of heart among you, my good men of faith, then share the fortune imparted to thee by the grace of our Savior. For the sake of our own learning, it is said, a little child shall lead them." Franklin dropped a paper note of generous amount into the hat. He walked over to stand next to Simon and Jasmine, who stood perfectly stunned and wide eyed.

Slowly, some of the children placed homemade toys near the grave. One by one, the head of each household dropped a coin or a paper note into the hat. One small boy, about seven years of age, threw his arms around Jasmine's waist and hugged her tightly. Still in a state of shock at the overwhelming generosity, she put her arms around him and sobbed.

Mr. Franklin's hat filled to the brim and overflowed. I counted the coins and paper notes. The total amount added up to more than enough for them to start a new life in Philadelphia.

-16-

Moonlight Dance

The harvest moon glowed red-orange as it greeted us on our way to the Moonlight Dance. With the first six-week's exams completed, every teenager in town was ready to rock the night away. My plan worked like a charm. Ronald Ripley arrived at Kate's house nearly half an hour early. I peeked over the bannister to see him dressed to the nines in a black tuxedo, complete with bow tie and black rimmed designer glasses.

I'd slept over the night before to make the finishing touches on Kate's dress. I told my parents I was going to the dance with Kate and Ronald, which was the truth. My admirable cause in making Kate the bell of the ball impressed my mother. She had dropped Kate and me at the salon earlier that day to get our facials, hair, and nails done. I was careful to keep my own dress less extravagant, so as not to overshadow Kate's special moment.

Ronald certainly didn't mind the idea of taking two dates to the dance. He stood agape as we each descended the stairs.

I wore a simple off-the-shoulder satin blue gown that complemented my eyes. Kate looked like a fairy tale princess in a white flowing gown with sparkling sequins. She looked stunning, just as I'd promised.

"Okay, smile," Marilou said.

The flash of the camera made me blink. "I hope my eyes weren't closed."

Ronald delivered on making special arrangements, ensuring we arrived in style. He provided us both with a wrist corsage, then offered us each an arm.

"Ladies, our carriage awaits," he said with a cocky grin, escorting us to a chauffeured-driven limousine parked in the driveway.

"I've never been in a limo before." Kate said, bouncing on the seat. "Gosh, I really do feel like a fairy tale princess now. Thanks Ronald."

"I just wanted you two to feel special tonight."

"Thanks, Ronald," I said. "This is really cool of you to take both of us."

Ronald straightened his bow tie. He placed a cigar in his mouth and spoke like a mob king, "Just sit back and enjoy da ride, ladies."

Ronald was in all his glory walking into the dance with a beautiful girl on each arm. Everyone complimented Kate on her dress, and she was quick to tell everyone I designed it for her.

I followed Kate's gaze to the other side of the room where Mike Coolsby—the ultra-cute drama star—headed right for her. Thinking quickly, I distracted Ronald by asking him to get refreshments. I was looking around for Johnny, when Mike walked past me and stopped in front of Kate. I stayed close enough to listen.

"Hi again," he said with a smile. "Kate? Right?"

"That would be me," Kate smiled back at him.

"You look great," he said, as he looked her up and down.

"Thanks. Anything's an improvement over bear stuffing." Kate blushed and fidgeted with her dress.

"Would you like to dance?" Mike asked as she glanced my way.

"Sure." Kate took his arm as they walked onto the dance floor.

I was watching my friend from a distance, when Johnny emerged from the crowd. After that, I only had eyes for him. We met in an embrace and kissed each other lightly on the lips. As we began to dance, a professional photographer offered a photo op and took a close-up.

Johnny held me close as we danced to a slow song. Our being together was all that mattered to me.

"Did you remember to bring a bag?" he asked.

"Yeah, I put one in my locker yesterday. How are we going to get there?"

"I borrowed a friend's car. I just told my parents I was spending the night with him."

"I told mine I was sleeping over with Kate again.

What about the fake IDs?"

"Took care of that, too," he said as sparkling lights and rainbow colors moved across our faces.

"Good." I leaned in to kiss him again.

"You're sure this is what you want?" he asked.

"Yes," I said, confidently. "Aren't you?"

"Yes. I love you, Nicole."

I smiled at that assurance. "I love you too." We kissed again, this time a little more passionately.

After we had secretly dated for weeks, attraction grew quickly into love, and we planned to elope that night. It was the only way to break the curse of racism surrounding us. I didn't tell Kate for I knew she'd try to talk me out of it. Johnny arranged to meet with a minister across state-lines in Ashville, Kentucky, to keep everything secret from his father.

As I rested my head on his shoulder, I saw Kate dancing with Mike. Our eyes met and we smiled. I mouthed to her *dreams really do come true.*

After her dream dance with Mike Coolsby, Kate relished his lingering attention.

Ronald Ripley arrived, carrying two plastic cups filled with red punch.

Perceiving disaster, I ran toward her. "Kate!"

In that brief second, Ronald took his eyes off where he was stepping, tripped on the train of another girl's dress, and fell forward. Punch splashed all over the front of Kate's dress. Her once-white gown now stained with various hues of pink, burgundy, and deep purple. Standing motionless with her mouth open in a state of shock, Kate stared down at her gown and watched as her dream turned into a nightmare. Red punch penetrated the fabric of her dress, creating large splotches from the top of the bodice to the hemline.

"Ronald, you clumsy moron!" she screamed.

"Oh, no, Kate, I'm so sorry." Ronald fumbled with his glasses, trying to steady himself on his feet.

One of the more popular girls in school started to laugh. "The clumsy oaf did it again!"

Kate ran to the locker room hoping to rescue the dress from any further staining. At least one friend, Sandy, thought to grab a can of cream soda and ran to catch up with her. I ran after them. Once in the locker room, I helped Kate take off the dress and placed it over the sink.

Sandy dabbed at it with a paper towel drenched in cream soda.

Kate went to her locker to change into gym shorts.

Sandy continued to dab, but with no luck. "You know what? Simple Green might work on this. I hear it takes out red wine on carpet."

"Simple Green?" I said, distraught that all of my hard work was now ruined. "This fabric is way too fine for that. I don't think cream soda is going to help either. We should ask my mom. She's really good at this kind of thing." I pulled out my cell phone and called her. It went to voice mail. I left a message for her to call Kate about the dress.

Johnny cracked open the locker room door and called out, "Nicole? Are you ready to go?"

"Be right there," I said, and went to my locker to retrieve my overnight bag. I stopped to check on Kate. "I left a message on Mom's voice mail to call you about the dress. Just make sure not to mention anything about Johnny and me. Okay?"

Kate grabbed my arm. "Wait, where are you going?"

I glanced over at Sandy, who was still working on the dress, then pulled Kate back into the locker area away from Sandy's earshot. "Johnny just wants to show me something. I'll be back later," I whispered.

"Then why are you taking a bag?" Kate whispered back. "And why are we whispering?"

"I just wanted to change into something more comfortable."

"Uh-huh," Kate said. "Nicole, I know you're up to something. What is it?"

"Don't worry," I said, still whispering. "Johnny's taking care of me. He's dropping me off at my house later tonight, so don't wait up for me."

Kate looked into my eyes, "You sure about this?"

"I've never been surer in my life. Cover for me, please?"

"Yeah, okay, go on, get out of here. Have a good time," Kate said, waving me on. "I'll just stay here with a ruined dress and go home with a freakin' nerd, the story of my life. No problem."

"Sorry about the dress. Hopefully, Mom will be able to save it." I slipped Johnny's letter jacket over my shoulders. "I've gotta go." I leaned in for a hug. "Thanks."

"Yeah, yeah, bye," Kate said, glancing down and pushing her toe against hardened gum on the floor. Just then, her cell phone rang. "It's your mom."

I waited to hear what Mother told her to do.

Kate gestured an okay sign and waved goodbye, while whispering, "It's okay. Go."

I slipped out the locker room door as quiet as a cat and met Johnny in the hall. He grabbed my bag, and we ran out the side entrance of the school to the parking lot.

Our plan worked. Next morning, I was Mrs. Johnny Beck. We spent the rest of the night and the next morning at a bed and breakfast.

As Johnny held me, he said, "I've been accepted at a university in the Northeast."

"That's fantastic, but when do you have to leave?" I asked.

"Not till the end of summer."

"What am I supposed to do?"

"You're totally smart enough to test out and graduate early or just get your G.E.D," he said.

"Will a college accept that?"

"Yes! We'll be living close to New York City, which

is the hub of the fashion industry."

I sat up with a realization. "Johnny, this could really work, but there's still the problem with our families."

"Once we're out of West Virginia, there's not much they can do."

"But what are we going to do in the meantime?"

"Lie low and stay undercover." He called downstairs to the service desk and arranged for a late checkout. After hanging up, he grabbed the blanket and threw it over our heads.

On the drive back to Charleston, I called Kate.

"Where have you been? You're mother's been calling here all morning. I've held her off as long as I can, and I was starting to get worried about you."

"I got her voice mails, and I've already called her back. We should be there in a little while."

"Are you still with Johnny?"

"No, I'm with Frosty the Snowman. Who do you think I'm with?"

"Hey, you're the one who left me with the messed up dress.

"I know. I'm sorry," I said in a lowered tone.

"Yeah, well, it's a good thing Mike Coolsby came to the rescue."

"Oh, really?" I asked.

"I'll tell you all about it when you get here."

"Johnny's dropping me off at your place. I told Mom I'd bring the dress home with me tonight."

"Okay. See you soon."

"Bye." I slipped the phone into my purse and snuggled next to Johnny for our last few minutes alone.

-17-

Constance in Philadelphia

A few months after my arrival to Philadelphia, Jasmine and I started working at my aunt and uncle's upholstery shop. I'm sure the two of us appeared more like giggly schoolgirls instead of the master's daughter and slave girl Southern society once forced upon us. As we walked the cobblestone streets, Jasmine shared her matchmaking thoughts with me.

"Simon says Henry Leverton comes by the shop often. Mr. Franklin likes the flag work he does and wants to get some made for the congressional meetings."

"Henry's very good," I said. "I've been learning a lot from him and my friend Betsy."

Jasmine examined my face close, raising one brow. "Henry?"

"What?" I blushed, swatting Jasmine's arm.

"You call him Henry now?" Jasmine said.

"What's wrong with that?"

"Nothing. Simon says Henry asks about you every time he's in the shop."

"Well, he's always nice to me," I said, adjusting

my hat.

"Um hmm!" Jasmine gave a wry grin.

"Do you really think he favors me?"

"Yes, ma'am! He sure do!" she said with a wide grin.

I put my gloved hand to my chin. "Really?"

"Sure as the sun shines," Jasmine said, and we both giggled.

A few months later, I arrived at the door of the recently acquired townhouse, located not far from the print shop. I wore an elaborate sack-back gown and a heavily embellished chapeau. My white wig piled high and cascading ringlets made me teeter. I turned, stiff necked, to blow a loving kiss goodbye to my husband. He waved from the carriage and signaled for the coachman to leave.

While waiting for Jasmine to answer, my heart raced. I held a large package and studied my regal silhouette that filled the oval stained-glass window.

Jasmine opened the door with an awestruck look on her face. "Well, if it isn't the newly wedded Miss Constance."

"That's Mrs. Henry Leverton now, my dear." I said and wiggled my gloved hand to show off the ring on my finger. "Oh Jaz, New York is such an exciting place."

"You look wonderful! Come in, I'm so glad to see you." She stepped aside to allow room for my broad skirt and me.

I chattered away and set the package on the table. I removed my hat and gloves, taking care to replace the ring on my finger. "I felt like a queen as we walked down the streets of New York City, Jaz. The hotel was magnificent. And the nicest thing about the city is they have a horse and carriage on every corner. Jaz, you can get almost anything you want there. It's amazing."

"Sounds exciting. Would you like some tea?"

"Yes, please, I have so much to tell you." I followed her into the kitchen. "We went to see Simon Boydell's Gallery. There were pictures of actors performing in several of Shakespeare's plays. Then we went to the theater and saw 'Hamlet.' I've never seen such a beautiful building before." My eyes widened. "Jaz, the chairs are red velvet."

Jasmine carried a modest tea set on a tray into the parlor. "Oh, tell me more. It sounds lovely. I love the arts. Come sit and have some tea. Sugar?"

"Please," I said, remembering our childhood days. I sat down and stirred my tea, then took a sip. "Mmm, this is delicious."

"Thank you. Mr. Franklin brought it with him from Boston and gave some to Simon. When you're done, I'll show you around."

"Oh, yes, please do. But first, you must tell me how you've been doing these past few months."

"Well, I've started laundering at the new hospital on the days I'm not working at the upholstery shop. It brings in a little extra income."

"Aren't you happier living here in a free colony?"

"Yes, of course," she said, remembering something in her pocket. "Oh, there's something I wanted to share with you. Simon brought home a London pamphlet Mr. Franklin gave him after a trip abroad." She unfolded the article and held it out for me to see.

"What's this?" I asked.

"It speaks in regards to a woman of color raised as an equal alongside her British cousins."

"Who is she?"

Jasmine read aloud. "Dido Elizabeth Belle is the daughter of an African slave woman and a Royal Navy Officer, Sir John Lindsay. While completing his duty, he placed her in the care of his uncle, the Earl of Mansfield, who raised her as a free woman, given the same privileged upbringing as her cousins. Dido Belle induced great compassion over the plight of slavery to her beloved uncle, Lord Mansfield, who serves as Lord Chief Justice of England and Wales. Lord Mansfield's ruling on the Zong Massacre, in England's Court of King's Bench, was a huge victory in the call for justice, making providential strides in the abolitionist movement."

I sat next to Jasmine, pulling the paper closer to see the artist rendition of a portrait, two young women, one darker, but both depicted as equals. "She's so beautiful," I said. "This reminds me of the

Biblical Queen Esther story."

"That's what everyone at church is saying. In fact, the Scripture reading was from the Book of Esther," Jasmine said, quoting the part she remembered, "and who knoweth whether thou art come to the kingdom for *such* a time as this?" She spoke passionately and with conviction, mesmerizing me in a way I'd never seen before. "They talked about how God used Dido Belle to save our people, just like he used Esther to save the Jews."

"Remarkable. God is truly amazing in the way He brings things about," I said, agreeing wholeheartedly.

We finished our tea and walked through every room on the main floor.

"I love your wallpaper. The papers in our house above the upholstery shop are simply dreadful. I can't wait to change them. Oh, I see you have a Franklin stove, and what a fine mantel." I ran my hand across the top. "Everyone is going to be so proud of you when I tell them how well you and Simon have done. Mother wants me to fill her in on the details when I return home this fall."

"You're going back home? But I thought—"

"Yes, well, Mother finally convinced Father he was just being a stubborn, old mule. Henry doesn't lay claim to any particular religion, but he still believes in God, the same as I. He just prefers to keep his faith on a more personal level." I patted my tummy. "I hope to have some exciting news to share with the family by then." I grinned sheepishly.

Jasmine gasped. "No! Already?"

"With the new upholstery shop in Jersey doing so well and all, we didn't feel the need to hold off."

"Oh, Constance, how wonderful!" She lay a palm on my belly.

"I haven't confirmed with the doctor yet, but I will soon. I love living in the city, Jaz. Life here is so much better. Don't you agree?"

"It's definitely better for us," she said. "Now that Simon's a master printer, we are doing well enough that my family can come live with us soon. In fact, perhaps they could come back with you. Or at least Mama and Pearlie anyway. I know the Captain may not want to leave yet. He feels it's his calling to help slaves to freedom. I hope someone else takes over his duties soon. He's getting on in years."

"Jaz that would be so perfect. If they lived here, you could have another baby."

Jasmine looked down, crossed her arms, and turned away.

"Oh, no, Miss Constance." She shook her head. "Doc Shaw said I shouldn't have any more children."

"He's just an old country doctor. You know they have wonderful doctors here. Maybe you could see mine."

"Simon doesn't want me going through that ever again. It was bad enough I had to go through it without him the first time."

"I know that was a devastating time for you," I said, patting her shoulder. "But, you shouldn't let it keep you from trying again. Just go see my doctor and see what he says. You never know. Things are better here in the city, and we have a hospital."

"Miss Constance, I appreciate your kindness, but no doctor will see a black woman. Free or not, it don't matter none to them. If it wasn't for your family paying Doc Shaw last time, I wouldn't be here today. The only way *I'll* get inside a hospital is to work there."

"You're right. I feel foolish for even suggesting it now." Looking past her shoulder, the package on the table came into focus. "But in the meantime, I have a surprise for you."

"What did you bring me?" She smiled, and the tension left her face.

I retrieved the package and carried it to her. "I've been working on this for a long time. I hope you like it."

Jasmine untied the string and opened the box. She gazed in awe at the beautiful hand-embroidered quilt. "Oh, Miss Constance, this is the most beautiful work I've ever seen." Her fingers moved along the seam line. "Such fine stitching and workmanship. You made this for me?"

"Of course. You were always a faithful servant, but more importantly, you are a loyal friend to me now. It's the least I could do. Consider it a belated wedding gift. I hope it goes with your bedroom ensemble."

"That shouldn't be a problem since there's not much up there anyway." Jasmine giggled. "I'm sure it'll go just fine with everything. Thank you so much." She embraced me again.

"Let's go put it on the bed, and then we can talk about doing something about that décor." We carried the quilt up the stairs together and entered the master bedroom.

As we spread the quilt out over the bed, I looked up and said, "That window could use some drapes. I remember seeing some old fabric at my uncle's shop. It's in the back storage area. I'm sure you could fetch it for a good price. Uncle Abram might even give it to you."

"I hadn't thought about that. I will look when I get back to work," Jasmine replied. "So how have things been at the shop in New Jersey?"

I tucked the end of the quilt behind the footboard. "Martha Washington came in the other day, looking for fabric to decorate the new mansion on the Potomac. We actually see General George Washington at church sometimes, and he comes into the shop for tailoring on special occasions."

"Really?"

Hooves clip clopping on the cobblestone street alerted me. I looked out the window to see Henry descending the carriage steps. I took Jasmine by the arm as we walked down the stairs. "These visits are far too rare now that you aren't living closer. I pray my efforts as an abolitionist will help bring an end to segregation."

Jasmine nodded. "And slavery will be abolished once and for all."

"Yes," I said, staring deep. I leaned in for a hug, and we held each other tight for a long time. My chin quivered as I struggled to hold back tears.

"I hope we see each other again soon," Jasmine said.

I kissed each of her cheeks. "That's how the French do it," I said, grinning, and we both giggled.

My husband waited, hand outstretched, to assist me. Before stepping into the carriage, I hesitated, turned back, and reached for Jasmine's hand once again. She held mine tight, her lips trembling. I sensed the pain of separation affected her as deeply as it did me. Marriage had changed things—forced apart the sisterly bond we shared—yet not for any other reason than circumstance and status. Our time together had now ended. War loomed, clouding my temporary happiness, and I did not know when I might see my friend again. Dabbing my cheeks, I climbed inside, looking back at Henry, who bowed and tipped his hat.

"Jasmine, always a pleasure. Please give my regards to Simon."

"I will. Goodbye, Mr. and Mrs. Leverton," Jasmine said, blinking away tears.

Henry stepped into the carriage and knocked his

cane against the roof, signaling the coachman. Jasmine held her palm out to me and mouthed the words—blood sisters. I pressed my hand to the window, earnestly watching her fade from view. As the carriage bumped along the cobblestone street, a sobering thought came to mind. *We may be free from slavery, but we still fight the slavery within our own hearts and minds.*

A few months later, my husband suffered a gunshot wound while serving in the Revolutionary War. He died despite all my best efforts to nurse him back to health. Shortly following his funeral, I received a letter from Simon informing me of Jasmine's death, an infection of unknown origin. I fell to my knees, heaving, overwhelmed. I refused to eat, for every time I did, nausea overtook me.

I found solace in work, while suffering through the loss of, not only my husband, but also my dearest friend. Left with debt and orders to fill, the upholstery shop became my haven. The solitude offered an escape. I pulled and tugged the twine in a sofa frame as tears streamed my face. Suddenly, anger overcame me. I screamed, grabbed a chair, and threw it across the room, splitting it in half. Shocked. What had I done? Running to inspect the chair, panting, amazed at my own strength. I covered my mouth, realizing the chair wasn't mine.

Nonetheless, I did some of my finest work during

this time. My good friend, Betsy Griscom, now Ross, had also suffered the loss of her husband. She often sent extra orders my way to help cover her own demand as she owned and operated another upholstery shop not far from mine. We continued our work for the SSS as well.

I left my cousin and her husband in charge of my business affairs, while I went to Philadelphia for Jasmine's funeral. I stayed with relatives a few days, which allowed time to gather Jasmine's belongings and send them home to her mother. Carrying a basket, I walked to the townhouse where Simon greeted me at the door.

"Miss Constance." He nodded and stepped aside for me to enter.

"Hello, Simon. I brought you a freshly baked pie, some fried chicken, and corn-on-the-cob."

"Thank you kindly, ma'am."

We sat at the small kitchen table and ate in silence, little to no eye contact between us. Though we rarely saw each other, I still found the need to brace my senses while around him. My desire did not wane, not even after my marriage to Henry. However, marriage did help stave my longings for him.

Simon finished eating, and said, "Thank you, Miss Constance. The food was delicious."

"You're more than welcome," I replied. I cleaned up and walked the stairs to the bedroom. A few minutes later, I carried a large bundle of dresses stacked on top a quilt down the stairs and placed them on the dining room table. "I'll take these back home to Tessa. I'm sure Pearlie will be ready to wear them soon."

"Oh, yes. Pearlie should be a fine young lady about now," Simon answered. He walked to the table and ran his hand across the quilt, the one I gave to Jasmine as a wedding gift. "She always loved this."

I drew in a deep breath, trying to focus on the task at hand. "You should keep it to stay warm next winter and for the special memories." My eyes squeezed shut when I thought about the painful reality he might experience without Jasmine. "I'm so sorry," I said, and began to cry. "I just miss her so much." A lump the size of a cannon ball came up in my throat and caused my words to squeak. "She was my dearest friend. I don't know how I'm going to get along without her."

"I know." Simon pulled me close and embraced me. I cried into his chest, while remembering the last time Henry had held me only a few weeks earlier. As my tears calmed, his hold lingered and Simon gently kissed my forehead. I closed my eyes to relish the warmth of his breath on my brow. Was this really happening? The man I had secretly longed for all these years now held me in his arms. My hands slid over his biceps. The curve of his muscles made my heart race. He lifted my chin with one finger and swiped my tears with his thumb, using the other hand to brush aside a fallen bang. I raised my eyes to meet his, and suddenly, we found ourselves locked in a passionate kiss. I pushed away and wiped my lips as if to somehow erase the shame. Hands shaking, I tried to reset the pins in my hair, but they dropped to the floor. The long strands fell to my shoulders, whisking against my skin, pulse racing.

Simon reached for me.

With a soft touch, I pushed his hand, but his fingers intertwined mine. I surrendered and melted into him. We kissed in a frenzy, desperate to devour each other. Simon pushed the dresses and quilt aside. They fell to the floor. He grasped my waist, lifting me onto the table. "Oh," I squeaked out a hushed yelp. His impulsive strength surprised me. He continued kissing my neck and chest while pulling up my dress, feeling my legs still covered in undergarments. I glanced at the window, relieved to see the drapes closed.

Hours later, I was home. I sat in my rocking chair near the fireplace sewing a star sampler. My cheeks flushed. An unexpected joy warmed my heart when an idea came to mind. I fumbled through my sewing basket for more thread and pulled out the list of symbols.

-18-

Grandma Goes Home

The morning after our visit to the farmstead, I received an unexpected phone call.

Kate blubbered over the phone, "She's dead!"

"Who's dead?"

"Grandma! She didn't wake up. She was supposed to pick me up for church this morning. When she didn't show, Mom and I went to check on her."

"I'm so sorry! I really loved your grandmother." I sniffed and grabbed a tissue, while trying to console her.

The pews at the funeral hall filled up fast. People stood in the back, while ushers gathered more chairs to place down the aisles. Kate stood near the coffin, a blank stare on her face. I sat in the front row next to Marilou, because she invited me, and to support Kate. Grandma Winnie looked peaceful in her open casket. The guilt that made me think it was all my fault didn't help either. I figured when she walked through the tunnel it was just too much for her.

Kate's Uncle Roy played "Amazing Grace" on the

bagpipes. "She always loved the pipes," Marilou said.

At least a hundred people came by the house to pay their respects. Most of them brought food. I stayed to help clean up and went to the kitchen with Kate.

"Going to the farmstead with your grandma that day was so much fun," I said, handing Kate a plate.

"Yeah," she said.

"I was looking forward to going back with her someday."

"Well, maybe we can go by ourselves," Kate suggested. "Grandma left me her car. I could drive."

"Cool! You think we should set up some sort of memorial for her?"

Kate nodded. "Grandma would like that."

Marilou walked in. "Grandma would like what?"

Kate turned to face her. "Nicole was saying how we should put some sort of memorial up for Grandma at the farmstead."

"She always loved that place," Marilou said, placing dirty cups and saucers on the counter near the sink. "By the way, I'm going to need help cleaning her house and putting things into storage. Nicole, would you be available to help out next week?"

I turned to face her. "Sure, any time after school, except Thursday."

Marilou reached inside the pantry and pulled out the coffee canister. "What's on Thursday?"

"The historical society meets at the library after

school."

"Oh, yes, I remember Grandma mentioning how both of you were delving into family history for a school project." As she filled the coffeemaker with water, Marilou placed a new filter inside and scooped coffee grounds into it.

Kate pulled out plastic wrap to cover a cake. "Yeah, but we found out a lot more than we expected."

"Grandma told me about those symbols on the star sampler. That sounds fascinating," Marilou said, filling a tray with coffee supplies. "Be sure and keep me posted on anything else you find out," she said as she carried the tray to the living room.

Kate and I finished putting away the food and cleaned the counters.

Marilou met us at Grandma Winnie's house a few days later. "Hey girls, I'm pooped and need a break. I left you some boxes in the bedroom. There's some fresh lemonade in the fridge. Just box up everything. I'll get the bed linens later." She grabbed her purse and left.

We went right to work in the bedroom. I packed the bookcase while Kate packed the closet. I sat a box on the bed and noticed an old Bible on the nightstand. Before placing it into the box, a photo fell onto the floor. I bent down to pick it up. Just out of curiosity, I began thumbing through the pages of the Bible and came across a piece of parchment. I unfolded it and squinted to make sense of the swirly writing. My eyes followed the top line from left to right, and I was able to read *Proctor and slaves*. I flipped the photo over and read the writing on the back.

"Pearlie Anne Miller, great granddaughter of Simon Miller, Jr.," I said under my breath. "Kate, come over here. You have to see this."

"What?" Kate fumbled with hangers, tossing them to the floor. She pushed the box aside and sat next to me.

I held the parchment up. "This looks like the lineage of the Proctor family slaves. Your grandmother told me the story on our way back home from the farmstead. You were sleeping in the back seat at the time. This is proof that the family secret is true."

Kate shook her head. "Wait. What family secret?"

"Great Aunt Constance had a secret love affair with Simon Miller after both of their spouses died. She got pregnant and moved back home to the farmstead to have the baby. Everybody thought it was her deceased husband's child, but when she gave birth to twins, the secret was out."

"What secret?"

"The twins, one was black and the other was white."

"Is that even possible?" Kate said.

"Simon Miller, Jr. was the black twin." I pointed to

the picture. "This is Pearlie Anne Miller, his great granddaughter. Grandma Winnie said Simon Miller's mother took the black baby to raise as a slave." I pointed to the parchment paper and read, "Look, this says Simon Miller, Jr. (Adopted orphan found in the fields). This proves my true connection to the family and my inheritance rights. Kate, this means that we really are related to each other."

Kate grasped her forehead. "Okay, wait, this is a lot to process. We should talk to the historical society people just to make sure."

"Good idea! We need to show this to Anna May." I put the parchment back in the Bible and slipped it into my backpack.

We finished packing, locked up, and went back to Kate's house. I told Marilou the whole story, then pulled out the Bible.

Marilou sat at the kitchen table, a stunned look on her face. "Wow, that's got to be one of the most unique stories I've ever heard."

"It's the truth," I said.

"I can't believe we're actually related," Kate said. "I mean, I've always thought of you like a sister anyway."

"Me too," I said, relieved she was finally getting it. "I can't wait to tell Mama and Grammy."

Marilou gasped, "Nicole, wait! You should get confirmation first. We don't want to mislead anyone."

"I guess you're right. That's probably best."

"Since tomorrow is Thursday, how about I meet you both at the library after school? I really want to hear Anna May's take on all of this," Marilou said.

"Okay." I picked up my backpack and reached for the Bible.

Marilou slapped her hand on top of it so fast I jerked my own fingers back. She slid the Bible from the table into her arms. "Since this belonged to Kate's grandmother, don't you think I should be the one to take care of it?"

"Oh, sure, of course! I don't know what I was thinking." I felt suspicious, but I decided to brush it off.

"I'll bring it to the library tomorrow," Marilou said.

"Come on, Cuz! I'll give you a ride home," Kate said, snatching the car keys.

Miss Fanny showed up at the library wearing a pink suit and pink shoes. She carried a matching purse. Her wide-brimmed pink hat sprouted a white feather plume. She even wore her teeth. A shimmering pink lipstick and coordinating nail polish completed the ensemble. An elderly gentleman, donning a navy pinstriped suit, accompanied her.

Anna May opened the meeting and asked about visitors.

Miss Fanny went first. "This is Fred Hewitt. We met at my brother's funeral. Fred has been going to my church for years now. Turns out *he* has an interest in genealogy, too."

I smiled, amazed at Miss Fanny's transformation.

"It's very nice to meet you Fred," Marilou said. "This is my first time too."

"My pleasure," Fred said.

She nudged Kate's arm. "Oh yeah, everybody, this is my mom, Marilou Walker."

"I'm Anna May, so nice to meet you." She leaned over and reached out her hand for a quick shake. "I've really enjoyed working with your daughter and Nicole."

"Yes, Kate's told me a lot I didn't know. I find the symbol interpretations to be fascinating."

Miss Fanny lifted a finger. "Well, if I could take another look at the sampler, I'll finish my interpretation."

"I have it right here." Kate reached inside her backpack.

Fanny took the sampler from her, adjusted her reading glasses, and looked at it intently with her brows pinched together. She reached inside her purse and pulled out a large magnifying glass. Her face looked enormous and distorted from the other side, and everyone laughed.

"Give me a break. I'm not the young chick I used to be," she said.

"Oh, no, Miss Fanny," Anna May said. "Your face looks hilarious from the other side of that magnifying glass." She took the magnifying glass and held it up to her own face. "See."

Miss Fanny laughed along with everyone else. "Oh, child, you can see every wrinkle."

"Don't worry, girl," Anna May said. "We all think you're beautiful just the way you are."

"You look pretty to me," Frank Hewitt said.

"Oh, ya'll are so sweet."

I glanced at Marilou. "Ms. Walker, did you bring the Bible with you? I'd like to show it to Anna May."

"Have it right here," she said, opening her tote bag.

Anna May's face brightened. "Oh, it's so exciting you found this! This could give us a lot of invaluable information." She took the Bible, sat down at a computer, and began to type the names on the parchment.

Miss Fanny continued looking through the magnifying glass. "Twin trees with black and white branches indicate a biracial heritage. The hammer shows masculine gender and it's on the black side, which means he was a slave. The tree with the ribbon shows a feminine side. It's above the other one, which indicates higher station. This last symbol shows two rivers flowing into the same tree. The roots grow deep at the confluence." Miss Fanny lowered the magnifying glass. "That was the last symbol. I hope this helps." She handed the sampler back to Kate, who covered it with tissue and slipped it inside her backpack.

"Thanks so much, Miss Fanny," I said. "You've helped to solve a mystery, and you've confirmed what I suspected all along."

Anna May smiled. "It looks like Kate and Nicole are related after all. The family branches definitely come together with this latest discovery."

"Welcome to the family, Cuz," Kate said, raising her hand to high-five me, but I ignored her and stared down at the floor.

Marilou remained stoic and reached for the Bible. "Thank you, Anna May. It was very nice meeting you." She grabbed her coat and told Kate to meet her at home.

"Mom, what's the rush?" Kate asked.

"I have an appointment to show a house. Go ahead and drop off Nicole, then come on home."

"No, don't bother," I said. "I've already called my dad to come get me."

"Why? I can take you home," Kate said.

"Please, just go. I've already called him. He's on his way."

"What's wrong? You're both acting weird," Kate asked.

Her mother left.

Without a word, I turned to leave, and I refused Kate's calls the rest of the evening.

The next day I struggled to keep myself on task. I pulled the wrong folder from my locker, and didn't realize it until I got to class. In between classes, I saw Kate in the hallway.

"Nicole!" She called out and moved toward me, but I just kept walking.

"Hey, Nikki! Wait a minute!" She yelled this time.

I stopped and looked back at her. "Don't call me Nikki."

That stopped her. I turned away and kept walking. At lunch, I tried to ignore her again, but she confronted me in line. She blocked my tray with a book, preventing me from moving it forward.

"Look, we need to talk."

I tried to walk around her, but she kept stepping in front of me. Not wanting to cause a scene, I rolled my eyes. "All right, meet me at the table outside near the tree."

Kate sat across from me at the table. "Okay, now will you please tell me what's going on?"

I shook my head, trying to think how to say what I needed to tell her. "It's just that...your family owned my family. We were your slaves."

"So? You're not slaves now. I don't think of you as my slave, Nicole, and I've never mistreated you or taken advantage of you like that. I'm not the one who owned anyone."

"When I told my mother and grandmother about it, Kate, you should have seen their faces."

"I really don't understand," Kate said, brows curled.

"That's because you're not black. I'm not sure how I feel about all this right now. I'm torn between you as my best friend, and my family feeling betrayed."

"Betrayed? How?"

"Your mother and grandmother had to have known all this time and just never said anything."

"I don't think that's true at all. You were with my grandmother at the farmstead. You know she was being honest about everything. If she had known you were related to us in any way, she would have accepted you and your entire family with open arms."

"But she had to know. She had the parchment with the names on it."

"She may have just discovered it herself. Or if she did know, maybe she didn't want to hurt you. That's why she left the paper in her Bible next to the bed. Maybe she was trying to figure out how to tell you."

"I'd probably believe you, if it weren't for the letter."

"What letter?"

"The one from the estate lawyer. He said your mother requested a letter of clarification to be sent to us. It says, we are not entitled to any inheritance from your grandmother's estate or from the farmstead."

"What?" Kate stood. "I had no idea she did that, Nicole. I swear!"

"It doesn't matter." I pushed forward to stand. "My family doesn't want me hanging out with you right now."

"Wait a sec. I really don't know what's going on here."

"Kate, at the library Anna May confirmed our connection to your family. Your mother heard the whole thing. She took your grandmother's Bible and left. Connect the dots. It's not that hard. Your mother is obviously worried my family is going to sue for inheritance rights. That's why she had the lawyer send us that letter to scare us away." I shook my head. "I've got to go."

"But we've been best friends since we were little."

"I know. Maybe things will cool off later, but I just can't be around you now." I grabbed my backpack. "I've got to study for a test." I didn't look back.

After the game that night, I sat alone in my bedroom texting Johnny, listening to music.

"Can I come over tonight?" He typed.

"Late, after everyone's in bed." I included a sleepy face emoticon.

"K." He typed in several hearts and a kiss face.

"Tap on the window. I'll let you in." I typed several hearts and kiss face too.

The caller ID showed Kate's number about fifty times. I missed her, but I hadn't said anything about getting married yet, so this gave me the time I needed to sort through all my emotions. Someone knocked on the door. I pushed my phone under my pillow. My mother entered and leaned on the wall.

"Nicole, your grandmother and I are thinking about bringing a lawsuit against the Proctor estate for our part of the inheritance."

"Mama, please don't do that. It'll just make things worse."

"But this could make a difference in your college choices."

"Mama, I'm smart and I have good grades. I think I'll have plenty of choices to get into college, and scholarships, too."

"Honey, times are hard now, and your daddy just got let go from the newspaper."

"Mama, I know. I'll be fine." I didn't dare mention I just married into one of the wealthiest families in town. Besides, there's no way Judge Beck could even fathom his son married to a biracial girl. I won't even go there.

Grammy came in to say her piece on the matter. "I know you think things is going be fine, but education is the key to your future. I don't want to see that jeopardized for anything. Besides, it's not just about you. It's for your sister and brother, too."

"Grammy, I know you're right, but I also know that if Kate's grandma were still alive she'd hate we were even thinking this way." Mother started to interrupt me, but I stopped her. "If she were hiding the truth, then why did she leave the proof in her

Bible where anyone could find it? I mean, she could have burned it. Kate has never mistreated me either. I really miss her." My chin quivered as tears swelled.

My mother took a deep breath, sat next to me on the bed, and put her arms around me. "Oh, now. Baby, I know you two have been friends since you were little. I don't want to stop that, but things have got to be resolved first."

"But if it's just about the money, why does that have to come between me and my best friend?"

Grammy sat on the other side. "It won't if things are worked out fairly. You have to understand what I went through growing up black. People calling me names I hope you never have to hear. Always looking over my shoulder, making sure I walked on the right side of the street. Having to go to a different public restroom and drink from the colored fountain."

"I know all about the Civil Rights Movement, Grammy, but times have changed. There are a few idiots like those racist skinheads, but most people in my generation don't treat each other that way anymore. You've got to let the past go, and give me the freedom to have my own friends, white, black, Indian, Hispanic, Asian, or whatever. Trust me to make my own choices." What was I saying? After I just went behind their backs and married a KKK leader's son? How could I possibly tell them the truth now?

Grammy didn't let up. Her words echoed loudly like a lion's roar. "But child, there's so much you don't understand. When I was growing up..."

Mother cut her off. "All right! Grammy go on now. Let me handle this." She shooed Grammy out the door.

"Nicole, honey, we can't allow ourselves to be lulled in our thinking here. Yes, it's true your generation is more open-minded and thank God for that. I have some lovely white women friends myself." She turned to face me and took hold of my hands. "Baby, we are a proud mixed race family, but you know as well as I do, there are people out there who hate us. I just want what's best for you and your brother and sister."

"Mama, according to our true heritage we are just as white as we are black, so what does it really matter?"

"You have a good point there, but I still feel we need to have some sort of restitution given in good faith. I think they should at least recognize our side of the family and include us in the lineage and inheritance."

Bargaining for sympathy, I said, "Well, if I can't see Kate, then can I see Johnny."

She shook her head. "Mmm-mmm, girl—you know that's nothing but trouble. His daddy will cause us a whole lot of problems."

"Why not?"

"You know he's the head of that white supremacist group."

"But Johnny isn't like him."

Mother shook her head and walked to the door. "I don't want to get into this right now."

"Fine, then. Close the door behind you." I rolled over in my bed.

"Goodnight, Nicole," she sighed. "I love you."

I didn't answer. Pulling out my phone, I started texting Johnny again.

-19-

Surprise Arrival

My reputation as a fine upholsterer afforded me the opportunity to travel with my friend Betsy Ross to the new home of George and Martha Washington. Along the way, we came to know each other even better. Having suffered the loss of our first husbands, this trip offered us focus on something else.

Mrs. Washington's keen eye aided us in our decorating efforts of Mount Vernon, while General Washington was away on military duty. We filled our days with sewing and our nights with delightful dinners and conversation. After a month of hard work, our task finally came to an end. Martha—as we'd grown accustomed to calling her—marveled at the quality of workmanship. We graciously said our goodbyes and boarded our respective stagecoaches. Instead of returning to New Jersey, I decided to go home to the farmstead for a long overdue visit. Upon my arrival, I fell ill.

"There's a fever going around the settlement," Mother said. "I think Doc Shaw should come and check on you."

I shook my head, as I lay in bed, pale from the persistent nausea. "No, Mother. I'll be fine."

She insisted, "I'm not willing to take any chances. I've already sent for him."

Doc Shaw pressed on my stomach several times. "Hmm!" He smiled with a glimmer in his eyes. "Well, it looks like your husband left you a parting gift."

"What do you mean?"

"You're with child, Mrs. Leverton," he said with a wink.

My mouth fell open. "A baby?"

Doc Shaw chuckled. "Don't be so surprised. This sort of thing happens all the time. I'm sorry to hear of your husband's unfortunate death, but he left his seed as a legacy to carry on after him."

"Oh, Constance! What a wonderful blessing from heaven," Mother said.

"You will have to remain confined to bed for a while yet. Drink plenty of fluids and try to get some food down. You're eating for two now." Doc Shaw closed his bag and stepped out the door. "I'll check on you again. Congratulations!"

"Thank you, Doc Shaw," I said, while staring blankly, stunned at the news.

After bathing, I stood in front of the mirror, rubbing my hands over my belly. My time with Simon happened only two weeks after my husband's death. Henry suffered for weeks prior to his death, but everyone assumed the baby was his. I couldn't recall our last intimate moment. Still, the question lingered. Who was the father?

I gave birth to a beautiful blonde, blue-eyed girl. Relieved, knowing she was Henry's child. What a fuss everyone made over her! Then, a sudden pain shot through my body. I grasped my stomach and screamed. Maggie bent down to take a look.

"Oh, it looks like you've got another one coming, Miss Constance."

Mother handed the baby girl to Tessa and sat down behind me to support my back. The pain intensified and I cried out as Maggie coached me along.

"Push! Push, Miss Constance!"

"Ahhhh!" The head appeared, and the baby fell into Maggie's arms.

Tessa stood at the foot of my bed staring down. "Oh, Miss Constance, what have you done?"

Mother moved out from behind me to see for herself.

With my legs spread wide, my body shook as the pain subsided, offering me blessed relief. I propped myself up on my elbows, still panting, not knowing what to say. My gown, now soaked, clung to my body.

"How can this be?" Mother said, astonished.

A tiny arm swayed in the dim light above the edge of my gown. My baby's cry called out to me, and instinct prompted me to reach for it. My eyes followed the arm down to the baby's body. I blinked and stared in disbelief, sweat dripping off my forehead.

Maggie stood, pinched brow, stern look.

My gaze rose to meet hers. With a hushed voice, I said the only thing that came to mind, "Simon."

"No!" Maggie gasped. "Dear God in heaven, not my boy. He would never do such a thing."

I fell back against my pillow as my head filled with streams of guilt. My eyes shifted about the room, desperate to find someone with compassion.

Mother covered her mouth, while Tessa tightened her fists and paced the floor.

"It's not what you think," I said, as I tried to sit up in bed. The baby boy lay swaddled securely next to me, his dark skin a sharp contrast to my own.

Tessa cried out, "Well, what is it then? You telling us Simon raped you?"

"No! No! Never! Simon would never do such a thing," I cried.

Tessa bent down, grabbed my shoulders, and shook me hard. "Did you sleep with my baby girl's man?"

"No! I swear! It wasn't like that at all!"

My mother grabbed Tessa from behind and pulled her back.

I fell back on the bed and drew my legs into a fetal position. I struggled to find my words.

"I swear it wasn't like any of that. We didn't mean for it to happen. It just happened."

Tessa's face grew hard, as she demanded to know more. "Mean for *what* to happen, Miss Constance?"

Maggie patted the baby on his back. "Yes, do tell us," she said in a softer yet suspicious tone.

I swallowed hard and tried to explain. "I … I'd just lost my dear Henry in the war and Simon had just lost Jasmine. We were both grieving and … we found ourselves in …"

"In what?" Tessa asked sternly.

Mother picked up the baby girl as she started to fuss.

The pain started to calm, and the bleeding slowed. I took a deep breath and continued. "I went to the townhouse to help pack up Jasmine's things. We talked about how much Jasmine meant to both of us, and I started to cry. Simon held me just to comfort me, but then…" I stopped for a moment and swallowed again.

Mother leaned in and asked, "And then what?"

"We," I stared blankly as tears pooled on my cheeks. My heartbeat quickened and forced me to breathe faster. "We couldn't stop." I covered my face with my hands, trying to hide my shame. "We didn't mean to sin. It just happened."

When I looked up, I saw Tessa at the window. Her eyes squeezed tight as she covered her mouth to muffle her inconsolable sobs. Guilt consumed me again, and I had to look away. My gaze found Maggie in silhouette, haloed by firelight. I sensed an unexpected peace as she hummed a spiritual and rocked gently to calm my baby boy in her arms.

"This child is a gift from God," she said, her cheeks now wet with tears.

What an odd thing to say in such a moment like this, and yet somehow I understood. A sweet comfort came over me, and my breathing slowed as my thoughts went out to her. *She may never see Simon, again,* I thought. *This baby is her son's firstborn.*

When Tessa turned to pace the floor again, my momentary glimpse of peace slipped away. "This isn't right. Jasmine tried to give Simon children. She can't help it if the first one died, but now here you be giving him babies?" She spun around to face me. "As if he's somehow your husband?"

Mother lay the baby girl down in the crib near the fireplace. She came to my side and bent down to check the bleeding. "Good. It's stopped now. Her face transformed to stoicism. "Tessa, I think it best for you to calm down now. What's done is done."

Tessa stared back at my mother with a fallen jaw. "What's done is done? Is that all this is to you?" She shook her head in disbelief. Her lips tightened, as did her stare. She turned and ran out of the bedchamber, slamming the door.

Once the tension in the room lightened, I leaned back against the headboard. Mother brought my baby girl to me, and I unwrapped the swaddling to study her body. "She's perfect."

"I thought the same thing when you were born."

I looked up at her, hoping to find forgiveness in her eyes. There was a glimmer of hope, but I knew better than to expect more from her in that moment.

Minutes later, Tessa returned. I noticed dirt on her dress and beads of sweat on her forehead, but she did seem calmer. She held out her arms to Maggie, who was still holding the baby boy. "Can I hold him?" she asked calmly. Maggie hesitated, but then handed over the baby.

Tessa looked at him, endearingly. "He's a part of Jasmine in as much as he's a part of Simon. This is the child Jasmine couldn't give her husband."

"I loved Jasmine, Tessa. I would never do anything to hurt her. She was my very best friend. You've got to believe me.

Tessa nodded. "She loved you too."

"We have to cover up the truth about this black baby," Mother said.

Maggie, in her most humble British servant's way, approached my mother with a suggestion. "Miss Susanna? Since he is my grandchild, and if it be fitting to you, I'd like to raise him as my own."

Mother looked at Tessa, who nodded in agreement.

"All right, then," Mother said. "Constance, you only gave birth to a baby girl today, understood?"

"Yes, Mother," I said.

"Not one word will be spoken about the true

father. This is our secret from here on out. It must never leave this room. Nobody needs to suffer any more."

Tessa looked at Maggie, and said, "You can tell everyone you found him in the fields. They'll think he was abandoned by one of the escaped slaves."

I handed my daughter to my mother and said, "Bring me my son."

Maggie took the black baby boy from Tessa and placed him in my arms.

I looked at him lovingly and stroked his cheek; cherishing the short time I had left to be his mother. Simon will never know of his son's birth. My brief moment of passionate despair and lustful disillusionment now fully disclosed must remain hidden. "Go in peace my child, my son." His tiny hand curled around my finger, which made me smile and cry at the same time. I kissed him on the forehead. Maggie reached for the small bundle, but before letting him go, I looked up at her with a tearful resolve.

"He was conceived in love."

"Yes, Miss Constance," Maggie nodded and reached again for the babe in my arms. I hesitated. Maggie left the room with a linen basket, which hid the precious life I once carried.

Mother called for Doc Shaw to come and examine me. He saw only one baby that night.

-20-

Secret Love

Unable to sleep, I turned and adjusted my pillow. A light tap on my bedroom window alerted me, and I jumped out of bed, knowing it was Johnny.

"Nicole," he whispered through the windowpane. I turned on the lamp, put on my robe, and opened the first-floor window.

"Everybody's in bed, Johnny," I whispered. My pulse quickened. "If my parents catch you here, they'll call the police. We'll both be in so much trouble."

Johnny leaned for a kiss. "I've missed you so much."

"I've missed you too." He climbed over the sill.

"We've got to keep quiet, or my parents' might hear us." The cold wind swept my hair back as I closed the window. I pulled Johnny close, and we shared another kiss, this time longer and more intense.

He fumbled in his coat pocket. "I've got something for you."

"What is it?" I smiled, looking down at his hand.

He pulled out a small box and opened it. "If you don't like it, we can get another one later." Inside the box was a ring of white gold with diamonds surrounding a larger one.

I gasped. "Oh, Johnny!" The ring sparkled in the dim lamplight.

"You're worth it," Johnny said. He adjusted a small pillow and lay back against the headboard. "So, what's up with you and Kate? I noticed something was going down today."

"It's a long story." I reclined beside him and pulled my terry robe over my legs, dotted with goosebumps.

"I've got time." He lifted his arm, and I rested my head on his shoulder.

"Well, it turns out we're related."

"How?"

I looked into his eyes. "Her family owned my ancestors as slaves."

"No way!"

"I *am* half black, Johnny."

"Oh yeah? You could have fooled me. You know that doesn't matter." Johnny stroked my cheek, kissed my nose.

"I wish everybody felt that way. My parents think we're entitled to some of the inheritance from Kate's grandmother's estate."

"Well, you do know there were black slave owners back then too."

"Yeah, Anna May gave me a little history lesson on that. Even the Quakers owned slaves in the beginning. And the first slave owner in the Colonies was actually a free black man who came over as an indentured servant."

"Whoa. You don't hear that being taught in schools."

"I know. Maybe if they did, we wouldn't have so many ignorant people like the Skinheads and the Black Panthers."

"So how are you related?"

"A plantation master's daughter had an affair with an indentured slave, who happened to be her maidservant's husband."

"Oooo ... sounds juicy. So how much money we talking about?"

"Enough for college, at least. According to my mom anyway."

"That doesn't sound too unreasonable."

"Really? If this were *your* family, you might not feel that way."

Johnny put his hand up in defense. "Whoa! You have to remember, we're talking about my dad now, king of the KKK!"

"Yeah, that's what I thought you'd say."

Johnny pulled my chin up with his finger. "Hey, come on now. I'm sorry. I didn't mean to hurt your feelings?"

"I know it's not you. Just your freakin' family."

"Right, and that's what you have to remember through all this. It's not you—just your freakin' family."

"Right," I snickered.

He pulled me closer to him. "Your hair smells good."

"It's jasmine shampoo."

"There's no place I'd rather be than right here with you." He kissed me again and reached to turn off the lamp.

A few hours later, Johnny roused. "Dang, I can't believe I fell asleep!" He sat up, slipped his feet into his sneakers, and bent to tie them.

"Hurry up. I don't want my parents to find you here."

"Okay, okay," he whispered back, rubbing his eyes, brushing back his hair.

I tightened the sash on my robe, while Johnny opened the window. He turned back and gave me a lingering kiss.

"Bye. Be careful on your way home."

"See you at school." Johnny climbed over the sill and ran out into the dark street.

-21-

Cousins and Old Flames

Conflicts with the British prevented safe travel back to New Jersey. My cousin sent me a letter confirming that British soldiers used the upholstery shop as a command post for a time. Too frightened to return on my own with a child, I remained at the farmstead for seven years, until the end of the war. There, I raised my daughter with the love and support of my family, watching over my son in secret. Maggie moved into the house as a nanny. Mother allowed her to bring my twin son with her, while he was still an infant.

"I think we should name him Simon Junior." I said, holding the babe in my arms.

Maggie bounced the baby girl on her shoulder. "Thank you, Miss Constance. That means so much to me."

I did nurse him on occasion, but only in secret. After weaning, Mother thought it best to separate us. I rarely saw him or spoke of him again.

Once the war ended and I knew it was safe to travel, I returned to New Jersey with my daughter,

Sidney. She knew of Simon, Junior only as a slave child, not her twin brother. I took her to visit her cousins and to pick up more fabric in Philadelphia.

The upholstery shop was on the same street as the print shop, and the inevitable happened. Sidney ran ahead, stopping to look at a doll in the window, while I caught up. It was then I saw him. My heart nearly jumped out of my chest, and I stopped breathing for a moment.

Simon stopped sweeping. He stared back at me.

I reached for Sidney's hand, tugging me along.

"Come on, Mother. Aunt Harriett is waiting."

This was her first time to meet her cousins in the Northern colonies, and she was excited. She knew nothing about Simon, her real father. I did remember that Maggie had shared stories with her when she mentioned him as her son. No one else knew the truth, except for the three women who attended me during the delivery, my mother, Maggie, and Tessa. My mind raced back to that day at the townhouse. The memories of those few hours we had spent alone together roused old feelings.

Simon stopped what he was doing. He looked down at Sidney, smiled, and returned to sweeping.

Though her coloring was light, like mine, I wondered whether he saw a part of himself in Sidney's face, her eyes perhaps. She did at times bear the same penetrating qualities. The tug of my hand prompted me to resume walking.

Simon stepped aside, allowing us to pass. The hem of my dress brushed his foot. Our eyes met. I wanted to hold him, comfort him. I wanted to be truthful, tell him about his children, both of them, but I didn't dare. Glancing away, I caught the image of a black woman peering at me through the print shop window. I shuddered and walked on, no hesitation. Pulling Sidney along the cobblestone street, I chastised myself, inciting sensibility. Seven years was a long time after all. On future trips, I made a point to take a carriage.

I stooped at one end of a settee to measure it, and the bell on the shop door jingled. A gentleman dressed in a black cloak, his back to me, waited at the counter. He turned, and I caught my breath.

"Miss Constance, it's so nice to see you again." He tipped his hat and bowed.

"Ma ... Master McClain! What brings you here?"

"Oh, please call me Matthew. I'm actually in town on family business, and thought I'd stop by to visit an old friend."

An old friend? That's how he thinks of me? "I can't remember the last time we saw each other."

"Well, I have kept in good company with your father. He told me about the loss of your husband." He removed his hat and held it over his heart. "He suffered an honorable death. God rest his soul."

"Thank you, Matthew. Please forgive me. I lived

at the farmstead for several years after he passed, but don't recall seeing you."

"No, I stayed near the back during church services and only saw your father for business, on occasion."

"Oh, I'm sorry I missed you afterwards."

"Yes, well, I felt it best to admire you from a distance."

I felt heat rise in my cheeks. "Admire me?"

"Yes, Constance. You're a wonderful mother, and your daughter is quite lovely."

"Thank you. Her name is Sidney. She's eight years old now."

"Already? Well, I must say the years have been kind to you."

"Thank you. What about you? Have you married?"

"Well, I was engaged once," he said, glancing away.

"Oh?" I wondered what happened, but dared not explore this without his offering an explanation first.

He cleared his throat. "Yes, well, she seemed to grow fond of another while I was away on business."

"Oh!" I said, softly. This sudden vulnerability endeared him to me. I found him attractive, sophisticated—not like before. He was different, more mature, and aware of others around him.

"I actually wish to employ your services."

"What can I do for you?"

"My brother is getting married, and I'm in need

of a new suit."

Over the next few weeks, Master McClain visited the shop for fittings, sometimes more than necessary. On certain occasions, I invited him to stay for tea and found him very engaging in conversation, especially in the arena of politics. I learned that his spending time with my father had impressed change on his views of slavery. He shared the same admiration for some of my favorite passages from John Woolman's book. His teachings along with the writings of Anthony Benezet, Thomas Paine, Granville Sharp, and John Wesley cultivated his support for abolitionism, which now grew steadily. In the meantime, my own feelings grew toward Matthew McClain.

During a fitting, a letter came from the farmstead. With Matthew as a friend of my family, I felt it appropriate to include him in the reading. "It's from Mother. To my dearest daughter Constance, Your father has taken ill. Doc Shaw visits almost daily, but there is little he can do. Your father requests your presence as soon as possible. I fear the worst is upon us. I look forward to seeing you and Sidney soon. Your loving mother, Susanna." I folded the letter. "Oh, dear."

"Constance, it's not proper for a woman to travel alone. Might I offer to accompany you in your travels?"

"No, that won't be necessary, Matthew. It's summer now, and the roads are not treacherous.

Besides, I've traveled alone on many occasions." I caught myself for a moment, regarding his concern for my safety. "I do see your point and appreciate the gesture." I gazed out the window with a blank stare.

"I'll leave you to your thoughts then." Starting for the door, he reached for his cane and hat. "Good day."

The bell jingle alerted me of his departure. "Matthew?"

He turned. "Yes?"

"I will seriously consider your offer."

He nodded and left.

-22-

Love Lost

I closed the window and peered through the blinds as Johnny made his way to his car parked down the street. *Yeah, that's all we'll do at school—see each other.* I took the ring off, placed it back in the box. The far back drawer of my nightstand made an excellent hiding spot. Snuggling in bed, I closed my eyes, and hoped for a few more minutes of sleep before my own alarm went off.

I hit the snooze button again, but heard my brother and sister arguing in the hallway, making it impossible for anyone to sleep. A sick feeling came over me. I sat up and held my stomach. Clasping my mouth, I bounded for the bathroom.

By the time I got to school, the gossip around campus bombarded me with the news about Johnny. My mind refused to believe it. I walked to my locker in a state of shock not knowing what to think or how to respond. All I could think about was finding Johnny. Where was he?

Suddenly, my cheerleading coach appeared before me. "Nicole, I'm so sorry to hear about Johnny. How awful. Are you all right? Is there anything I can do for you?"

I stared at her in disbelief and shook my head. "What? What happened?"

"You haven't heard?"

The intercom cracked and Principal Ripley's voice streamed out. "Ladies and gentlemen, I have a special announcement. Just a few minutes ago, I received word that Johnny Beck, the captain of our football team, died in an automobile accident sometime early this morning. I know this comes as a shock to many of you. We are taking steps to add grief counselors on campus. If any of you feel the need to go home, please check out at the front desk first. My deepest sympathy goes out to the Beck family."

Johnny? Dead? My books tumbled to the floor as I collapsed to my knees in uncontrollable sobs.

"No!"

A familiar embrace warmed my shoulders and rocked me with a gentle motion. I recognized Kate's fingernail polish through my watery daze. A crowd gathered as Kate helped me to my feet. Pushing past the crowd, we walked out of school, still clinging to each other. Marilou met us at the curb and drove me home.

It took both her and Kate to help me out of the car and into the house. Mother and Grammy heard the commotion in the living room and came running.

"What's going on here? Mother demanded.

Marilou tried to explain things, while Kate helped

me to the bathroom. The cool water soothed my red, swollen eyes. I dried off with a towel, but started to cry into it. A lump swelled in my throat, making it difficult to swallow. I stumbled to the bed and collapsed.

The police concluded that Johnny swerved the car to avoid hitting a deer and ran head on into a tree, killing him instantly. In the days that followed, grief engulfed me. I sat on the couch, a tissue box in my lap, and watched the news. Reporters interviewed the Beck family, asking pointed questions. Why was Johnny out in the middle of the night? Where did he go? Who did he see? His parents confirmed they didn't know, but added that Johnny wasn't the partying type. I worried what might happen if they discovered Johnny was with me that night.

My eyes narrowed when red lights glared through the living room window, and a surge of adrenalin pulsed through my veins. My head throbbed. Mother opened the door, and I leaned over to listen.

"Does Nicole Durham live here?" the officer asked.

"Yes, she's right here," Mother said, moving aside to let them in.

I stood, pulling my robe tight around my waist. "I'm Nicole."

The officers remained impersonal and cold. "Miss Durham, did you know Johnny Beck?"

"Yes."

"Do you know that he died in a motor vehicle accident earlier this week?"

"Well, yeah. It's been all over the news."

The officer seemed indifferent to my tone. "How well did you know Johnny Beck?"

"We dated."

"How long?"

"A couple of months, I guess." I shifted my gaze to my mother. Her eyelids at half-mast let me know to expect a discussion later.

"Did you attend the Moonlight Dance with Johnny Beck?"

"I met him there."

"Did you leave the dance with him?"

Oh, God! How do I say this? "Yes, I went for a ride in his car."

"Where did you go?

"We drove around a while, then he dropped me off at Kate's house." I left out the part about going across state lines, getting married.

"Would that be Kate Walker?"

"Yeah, we actually went to the dance together with Ronald Ripley."

"Why didn't you go with Johnny Beck?"

"Because his father told him he couldn't date me anymore."

"And why was that?"

I stood, mouth agape, not believing what the

officer was asking.

Mother pointed to the family photo on the wall. "Do you really need to ask?"

The officer nodded. "I understand." He jotted something in his notes, and then continued. "Would you say you and Johnny were close?"

"Yeah, we really liked each other a lot." I pressed the tissue to my eye.

The officer turned to his partner. "Any more questions?"

"No," his partner said.

"Thank you for your time, Miss Durham. Sorry for the loss of your—friend."

Mother closed the door behind them and turned. "It's time to come clean, young lady."

I shook my head. "Not now, Mama. I can't eat. I can't sleep, and I'm not ready to talk to you about this yet." I started for my room.

"What about school?"

I paused and looked back. "No way am I ready for that either!"

Though Johnny and I had taken every precaution to keep things secret, it seemed as though the entire student body and faculty knew about us. The Moonlight Dance, no doubt, was a field day for the gossips. Pictures of Johnny's car wrapped around the tree trunk, and the one taken of us on the dance floor, flashed across the TV screen and in online news feeds for days, which only compounded my grief. My phone filled with texts messages and emails, most of them sympathetic, some unkind, hateful. Johnny's Facebook news feeds and mine filled with similar sentiments.

One girl's text said, "Johnny would never date a hoe like you."

I chose to ignore her and blocked her number. My Facebook page had a lot more hate messages though and trolls, so I deleted my account entirely. The thought of going off grid wasn't a hard decision at that point. I wanted to disappear forever. At times, I wished I could have died.

Three weeks passed. I tried to attend classes again. I never told Kate about my getting married. Grieving for Johnny was all I could handle, one day at a time, one foot in front of the other. Going back to class proved to be too much, causing me to burst into tears. The extra-curricular activities I always loved participating in, I left unattended. I wore Johnny's ring on a silver chain, careful to keep it hidden under my clothes.

On Halloween, Dad took Shelby and Jackson around the neighborhood. I stayed home. Kate arrived dressed up like a pumpkin. I opened the door, didn't crack a smile, and tossed some candy her way. "You look ridiculous."

She caught the candy in her bag. "Well, I was hoping you might come with me."

"Where?" I said flatly.

"Sandy's house. She's having a party, remember?"

"And how would I know this? I haven't been to school in a month."

"All right, I just thought I'd ask."

A small group of children lingered at the edge of the driveway. "There's another group coming. Anything else?"

"Well, uh ... you want to go to the farmstead again?"

I paused. A surge of excitement caught me off guard. "When?"

"This weekend," Kate said with a sly grin.

I took a deep breath. The small group of children descended upon us, surrounding Kate.

One obnoxious kid pointed at her. "Hey look. It's the great pumpkin. Hahahahaha!"

I tossed candy into their bags, trying to at least smile and act happy for them. Kate hung back, waiting for my answer.

The last child skipped away, and I reached for the door. "Okay, I'll go."

Kate bounced on her feet. "Great! I'll pick you up about nine on Saturday."

"Okay. Have fun at the party."

"Sure you don't want to come?"

"What? And miss all this?"

Kate laughed. "I've missed your sick sense of humor." She tossed me a piece of candy.

I missed and let our dog, Sugar, lap it up. "Yeah, well, I'll see you then."

On Saturday, a honk in the driveway alerted me. I opened my bedroom window and waved. "Be right there," I called out.

Although it was a month after Johnny's death, I still found myself crying every day and struggling through the grief counseling sessions.

I made it to the car. "What took you so long?" Kate asked.

"My stomach's a little messed up."

"Sure you're up for this?"

"I'll be fine. It's probably just a bug. Besides, I've been looking forward to this all week. I feel like, in a way, we're going to see Grandma Winnie again. Does that sound weird?"

"Not really. I feel the same. Just hope Uncle Eyrie remembers us. It's been weeks since we saw him last." Kate backed out of the driveway.

"Yeah, I hope he can hear us," I giggled.

Amazed Uncle Eyrie remembered us, we climbed the attic stairs and started rummaging through old boxes. I spotted a dusty chest in the corner. My curious nature drew me to it. *No keyhole.* Pulling the lid up, I waved the dust away and coughed. I got down on my knees to peruse the contents, and caught the fresh scent of cedar. Moving tissue aside, an antique wedding dress emerged. "Oh." I ran my fingers over the lace appliqué and pearl beading on the silk bodice. Under the dress, I found a quilt, another exquisite piece of work.

"Look what I found," I called out to Kate. "I bet this is the quilt Constance made for Jasmine."

Kate joined me beside the old chest. "It looks pretty good for being so old." She left me holding the quilt to continue her search. "I think I found some more journals."

"Who wrote them?" I asked, gently packing the quilt and dress back into the chest.

Kate sat to flip through one of the books. "I don't know yet."

I felt for the hidden lever and pulled it. The doorway to the hidden room cracked open. "I'm going to check out this room."

"Okay! I might need you to help me in a bit. This is hard to read."

A few moments later I called out, "Kate, come look at this."

"What is it? I'm reading something very interesting right now about Simon Miller, Jr."

"Come look."

Kate entered the hidden room, where I held a framed black-and-white photograph of a steamboat captain standing at the wheel. "Is that Simon Miller, Jr.?" she asked.

"I don't know, but I bet the name is written on the back." I flipped the frame and carefully removed the photo. On the backside was some faded writing. I squinted and read it aloud. "1862 Captain Proctor of the Steamboat Susanna."

"1862? Wasn't that during the Civil War?" Kate asked.

"Yeah, it started that year."

"One of the journal entries I read said that he transported slaves across the river to freedom during the war."

"This proves our involvement with the Underground Railroad. What else did you find?"

"One journal entry said Master William Proctor entrusted certain slaves to do business for him at the tobacco warehouses. He taught them how to read, write, and do simple math, which means Simon was most likely literate. I bet he kept a Captain's log."

I looked around the room, spotting an old chest of drawers. My pulse grew faster with a rush of anticipation. I set the photo down and pulled open the top drawer. Pushing the contents from side to side, I did a quick search. "I'll keep looking around," I said, moving down to the second drawer.

"I'm going to take the journals I found and put them in the car," Kate said.

"Cool! I'll meet you downstairs in a little bit."

I searched the third drawer, still nothing much. The bottom drawer stuck. I tugged hard, working it side to side until it shimmied free. Reaching inside, I picked up a leather-bound book, flipped it open and read the words, "Ship's Log Steamboat Susanna" by

Captain Simon Proctor.

"This is it." I retrieved a smaller book titled, "The Journal of John Woolman." Replacing the drawer, I carried the books downstairs to the mudroom. As I walked through the kitchen, I heard voices that sounded like my mother and Marilou. "Mama?" I said, now entering the dining room.

"Hi, Honey," Mother said. "Come on over here and enjoy some lunch."

"What are you doing here?"

Mother put one hand on her hip. "Oh what? Is it just not cool to have lunch with your mama?"

"Uh, no," I said, but caught myself. "I mean, yes! It's okay." I sat next to Kate, wondering why our mothers were getting along now. Marilou set napkins and plastic ware next to our plates. "Luella's never been to the farmstead. And after telling her all about it, I thought it would be nice to bring her out here, let her see the place."

Luella scooped potato salad and corn casserole onto each plate. "Yes, I find the whole story fascinating. And since it is part of our family heritage, too, I really wanted to see it." She filled Uncle Eyrie's glass with lemonade.

"This is the best lunch I've had in a long time," he said, stuffing a napkin into the neck of his shirt. "Thank you, ladies, for bringing it all the way out here."

"You're very welcome, Eyrie. It's our pleasure,"

Mother said.

I waved. "Wait a minute. What's happening here? Last thing I knew you two weren't even on speaking terms."

Marilou interrupted, "Well, we talked things over and decided to do what was best for the family."

"The *whole* family," Mother said.

"Okay," I said and decided not to pursue it.

"We found some more journals up in the attic today," Kate said.

I swallowed a bit of corn casserole. "And I found an old photo of Simon Miller, Jr."

"Oh, I'd love to see it," Mother said.

"It's right here." I pulled the photo from the book.

Mother held it carefully. "Oh, my goodness. I can't believe it's so well preserved."

"Turn it over."

She flipped the photo, eyes darting across the back. "This proves our involvement with the Underground Railroad, too."

"Yes," Marilou said excitedly. "I think the historical society will be *very* interested."

Mother looked at the photo intently. "When was he born?

"Around 1777, I believe," Marilou said.

Quickly calculating, Mother replied, "He was in his mid-80's and still working as a steamboat captain?"

"About 85, I suspect."

"That is amazing. Put this in a safe place," my mother said, handing me the photo. "I don't want it to get damaged."

I tucked it carefully inside the captain's logbook, and finished eating.

"Well, girls, let's eat up, and then I want to see that secret room and the tunnel," Mother said.

After cleaning up, I led them down the creaking stairs to the basement and found the chain to turn on the light.

Everyone waved away the dust and coughed while I ran my hand along the wall in search of the handle. My fingers slipped over cold metal and wrapped around the oblong lever. I pulled it, and the wall opened.

"Oh, my goodness," Mother gasped. "No one would've suspected a secret tunnel, so ingenious. This is amazing." She stepped back a bit when she saw a mouse crawling along the baseboard. "Oookay, I think I've seen enough. Let's go."

"It's that way." I pointed.

Mother turned the flashlight toward the black hole. "No way. I'm not going in there."

"Mama, it's really cool when you come up on the other side."

"I don't care about no cool. Is this safe? Are you kidding me?"

"Girls, what if this were to cave in?" Marilou said.

"We walked through it with Grandma. It was

perfectly safe then," Kate said.

I led the way into the tunnel, Mother behind me. The others followed.

"I don't know about this, Nicole," Mother said.

"You're okay, Luella. I'm right behind you," Marilou said.

"Oh that's just great, Marilou. If this place caves in, I'm the first to go."

"Well, then, how'd you get so lucky?"

"Oh—ha, ha!"

"No, that means I'll be stuck here to dig us out," Marilou said.

Kate whispered, "Would you two pipe down? All this noise is going to make the walls cave in for sure."

I turned. "Mama, don't worry. Everything's going to be fine. Trust me."

Mother pulled my shoulder back. "Who are you and what have you done with my daughter?"

I smirked and turned back around.

She patted me on the back. "All right, baby, we'll just whisper. You lead the way. I'll follow."

"The ladder's just ahead," I said. "We should be out of here soon." I felt a tug on my belt and realized she was holding on.

"Good! This tunnel is really starting to give me the creeps," she said.

We reached the ladder, and I stepped aside to allow Mother to climb up first.

"When you get to the top, you've got to push

really hard. The hatch sticks," I said.

"Great, Marilou. You'd better come with me, then. I don't know if I'm strong enough to push that hatch all by myself."

"Okay, I'm right behind you. Hope this ladder's strong enough for both of us."

Kate held it steady.

"Okay Luella, let's just give it one big push," Marilou said. Both grunted, and the hatch pushed open slightly with a tiny stream of daylight piercing into the tunnel.

I looked up and saw Marilou peer out. "Somebody's out there," she whispered.

"Wait. Isn't that Judge Beck?" Mother whispered.

"Yes, and the other guy is Adam Myers. He's over the historical society."

Kate and I looked at each other with raised brows.

Marilou whispered, "I've got to get closer and hear what they're saying."

"Be careful!" Mother warned.

Marilou raised the hatch halfway up, climbed out quietly, and hid behind a barrel.

"Mom, what's going on?" I whispered.

"I don't know. Just wait," she said. After a few agonizing minutes, she pulled the hatch open all the way. "It's okay. They're gone." We climbed out onto the barn floor. She paced outside the stall. "If the historical society sells this land, Judge Beck will tear down the farmhouse and the barn. Everything this house and land has ever stood for will be lost."

"But I thought they said something about building a new museum," Mother said. "If that's the case, they could take everything from the farmhouse and just put it over there."

"No, Luella, you don't understand. Once Judge Beck gets his hands on this land, he'll wipe out any semblance of history we have left in this town."

"Judge Beck wants to tear down the farmhouse?" I asked.

"To build high-priced houses," Marilou said.

"We can't let him do that," Kate said. "This farmstead means too much to our family. The historical society will be making a big mistake if they sell it."

"All right then, let's say you're right," my mother said. "If the land isn't sold, then how much money is it going to take to restore this place and make it ready for historical tours?"

Marilou replied, "Well, we'd have to get it appraised. Kate's right, though. This land has been in our family for generations, and we're just now coming to find out its true value. You can't put a dollar sign on that, Luella."

"But what can we do now?" I asked.

Marilou raised her finger. "Grandma's will said the historical society can't do anything until Uncle Eyrie either dies or can no longer care for himself and live here."

Kate got an idea. “Why don’t we join the historical society? That way we can vote not to sell the farmstead to Judge Beck.”

“That’s it!” I said. “Then we can help persuade the other members not to sell either.”

“Sounds like a plan,” Marilou said, grinning. “Let’s go girls.”

Unfortunately, a phone inquiry into joining the historical society throttled that plan.

We entered the living room slowly, and I slouched into a chair.

Uncle Eyrie turned off the TV and looked at each of us. “Why the long faces?”

Mother explained. “Uncle Eyrie, we can’t join the historical society here because we are already members of the Charleston Historical Society. Apparently, it's against the rules to join more than one organization.”

“Why did you want to join anyway?” he asked.

“Because they are thinking about selling this place, and we wanted to vote no to stop them,” Marilou said, “The guy who wants to buy it will tear down the farmhouse and the barn and build fancy new houses along the river.”

“But this is my home,” he said. “They can’t do that.”

She patted his shoulder to reassure him. “We know. That’s why we’re doing all we can to stop them, Uncle Eyrie. Don’t worry. As long as you’re living here, the will states they can't force you out of your home. But in the meantime, I think we should contact a lawyer."

Mother got an idea. "Why don't we contact the Charleston Historical Society and see if they can help? I bet Anna May will know what to do."

-23-

Change of Heart

I decided not to complicate my life with Matthew McClain and declined his offer to accompany me home. Upon our arrival, Mother greeted us at the front porch along with Etta.

Sidney jumped from the carriage and ran to her. “Grandmama! I’ve missed you so much.”

Mother met her at the bottom step and embraced her. “Oh, I’ve missed you too, my darling girl.” She stood and kissed my cheek. “How was your trip, dear?”

“As well as can be expected under such circumstances, I suppose.” I removed my hat and gloves, handing them to Etta.

“Welcome home, Miss Constance,” she said.

“Thank you, Etta. I'm glad to be back,” I said, turning back to mother. “How is Father?”

“Where is Grandpapa?” Sidney interrupted.

Mother said, “Your grandpapa is not feeling well just now, but you can see him later. Now run along. The dolls are waiting to play tea party.”

“Oh, I’ve missed playing with them,” she said and trotted up the stairs.

"Where's Elizabeth?" I asked.

"She'll be along soon," Mother said.

"Is Father awake? Can I see him now?"

"I was just about to take him some broth. Come with me."

We entered the master bedchamber, where Father lay sleeping. I carried a tray, while Mother lit the lantern next to the bed. Father roused and blinked.

"Constance?" he said, as he reached out, his arms weak and shaky. I set the tray on a small table near the bed and took his hand.

"I've missed you so," I said with teary affection. The moistness on my cheeks dropped to the sheet.

"I'm so glad to see you," he said, gasping. "This is a wonderful surprise. Did Sidney come with you?"

"Yes, but I want her to wait until you're up to seeing her."

"Oh, bother. I'm feeling better already." He gasped and coughed again, this time more heavily.

Mother held out a teaspoon of medicinal liquid. "Here you go, dear."

"Not again!" He murmured to me. "She makes me take this horrid stuff all day long."

"You know Doc Shaw said it's good for you," Mother admonished.

"Yes, well, he doesn't have to drink it." She pushed the spoon toward him. He pursed his lips, squeezing his eyes until the sharp taste subsided.

"Uh!" He shook his head. "Please tell me I don't have to take anymore."

"Only at bedtime," Mother said.

He reached out to pat her graying hair. "Whatever you say, dear."

"We just want you to get better," I said.

"Well, I believe you'll find me up and running strong in no time. Where is Sidney?"

"She's playing."

"I shall see her later on today then."

"We'll see," I said. "You need to get your strength back."

"Oh, nonsense, I'm not dead yet. I have too much to do. There's still plenty of fight in this old man." He wheezed. A deep rasp grew into a full-blown coughing fit. Mother grabbed a warmed towel. She laced it with eucalyptus oil and placed it against his chest, while rubbing his back until the cough subsided.

I stepped out to clear my thoughts and decided to take a walk. I had never seen my father in such a weakened state. Distant gunfire reminded me to stay on the path. Through the trees, the back of a cloaked, short person came into view. The figure bent down on one knee to position for the kill, and one well-directed shot rang out. Boots brushed past foliage as the person ran toward the mark and picked up the limp body of a rabbit.

"You're a good marksman," I called out. The person turned to face me. "Elizabeth?"

"Sister!" Elizabeth dropped her prey and ran to me. We embraced. "When did you get here?"

"Just today."

"And Sidney?"

"Yes, she's at the house. My you're quite the frontier woman now."

"Well, with Father fallen ill, somebody's got to keep food on the table." She retrieved the rabbit, and we walked back to the house.

"I fear Father may not recover."

"Ah! He's a tough old bird. I don't think he'll be down long now that you and Sidney are home."

"I hope you're right." We entered through the back door, and Elizabeth stretched the furry carcass across the preparation table for the cook to skin.

"Oh, that makes two in one day. We having rabbit stew tonight," Etta said.

Sidney ran through the dining room and gave Elizabeth a big hug. "I've missed you."

"Hey, you've grown," Elizabeth said, and handed her a basket. "You want to help me pick some vegetables for supper tonight."

"Sure," Sidney said.

"Miss Elizabeth," Maggie cried at the back door. "Come quick, please. The foreman's beating my boy." Her British accent still intrigued me after all these years.

"Oh, no, those beetle-heads never listen to me." She ran out the door and followed Maggie to the barn.

"Stay here, Sidney," I said, taking off after them. I arrived upon the scene with Elizabeth standing her ground, straddled over a slave boy who huddled beneath her.

"I told you to stop hurting these boys. They're doing the best work they can."

"Lazy bantlings are nothing but trouble, Ma'am. Master William—"

"Shut your bone box and leave my father out of this. Master William left me in charge until he reaches a full recovery, so don't you go trying nothing behind my back here. I'll not have any slave whipped on my watch." She stepped forward and got right in his face. "Are you hearing me right?"

"Yes, ma'am. I'm just trying to do my job."

"Well, you can do your job without all the bluster."

The foreman muttered, "I'll give the durgen a cold pig bath next time."

"I don't want to hear another word about it. Get on with your work." The foreman threw down the whip and stomped away. Elizabeth turned around to help the slave boy to his feet. "Go on now and try to stay out of trouble." She slapped her hat on his back as he trotted away.

"Bless you, Miss Elizabeth," Maggie said. "Thank you so much for your kindness."

I looked at her, admirably. "Elizabeth! I can't believe you stood up to him like that!"

A crooked grin crossed her face.

"Weren't you scared?" I asked.

"Heck no! These guys aren't going to hurt me. They need their jobs too bad."

"Well, you've certainly learned a lot about managing a farm."

"Can't say it wasn't forced on me. Thomas went off to the university, and George married some Southern belle down in South Carolina."

We walked back toward the house. "I'm sorry I haven't been here to help more."

"Ah, I don't mind. This is home. I love it here. I don't ever want to leave. I'm glad I never married. Father's just happy one of his children stayed to take care of this place."

"I'm so proud of you."

"Thanks." She bumped my shoulder in a playful gesture, but nearly pushed me to the ground. Her strength and confidence amazed me.

Over the ensuing weeks, Elizabeth taught Sidney how to hunt and fish, two skills most children raised in the more cultured Northern colonies rarely needed. Yet it never hurt to know.

Father's condition grew worse. Mother and I took shifts, staying by his side day and night. We feared the worst and prayed in earnest for his recovery. The medicine bottle was almost empty, and though it only seemed to help a little, it did offer him some relief. Mother sent me to town to retrieve more from Doc

Shaw. I took Sidney.

Andrew waited at the porch to help us into the carriage. A slave boy about Sidney's age sat on the front bench next to him. Something about this child seemed familiar. He looked directly at me with that same penetrating stare, the same kind of stare that saw right through to my soul, and I knew at once. Memories flooded back from the deep recesses of my mind. Was this the twin I gave to Maggie when I gave birth? My son? I covered my mouth. The last time I saw him, he was still a babe. Once discharged into Maggie's care, I never saw him again. Mother forbade me to speak of him or to inquire about him anymore. I dismissed him from my presence entirely as if he had never existed.

My heart throbbed as I recalled the events surrounding his birth. I swallowed hard as a feeling of nausea stirred in the pit of my stomach. Here I lived with wealth and nobility, while my own flesh and blood lived impoverished and disgraced. How could I let this happen to my own child, my son? I pressed against my chest and tried to breathe in the fresh air to calm my nerves. I reminded myself and knew in my heart that no one—not even my good friend Betsy—could ever find out. Was there nothing else I could do for him? And what about Sidney? No, she could never know she had a twin brother.

Andrew stopped the carriage in front of Doc Shaw's office across from the general store. I climbed out after Sidney and glanced over at the boy. His piercing eyes, strong jaw line, and well-balanced frame reminded me of Simon. The office door opened and the jingling of a bell drew my attention to the task. "Andrew, meet us in front of the general store. I have to pick up some things."

"Yes ma'am, Miss Constance," he said, slapping the reins.

"Come along, Sidney."

We entered the doctor's office and waited for an unusually long time. A strong medicinal smell filled the air. I swallowed, nauseous. Finally, Doc Shaw walked through some curtains. "I'm sorry it took longer than expected. So many folks suffer with the same ailments right now that I decided to make a larger batch." He wrapped the dark brown bottle in a piece of brown paper and tied it off with string.

I placed a small wooden box of cigars—the preferred form of payment—on the desk. He handed me the bottle. "Thank you, Doc Shaw." A soothing warmth penetrated through the paper.

"Please tell your mother I'll come tomorrow to check on Master William."

"I will. Thank you again." I followed Sidney out the door and took her hand to walk across the road to the general store.

Mrs. Willis greeted me kindly. "Why Constance, I haven't seen you here in what? A year or more? How are you?"

"We are all well, except for my father."

"Oh, yes, I'm so sorry. Our prayers are with you."

"Thank you. Is our package ready?"

"Yes, I have it right here." She pulled it out from under the counter and handed it to me. "Will there be anything else?"

Sidney pulled my dress, "Mother? Can I have one of those?"

"Why Sidney, I didn't even see you standing there?" Mrs. Willis said. "My goodness, you have grown."

"Hello Mrs. Willis," Sidney said with a curtsy.

"Oh my and how lady-like, just like her mother." She placed a hand on the container. "These are sugarplums, fresh made. Two on a stick for a farthing."

I smiled and nodded at Sidney. "Yes, you may have one, dear."

She pointed to a red piece. "Can I have that one, please?"

"You sure can, honey." Mrs. Willis stabbed at two sugarplums and handed them on a stick to her. "Here you go, sweetheart. Shall I put this on account?"

"Yes, please. It was nice to see you again." We stepped out onto the boardwalk where Andrew and the carriage waited.

The slave boy, whom I now realized was Simon Jr., stepped in front of Sidney. "Can I taste that?"

Sidney stood there with her red lips parted. "What?"

I stared at him, making note of his demeanor, questioning, whether he knew of his connection to Sidney. Why else would he make such a brazen request? Did Maggie tell him? Surely not.

Andrew grabbed him by the shirt and pulled him back, "Boy, what's the matter with you? You don't be acting like that. Now say you're sorry to Miss Sidney," he said, releasing his hold.

"I just want to know what it tastes like," he said.

The leering eyes of passersby alarmed me. "Let's just go now, Andrew. Sidney, get into the carriage."

Simon Jr. snatched the stick and ran off. I knew he risked a severe punishment. "Andrew! Go after him!"

"Best we leave him," Miss Constance. "He can find his way back to the farm on his own. And when he do, I'll be sure he gets a whipping he ain't never to forget."

A child screamed. Mr. Willis appeared from around the corner, dragging Simon Jr. by the neck. "Is this here your Negro, Miss Constance?"

"Oh, yes. Thank you, Mr. Willis. I'll take care of him from here."

Mr. Willis pushed Simon Jr. to the ground in front of him. He reached for a whip that hung near the front door and said, "This boy needs to learn his place." The whip snapped against the boards next to Simon Jr., who panted in anguish. The next strike hit across his back. He screamed and curled into a ball.

Every motherly instinct within me wanted to

protect my child. Like an angry she-bear, I wanted to kill Mr. Willis. I held Sidney close and shielded her eyes. Blood splattered against the hem of my dress. I watched in horror as the small boy huddled at my feet. He scooted about the floor trying to miss the whip.

"Please, stop! Mr. Willis, that's enough now! He's just a boy!"

"No Ma'am, Miss Constance. This boy needs to know he's done wrong." He thrashed the whip again, and blood splashed against my face and dress.

I held my arm up to block any more from hitting me and yelled, "Stop!"

Simon Jr. put his face to the floorboard, trembling, gasping through sobs.

"Enough!" A man's voice boomed.

Willis stopped midway to thrashing and looked out above the crowd. "Who said that?"

I turned, sifting through the crowd until I spied a red bandanna. My eyes moved upward to the neck and chin to see the familiar face of Matthew McClain come into view.

He stepped forward. "Now see here. This is just a child." He took hold of the whip and wrestled it away from Mr. Willis. "Have you no sense of common decency? There are women and children bearing witness to this."

Willis wiped the blood off his face with his sleeve. "Why, he's just a slave. What do you care?"

McClain bent down to check on the boy, who flinched at his touch. "Here now, I'm not going to hurt you." He helped the lad to his feet. "What's your name?"

Simon Jr. stood there, shaking, bleeding, not saying a word.

McClain took his finger and dabbed lightly against a wound on the child's cheek. He stood up and held his hand out to show the crowd. "What color is this blood?"

Another child called out. "Red!" His mother shushed him quickly.

"That's right! This child might be a slave to you, but his blood runs as red as yours and mine. And it's the same color as the very Savior we all say we serve."

The crowd murmured and began to disperse.

McClain looked back at Willis. "And his pain runs as deep."

Willis spit on the ground, and pointed to Simon Jr. "Get him out of here," he said, turning to leave.

Andrew picked the boy up and set him on the carriage bench.

Mathew McClain helped Sidney into the carriage and then assisted me. I reached out for his hand, squeezed it tight, and said, "Thank you. From the bottom of my heart, thank you."

"I just did what was right," he said.

"You are welcome at our home anytime." The carriage started rolling. I sat up to look back at him.

"Come for supper?"

"I just might do that," he said, grinning and adjusting his hat.

Halfway home, I helped Simon Jr. climb down into the carriage and dressed his wounds using strips of my petticoats. "I'm so sorry he did this to you."

Simon Jr. sniffed. "I just wanted to taste it. I'm sorry, Miss Sidney."

"It's okay," Sidney said.

"I ain't never got no candy before." The boy swallowed. "But it sure was good," he said, licking his lips.

I wiped his brow. "I've got an idea. Maybe next time we can get two sugarplum sticks and give Simon Jr. one on the way home when nobody's looking." A few minutes later, he fell asleep, his head in my lap.

Just before we reached the entrance to the farmstead, Sidney asked, "Is Master McClain going to be my father?"

"Sidney Alise, you know better than to ask such a presumptuous question."

"It's just that I never knew my real father. Don't you think he'd make a good one?"

I looked away, avoiding eye contact, making no further comment. Certainly, Matthew McClain had won my respect that day. I hoped Sidney didn't notice my lingering smile.

-24-

The Luncheon

At the Charleston Public Library, the women of the historical society, including me, planned a campaign to save the farmstead. Anna May opened the meeting.

"The agenda for the Ravenswood Historical Society meeting was posted online today, and is scheduled for next month at the local library. Our only concern on the agenda today is the vote to sell the farmstead to a construction company owned by Judge Beck." She handed some papers to Kate and me, and we passed them out to everyone.

Dad arrived and sat next to Mother.

Anna May continued. "My plan is to change the voters' minds. From what I've found on the website, they show nine board members who make all the decisions. Out of those nine, six lean toward a *yes* vote to sell the farmstead. Two are undecided, and one remains anonymous, voting absentee, a ghost voter. It could be anyone, even Judge Beck himself. Who knows? The main thing is to give the community a positive image on the value of the farmstead and its history. How are the plans for our Pioneer Days

Festival at the farm coming along? I think we should use this opportunity to raise funds for renovations. Kate, have you heard back from the reenactment group?"

"Yes. They are ready and willing to do a full reenactment of the battle between Chief Cornstalk and Colonel Andrew Lewis at Point Pleasant."

"Good." Anna May turned to my mother. "Ms. Proctor, have you heard back from the Trail Riders Club?"

"Yes. They said they can organize all-day wagon rides that will take our guests on the original path Benjamin Franklin took from the General Store to the farmstead."

"Miss Fanny, what have you heard?" asked Anna May.

"I contacted the quilting club. They will be glad to do demonstrations on how to make flags and star samplers."

"Very good." Anna May glanced around the room and pointed. "Nicole, how's the design for the flyer coming?"

"Almost done," I said. "Just have to make copies and get them out to our volunteer distributors."

My dad raised his hand. "Hi, I'm Sam Durham, Nicole's father. I do freelance work for local newspapers, and I'd be glad to donate my services for a cover story on the history of the farmstead, to help raise awareness."

Mom smiled and patted his arm.

Marilou pushed her hand up and waved. "I've contacted a structural engineer to make sure the tunnel is safe to show. He should be out tomorrow."

Mother sat forward. "Maybe we could have a tour set up and charge a small donation, where people can see the attic and the secret room. We can take them downstairs to the basement, walk them through the tunnel and on out to the barn."

"We could have wagon rides to the barn," I said, "and walk them through the tunnel from that direction to reenact how the slaves actually experienced it."

"Those are all great ideas." Anna May's eyes sparkled with excitement.

"Sure hope that tunnel's in good enough shape. I should know by tomorrow," Marilou said.

"Good work, ladies and gentleman," Anna May said. "The owner of the tearoom decided to waive the rental fee and provide the food free of charge."

"Oh, wow!" I said, and clapped along with everyone else.

"This is good news, finding such community support. I've sent a personal invitation to every board member of the Ravenswood Historical Society. So far, six of them responded positively. Now remember there are nine total, but one is the ghost member. I'm hoping the other two will respond soon. Are we all ready to go this Saturday to pass out flyers, door to door, before the luncheon?"

The group acknowledged with nods and *yes*.

"Then we will meet here at the library parking lot at eight AM sharp. It takes a while to get there, and we want enough time to pass out and post flyers around the town square."

Dad asked to borrow a computer and followed Anna May to her office after the meeting. Minutes later, he rejoined the small group that lingered behind to chat. "I can meet the deadlines for both the *Charleston Gazette* and the *Ravenswood Times*," he confirmed.

"Thanks so much for doing this, Mr. Durham. This will help a lot," said Anna May.

On the way home, Dad explained his plan for work. "Bob said he can't let me come into the office every day, but he can pay me for freelance work under a pseudonym."

"That's brilliant, honey," Mother said.

"Well, it should help keep the bills paid for a while, anyway. The unemployment won't last for long."

"Can you come to the festival with us?" Mom asked.

"I'm not sure. It depends on whether or not I have an assignment. Right now I have to take anything I can get."

Saturday came early. Kate and I rode together

and led the way, while Marilou, Mother, and Grammy, followed. Anna May had picked up Miss Fanny a little earlier and forged ahead, along with two more cars filled with volunteers.

When we arrived at the tearoom in Ravenswood, I handed each volunteer a stack of flyers.

Fanny and Grammy stayed at the tearoom with other volunteers to help decorate.

Anna May handed them a list telling them where to set place cards in a planned pattern on the tables. There were extra tables, additional seating for city officials and members of the press, both locally and from Charleston.

Anna May and I, with a few others, left to put up flyers in the town square. We hit every shop window, the library, bank bulletin boards, the corner deli, a convenience store, and quite a few telephone poles.

"Thank goodness Ravenswood is a small town," Anna May said, as we walked back to finish preparations for the luncheon.

We arrived back at the tearoom with enough time to relax and drink iced tea.

A few minutes later, our guests made their way through a set of double doors. A head table and several round tables covered with white linen displayed beautiful country rose patterned china, crystal stemware, silverware and a color-coordinated napkin folded atop each plate.

Fanny sipped hot tea, while chatting with two

Ravenswood Historical Society board members.

Anna May perused the room, pleased that her strategy seemed to be working. At least one historical society member adequately covered each board member. She bent over and whispered in my ear. "I notice only five board members are here. They happen to be five out of the six board members who have already decided to vote for selling the farmstead. I'm concerned about the other two undecided voters."

I whispered back. "I hope they get here soon."

She walked to the podium and tapped the microphone. Feedback squealed through the amplifier. "Welcome to the historical society luncheon. We appreciate your attendance. This gives us an opportunity to share our concerns regarding the current ballot involving the sale of the farmstead once known as Washington's Woods. I see not all our guests have arrived, so we'll allow a little more time before proceeding. In the meantime, please feel free to enjoy the wonderful tea. Our food should be served shortly."

Anna May sat and introduced herself to the ladies at her table. Shortly after that, an unexpected entourage of men arrived and barged through the double doors. Judge Beck, along with his lawyer, the manager of Beck Construction Company, Alan Myers, the historical society president, and the other two undecided voters, walked into the room as if they owned the place. With six men in all, Judge Beck took a seat at an unoccupied table intended for the press. The other men took seats as well. Anna May's face turned a bit pale as she leered at Judge Beck with steely eyes. Lunch arrived, and she went to the podium to introduce herself. She explained the purpose for the luncheon, careful to remain cordial.

"We are surprised to have some unexpected guests with us today. The honorable Judge Beck has graced us with his presence." Everyone clapped, and Judge Beck smiled and waved. Then Anna May introduced Kate and me.

"Our two main speakers today are both from the Charleston area. They started researching their family heritage as a history class project and found out much more than they could have imagined. I think you'll find their story fascinating. Here are Nicole Durham and Kate Walker." The crowd clapped generously.

Kate told her part of the story first, finishing with a tribute to her grandmother. "My grandmother once told me it's in the weaving of your heritage that you find out who you really are. When I think about that now, I wonder if Grandma Winnie knew more about our family than she let on. But now I've come to understand it in another way. Our lives are woven together, a lot like this star sampler."

I helped Kate hold up the sampler, now mounted in a new frame, as she began. "This isn't just about my family. It's about all families in America, and it's about freedom for all people. Each of us is like the threads on a sampler. We may come from different ethnic backgrounds, but we are all woven together to make one perfect piece." The small crowd applauded.

I finished by saying, "I hope you can see how much this farmstead means to the Durham-Miller families, as well as the Proctor-Walker families. Our lives came together in friendship first, but then we discovered a rich heritage. It also means a lot to this community and our entire country. I think a historical landmark of this nature would be a tourist's magnet. Along with the secret tunnel, we recently found linking evidence involving the Underground Railroad."

Kate interrupted, "Yeah, you gotta admit that part's really cool." The crowd applauded as we left the podium. Anna May began to introduce the last speaker, but she was interrupted.

Judge Beck stood, "Please excuse me. I just wanted to say one thing. We have our own tee time to make here in a few minutes, and I wanted to share a quick update."

"By all means then, go right ahead," Anna May said, stepping back from the microphone.

Judge Beck continued. "Thank you. I can just say it from here. Folks, I want all the board members to know that someone made a large donation toward the new building fund. That, along with the profit from selling the land, is more than enough to complete the plans for a brand new museum closer to town. We have plans to represent and display all the farmstead archives, including that lovely star sampler, if the family will permit it. The architect said he could even recreate the secret tunnel, a far safer exhibit than the present two hundred year-old structure. Thank you for your time, folks. This was a lovely luncheon, ladies, but I think we're still full from our breakfast. I'll see everyone at the board meeting." He smiled and waved goodbye in the usual political manner again. The entourage of men sidled Judge Beck as he left through the double doors. Laughter followed them as they walked away.

Anna May said, "Well, he certainly knows how to crash a party." Some chuckling in the crowd dissipated once the food arrived.

The sumptuous aroma of baked cordon bleu chicken wafted through the tearoom, which for some reason made me nauseous. I leaned over and whispered to Kate, "I think I'm going to be sick."

"Oh, no, come on," Kate said.

We snaked around tables to the restroom at the same time Miss Fanny pushed the door open. I rushed passed her. A moment later, I walked back to my seat and saw Miss Fanny standing next to the fish tank.

"Is everything all right?"

"Well, not exactly," she said, wryly, her eyes shifting to the tank.

I looked down and noticed her teeth resting serenely at the bottom of the tank. "Oh, my!"

"Just give me a minute. I can fish them out."

"It's probably best that we not draw attention to this. Follow me. We'll figure out how to get them later."

We got back to the table. Marilou noticed Miss Fanny's upper lip caved inward. "Miss Fanny, where are your teeth?" she whispered.

Miss Fanny pointed. Marilou followed her finger's direction. She nodded, maintained her composure, and managed to remain expressionless. The teeth now lay at the bottom of the tank, a scavenger fish sucking on them. The lionfish flared into attack mode, while smaller fish poked at them upon closer inspection.

My mother tightened her lips to keep from laughing. "Lord, have mercy," she whispered, trying her best not to snicker.

Anna May approached the microphone. "I would like to introduce Ms. Marilou Walker of the original farmstead lineage." The crowd applauded.

Marilou leaned over and whispered to Fanny, "Don't talk to anyone or say anything." She smiled and walked to the podium. "I just want to let you all know that the structural engineer confirmed the tunnel is still structurally sound. We just needed to replace a couple of beams. We'll offer tours of the house and the tunnel during the Pioneer Days Festival. The visitors' tunnel tour from the barn to the house will enable them to experience what it was like to be a slave and use the Underground Railroad system. We also have a real steamboat coming to give ferry rides across the river. It is exciting that people of this generation will be able to experience what it was like living at the old farmstead during Civil War times. Please help us spread the word. I cannot see how a brand new structure could possibly replicate the value of this historical site. You can't replace the grain of worn wood on the steps of a colonial manor or the true ambiance of a two-hundred-year-old barn. Instead of making this another amusement park, let's keep history alive by preserving the past and giving future generations the chance to walk in their ancestral shoes."

Anna May adjourned the meeting. The crowd applauded and mingled afterward during which time Mother and I discreetly retrieved Fanny's teeth from the fish tank.

She wrapped them in a napkin. "Now we can't get them sterilized until we get back home. Just fake a smile for the cameras. Think you can do that?"

"I'll try," Miss Fanny said.

Reporters from the *Ravenswood Times* and *Charleston Gazette* took photos and did short interviews with Marilou.

Anna May showed us the paper. "Good thing those pictures are small," she said. "Miss Fanny has her tongue sticking out in every one of them."

-25-

A Guest for Supper

Pearlie, Jasmine's younger sister, assisted Sidney and me with washing and dressing, while I filled Mother in on what happened in town.

Mother hung her head. "Poor Simon Jr. But how noble of Master McClain. Hearing about his change of heart will please your father. He sat up and ate his entire breakfast this morning. He even asked me to prepare him a bath later this afternoon."

"Do you think he might join us for supper? I invited Matthew."

"Oh, it may be too soon for that yet. We shall have to see how things progress today." Mother twisted the handkerchief she held in her hand and cocked her head as if to inquire. "How nice that... Matthew is coming. Does this mean he will be calling on you again?"

"Mother!" I glared.

"Oh, all right, dear."

"I may have softened toward him, but that doesn't in any way reflect romantic notions."

"Well, you can't blame a mother for trying. I only want what's best for you and Sidney."

"I know."

"It's been eight years since Henry died. Don't you think it's time to get on with your life?"

"I think I've done quite well on my own. I don't really need a man now."

"But what about Sidney? A child needs a father."

"Her grandfather fills that role well enough."

Mother held onto my shoulders. "You've had to be strong on your own for so long now, and I'm very proud of you. Maybe it's time to let someone else help carry the burden—not *for* you, but *with* you."

In my heart, I knew she was right. I walked to the window, pulling my shawl tight. My knee bumped against the wall, and I looked down at my booted foot, scuffed and muddy. The creak of the door closing let me know my mother had left, and a sense of loneliness came over me. I stayed there for a long time pondering about life, the past, the present, and Matthew McClain.

Later that day, Sidney and I sat on the back porch. I churned butter, while she snapped peas. Mother walked past us with a bucket of soapy water. She carried it to the garden, dumped it, and returned to the porch. Wiping her brow, she said, "Your father is starting to get his strength back and will be joining us for supper tonight."

"I miss Grandpapa," Sidney said, clapping her hands.

I stopped churning. "Sidney, he's not completely

well yet. We must give him plenty of time to recuperate. Mother, could you hand me that bowl, please."

"Yes." She set the bucket next to the steps, pushing the bowl toward me. "We have to keep him calm, or he'll end up in bed again," she said.

The shadow of a horse and rider caught my attention. Matthew McClain appeared atop his steed, and I nearly lost my breath for a split second. The large butter bowl on my lap prevented me from standing. He dismounted and removed his hat. "Ladies, good day."

"Good day, Master McClain. Uh, I mean Matthew," I said, while wiping my hands against my apron. "I'm afraid you've caught us in the middle of preparations. Supper won't be ready for quite some time."

"I wanted to check on Master William, if he's up for a visit." He started for the steps, but a sudden downpour of gray water drenched him.

I gasped, realizing Father's bath water now dripped from Matthew's hair and upper garments. He stood flapping his arms in an attempt to shake off some. I raised my hand, but stopped short of covering my lips with butter. "Oh, my goodness! I'm so sorry." McClain's face clouded as he slapped his hat against his legs. In the awkward moment, I yelled up to the window. "Willow! Bring down one of Father's shirts."

Mother retrieved a towel and handed it to him.

"Here you are, sir. Kindly remove your shirt, and I will make sure it is cleaned and returned to you later this week."

"Thank you," he said, rubbing his head and face.

I looked for a way to escape the embarrassment. My bodice stained, hair frayed. I needed to gather my thoughts, dress for the evening. *But wait! Was he here to see Father or me? On the other hand, was Father a mere excuse?* Then I remembered I was the one who had invited him to supper. I felt my cheeks flush, and I turned away at such a girlish reaction. Patting the butter into a thick ball, I said, "I'd better get to the kitchen or this heat will..." I paused as he removed his shirt revealing a firm, muscular upper body. The creamy concoction oozed between my fingers. "...melt my butter," I said, breathless, the mist on my face reflecting more than the day's heat.

I shook my head to regain my senses, stood, and reached for the knob. My fingers slipped, but the door opened on its own. Willow stood at the threshold, carrying a folded shirt in her arms. I whisked past her.

I took my time getting ready for dinner. As I descended the stairs to the foyer, a sweet cigar aroma greeted me. Men jesting in low mumbles flowed from the study. A slight pull on my arm drew my attention away.

"Mother, Simon Jr. is asking for you," Sidney said, trotting ahead. I followed her to the kitchen, where Etta and Willow finished last minute dinner preparations. The enticing smells made my stomach growl a bit. At the back door, Simon Jr. stood next to Maggie, who held out a cornhusk doll to Sidney.

"Beggin' your pardon, Miss Constance. Simon Jr. told me about what happened in town today, and I just wanted to thank you for all you did for him. I made this doll for Miss Sidney. We are truly sorry for the trouble he caused you."

"Oh, Maggie," I shook my head in wonder at her humility after all I had put her through. "Of course, I couldn't allow such cruel treatment. Surely, you know me better than that by now."

"Yes, Miss Constance." She nodded with a slight curtsy. "Simon Jr. will not bring you anymore trouble." She nudged the little boy's shoulder.

Simon Jr. glanced at Maggie and back at me. "Yes, ma'am. I promise to be good from now on."

"Well then. Everything's just fine." I nodded. "Sidney?" I looked at her with a raised brow.

Her eyes darted between Maggie and me as she reached for the cornhusk doll. "Thank you," she said sweetly.

Maggie smiled, nodded, and curtsied again. "You're welcome, Miss Sidney. I'm glad you like it." She turned to leave and pulled on Simon Jr.'s arm for him to follow.

He looked back at me, gleam in his eye, and a grin as if asking, *Did I do good?* I smiled back.

The dinner conversation included an amusing

rendition of the events in town earlier that day. Laughing helped alleviate my fears. It turned out that Matthew McClain was quite the storyteller with an appealing sense of humor. He asked me to take a stroll with him after dinner. Sidney tried to follow, but Father intervened.

"Come play checkers with me, little one."

"Grandpapa, I'm eight years old now," she said, hands on hips.

"Oh, of course, how silly of me, but I bet I can still beat you at checkers."

"I bet you can't," she said, running into the parlor.

I walked the path to the gazebo, Matthew following close behind. We came to a clearing, which offered a spectacular view of the sunset over the river. My pulse quickened as his hand enfolded mine.

"I hope you don't find this too presumptuous of me," he said.

I fixed my eyes on his. "Not at all." My mouth creased, his gaze lingered. I did not resist his affections.

-26-

Pioneer Days Festival

Hundreds of people filtered through the farmstead on a colorful fall day. Reenactments of the war between Colonel Lewis and Chief Cornstalk included a morning and an early afternoon show at the battle's actual location in Point Pleasant. Wagons carried visitors from the original general store, located near the town square, to the farmstead, and included the story about Benjamin Franklin's visit.

Inside the farmhouse, we roped off the living room area where Uncle Eyrie stayed, covering the doorways to ensure his privacy. Tunnel tours started from the barn and went in one direction only, finishing up at the farmhouse attic. A steamboat, which offered a horn blast heard for several miles, completed the Underground Railroad experience. Pioneer-style tents, ranked in rows on the grounds, included people dressed in period costume. Women cooked in iron kettles over open fires while others sat next to looms and quilted. Men whittled small wooden toys and musical instruments, while a blacksmith pounded on horseshoes. Artisans crafted their wares. Pony rides and a petting zoo with goats and piglets entertained the children. Musicians played folk music on homemade fiddles, dulcimers and guitars.

At one of the open-sided tents, a hunter held up a wild turkey he shot with his musket. He wanted to demonstrate how to pluck it and prepare it for cooking, but Anna May, donning vintage dress herself, arrived just in time to stop him.

"Kind sir, please put away the bird," she said regally. "Your efforts are most noble; however, such a demonstration might disturb some of our younger guests." She patted his shoulder and smiled. "Save your turkey for a good dinner at home."

"As you wish, madam." He nodded and placed the bird in a cooler hidden behind a burlap curtain.

I followed Anna May through the crowd, past the old smokehouse—with real meat hanging from the beams—to the registration booth. She leaned over Mother and asked, "How are donations coming?"

Mother smiled. "Pretty good, but I haven't had a chance to count this afternoon's take yet."

"Okay. Let me know if you need a break," Anna May said.

"All right, Marilou should be back in about ten minutes."

Kate and I helped conduct the tours, both of us dressed in period costume. I dyed and redesigned Kate's princess dress into a fancy colonial style dress. We swapped off, taking groups of ten at a time. Some folks found it so fascinating they went through twice.

I stood at the bottom of the ladder in the tunnel holding a lantern, dressed like a house servant, and greeted guests as they descended.

"Shh, keep quiet. Follow me, please." I whispered to my followers as I led them through the tunnel, now well lighted. I pulled the latch and opened the hidden doorway to the basement, and Kate greeted them with a welcome speech much like the one Susanna had offered long ago. Kate led them to the attic to show the hidden room while sharing the story of how slaves escaped. The Daughters of the American Revolution handed out material at the conclusion of each tour.

All the board members of the Ravenswood Historical Society showed up. Many expressed their appreciation and gave positive feedback. Four out of the five that attended the luncheon changed their minds.

One board member said, "I can't see a brand new building recreating anything like this. It's fabulous."

Marilou said, "We can do this annually to keep funds coming in to maintain the farmstead."

"What a great idea," said another. "I've met folks from Kentucky, Tennessee, Ohio, and even Pennsylvania. All the hotels in town are full. It's really good for business."

At the end of the day, we all sat around the dining room table, while Mother and Marilou finished counting the donations and handed Anna May a paper note with the total amount.

Her eyes widened. "We made almost twenty thousand dollars in donations for the historical society renovation and rejuvenation fund."

"In one day?" Kate asked. She raised her arms in victory. "Yahoo!"

We all did a joy dance around the room.

"The most important thing is, we got the word out about the farmstead," Anna May said. "I think that's going to make the biggest difference in creating public interest."

"Maybe," I suggested, "we can continue public awareness by placing a thank you letter in all the newspapers."

"That's a great idea, honey." Mother said.

Kate bumped my hip. "Way to go."

Miss Fanny awakened from a nap, still a bit groggy. "Can I help with anything?"

Mother said, "Miss Fanny, you just keep sitting right there and keep your teeth in your mouth."

I stopped laughing when stabbing pain forced me to double over. "Ah!"

"Nicole, what's wrong!" Mother cried.

"I don't know! Ow!" I grabbed my stomach, squinted my eyes, and collapsed to the floor.

Mother screamed, "Someone call 911!"

Kate ran to my side. "Nicole?"

"They don't have 911 services out this far," Marilou said, holding the door open.

"Then where's the nearest hospital?" Mother demanded.

Anna May grabbed her keys. "Come on, I saw one on the way into town today."

The shadow of her figure walking toward the door grew dimmer, while Mother and Kate picked up my limp arms and helped me to the car. I stumbled along, trying to speak, but nothing came out. My head pounded, and I blacked out.

I awoke in the emergency room and blinked to focus on the IV protruding from my arm. "What happened?"

Kate sat next to me. "You passed out, Nicole."

Marilou touched my arm. "Welcome back."

Mother stroked my head. "How you feeling, baby?"

"My stomach is sore." I tried to turn over, but it hurt too much. I looked around the room.

"It'd be nice if they at least had a TV in here," Kate said.

"Not in the ER, Kate. It messes with the medical instruments." Marilou reminded her.

Mother helped me sit up. "Careful now."

"Ah, I'm good." I squirmed a bit.

A doctor and a nurse breezed into the room. "Hello, I'm Doctor Thompson. How are you feeling?"

"I'm okay. I guess."

"I'm just going to examine your abdomen." He moved the blankets down, pulled my gown up, and pressed gently.

"Ow!"

"Tender?" Dr. Thompson asked.

I tried to adjust my position. "Yeah."

Dr. Thompson held the stethoscope to my abdomen and listened. "Hmm!" He glanced around the room. "Ladies, would you mind going back to the waiting room for a moment? I need to conduct one other test and there's simply not enough room in here."

"I'm her mother. Can I stay?"

Dr. Thompson said, "We'll call you back in just a few minutes."

Marilou gently nudged my mother to move along.

The doctor pulled down an instrument from the wall and flipped a switch.

The nurse closed the door and returned, holding a plastic bottle. "This might be a little chilly." She squirted some gel onto my belly. I cringed at the cold.

Placing the round bulb of the instrument over the gel, Dr. Thompson rubbed it gently in circles across my abdomen. After a moment, a pulsating rhythm throbbed from the speakers.

"That's your baby's heartbeat," he said.

"What?"

"You're pregnant," the doctor confirmed.

"A baby?"

"When was your last period?" he asked.

I thought for a moment and said, "I guess a

month, maybe a little longer."

"And the last time you had intercourse?"

I stared blankly in a mesmerized dream-like state. "Uh, just over a month." I recalled the night Johnny and I eloped, and then the night Johnny was killed.

"That's about right for the size of your uterus. Your baby is doing well. You're almost six weeks along." Dr. Thompson wiped off the gel and removed his gloves.

"Then why am I so sick all the time?"

"It's quite common to experience extreme nausea. You are very dehydrated, however. I want you to stay overnight to build up your fluids. Of course, if you choose to terminate this pregnancy, you will need to decide as soon as possible. The procedure should be done before you reach the second trimester or shortly thereafter."

"When's that going to be?"

"Another month or so—give or take a couple of weeks," Dr. Thompson said.

"I need to talk to my mother. Can my friends come back in, too?"

"Yes, of course. But first, I need to know if I'm at liberty to speak about your condition in front of your mother and friends."

"No," I blurted. "I have to tell them first."

"I understand." He nodded. "I'm going to reserve a hospital room for you, then. The nurse will come get you when it's ready." Dr. Thompson left the room. The nurse followed.

Marilou, Kate and my mother returned. I told them about Johnny and me eloping, and then about the baby.

Mother almost fainted at the news, but Marilou caught her and helped her sit down in a chair. "Come on, girl. You've got to be strong now."

"My baby's having a baby," Mother said. "Oh, God, how can this be happening?"

Kate stood at the end of the bed, a blank look on her face. "How come you never said anything?"

"I don't know, Kate. I guess with everything happening in our families, it just seemed like too much."

My mother grabbed my arms and shook me. "Nicole, you can't have this baby. Judge Beck will kill you once he finds out."

"Mama, I knew who he was when I married Johnny. I just didn't know I was going to lose him. And I sure didn't know I was pregnant."

Marilou gently pulled my mother back. "Come on now. A baby can change people. This just might be what the good Lord planned all along."

"Oh, that's easy for you to say. It's not your child who's pregnant!" Mother snapped. Her hand trembled as she covered her mouth. "I'm sorry." Her face contorted. "I'm just scared," she cried.

Marilou embraced my mother and rocked her. "It's going to be all right."

I was too exhausted to cry or say anything. The news of my pregnancy started to sink in, and I now faced a decision that would alter the course of my life.

An hour or so later, my mother called my father to let him know we were staying overnight with Marilou. That was true, for the most part—they did stay with us.

We arrived home the next day, and Mother decided to let the dust settle a while before telling him anything.

I sat in a living room chair tapping my fingers on the arm, and Grammy relaxed in her recliner. She didn't know about the pregnancy yet, since Anna May had brought her home after leading everyone to the emergency room. My dad sat on the couch while Mother broke the news. He shook his head and ran his hands through his hair.

Grammy placed a hand on one cheek. "Oh, Lord, have mercy."

After a long pause Mother asked, "Sam? What are you thinking?"

He rubbed his chin. "Nicole, what are you going to do?"

"What do you mean?"

His eyes squinted, piercing right through me. "You know what I mean. Are you going to have this baby, or not?"

"Uh, I hadn't really thought that far ahead yet."

He raised his voice. "If you know what's good for you, you won't say a word to anyone and just get rid of it! We don't even have insurance right now!"

I shrunk back into my chair, surprised at his abrupt reaction.

"Sam!" Mother shouted.

"What?!" he shouted back. "If Judge Beck finds out she's carrying his son's baby, he's going to have us all killed."

My mother put her arms around my shoulders. "I can't believe you would even suggest such a thing."

Dad continued his rant. "You can't have this baby!"

My face contorted, and I ran to my bedroom. A few minutes later, the front door slammed so hard it made the window shake in my bedroom. Pounding footsteps just outside my window made me curious. I peeked through the blinds to see my dad stomping to the car.

"Nicole?" Mother knocked. "Open the door, honey."

"I don't want to talk about it." She knocked repeatedly, but finally gave up and left. I decided to call Kate and talk things out.

After a good cry, I said goodbye and walked across the hall to the bathroom to wash my face. The cool water relieved the redness around my eyes. Thirst drove me to the kitchen for a glass of water. I turned around and there stood Mom. "Oh, you startled me."

"Your daddy's not here, so you don't need to hide." Stress lined her forehead.

"What does he expect me to do, Mama? I loved Johnny and this is our baby. It's all I have left of him." My chin quivered.

"Honey, Daddy just needs time to figure all this out. He's in a state of shock, like the rest of us. This is the last thing we expected. A pregnant teenage daughter was nowhere on my radar. You have always been a good girl, a straight A student. Baby, you're way too smart for this."

"Oh, so loving Johnny makes me stupid, now?"

"No, it doesn't make you stupid." Her voice softened, her face relaxed. "It just makes you a woman much sooner than you needed to be."

She put her arms around my waist and walked me to the bedroom.

Dad returned home later.

I peeked through my blinds and saw him practically fall out of a taxi in the pouring rain.

My eyes followed him all the way to the porch.

"I'm singin' in the rain, just singin' in the rain." He stumbled on the front steps, where Mother met him on the porch. "Hello, my love." He grabbed her and forced her to dance with him. "I'm hap-happy again!" He hiccupped. "Oh, 'scuse me."

Mother pushed him away. "Over ten years of

sobriety and it's come down to this?" Dad pushed his hair back and looked at her with a sheepish grin. She shook her head and gave up trying to reason with him. "Come on, let's get you out of these wet clothes."

All those years and I blew it for him in one day. I sank into my bed, guilt hounding my conscience. My grief for Johnny surfaced and the realization of what I'd done to my family and to my father now overwhelmed me. With loud sobs, I cried into my pillow.

Sunday, Grammy prepared breakfast for everyone. Shelby and Jackson dressed for church, while I struggled through my morning ritual to upchuck in the toilet. I imagined the guilt about falling off the wagon the night before loomed in my dad's subconscious, along with a pounding hangover. I came out of the bathroom just in time to see Grammy going into the master bedroom. She slapped her hands together in an attempt to wake my father. I rushed to the door and poked my head inside.

"Uh, please be quiet." He turned over and smashed the pillow to his head.

Grammy persisted, "Get up now. Your redemption draweth nigh."

"Go away," he groaned.

"The Lord Jesus has got something good for you today. I'm not going to leave until you get up," Grammy persisted.

Mother walked in past me. "Grammy, maybe this isn't such a good idea."

Grammy started singing. "Amazing grace, how sweet the sound ..."

My father rolled and grabbed another pillow. "Turn her off, please."

I started to snicker, covering my mouth.

"That saved a wretch like me..." Grammy belted it out.

"Oh, dear God! Save me!" he pleaded.

"He hears you, child. Keep on praying now," Grammy said with relentless determination.

Mother snatched the pillow away. "You'd better get up. You know once she gets started, there's no stopping her."

My father sat up. "Aspirin," he said, eyes half closed. Mother retrieved the bottle of pain reliever from the bathroom, dropped two tablets into his hand. Tossing the pills in his mouth, he grabbed a water bottle on the nightstand and jugged down a few gulps.

"I once was lost, but now I am found. Was blind but now I see," Grammy finally stopped singing.

"Thank God," he said, pressing his hand to his forehead.

"Got some fresh coffee brewing. We leave in thirty minutes," Grammy announced as she walked past me, singing. "Oh, victory in Jesus, my savior forever ..."

My father stared at the pulpit in a fogged stupor, hands folded. I sat a few seats away, still hurt and upset about the harsh words from him the night before. The zealous mixed race worshipers cried out "Amen" and "Hallelujah." My father rubbed his eyes and temples.

"How many times did the Lord say to forgive our brothers and sisters?" Bishop Jacobson called out to his three hundred plus parishioners. "Seventy times seven" echoed across the congregation. "My grace is sufficient for thee," he continued.

I reached inside my pocket to find Johnny's ring and rolled it in my fingers. The thought of telling his parents about the baby made me shudder. My father's words barreled through my head like a freight train. *Maybe he's right. Maybe I should just get rid of it.*

-27-

Fire and Ash

Sometime in the middle of the night, I awoke to screams, clanking pots and pans.

"Fire! Fire!" Andrew yelled, banging against the front door. Just as Etta opened it, I reached the top of the stairs.

"Tell Master the crops is on fire." Andrew left, and I ran to wake up Mother and Father, while screaming back at Etta.

"Come help me wake the others."

"Father! Mother! The crops are on fire!" Father, now fully recovered, pulled on his trousers.

I ran to my bedchamber and threw on a work dress.

Sidney roused and walked across the hallway wiping her eyes. "What's wrong?"

"Get dressed and fetch a bucket. We've a fire to put out." I stopped at the kitchen and gathered as many pots as I could carry to the river.

Elizabeth and Sidney formed a line with the slaves, while I dipped pots into the river to fill barrels. Father drove the horses close to the fire, while slaves tilted the barrels to drown the flames.

Another scream came from the house. I craned my neck to see a group of men on horseback. They surrounded two slaves tied together. A rope hung over the branch of a tree. Sidney started for the house.

"No! Sidney, stay with Etta." I ran toward the house, and Elizabeth pulled my arm.

"Follow me!" We ran to the backdoor and through the house. She took the pistol out of the parlor desk drawer and placed it in my hand. I turned it over, unsure of what to do, much less how to use it. "That's Willis and his gang. They must have set the fire. We can't fight them unarmed." The spark of excitement in her eyes scared me. She ran through the house to retrieve her musket.

I moved the pistol from one hand to the other. "Shouldn't we wait for Father?"

"He's too far away. He'll never get here in time." She glared back at me. "If we don't do something to stop them, they're going to kill our slaves." She cracked the front door, poked the rifle tip out, turned her head toward me, and said, "Ready to show 'em what we're made of, sis?"

I swallowed, adjusting my hold on the pistol as she opened the door. Elizabeth stepped out onto the front porch, and I positioned myself beside her.

"Hold it right there, Willis!" she called.

The mob of men laughed. Mr. Willis yelled. "Well, what have we got here?" He turned his horse to face us.

"Just let our slaves go, and there won't be any trouble."

"Not this time. Everybody knows you're all a bunch of slave lovers, and we're not going to stand for it anymore. Are we, boys?"

Several men yelled out, "No ... no more." One of them screamed, "String 'em up."

"These are our field hands. We bought and paid for them. You don't have the right to come on our land and kill them."

"We'll see about that. Pull 'em up, boys!" The other mob members rallied around Willis. They placed a noose around the neck of a slave with his hands tied behind him. The rope tightened and pulled his body away from the ground. His feet dangled as he gagged and struggled to free his arms.

Elizabeth cocked the lever and aimed. A shot rang out. Her perfect marksmanship cut the rope, dropping the slave to the ground. "Get off our land! I'm not going to tell you again," she said, while reloading.

Willis pulled back on the reins of his horse. "No woman tells me what to do."

I held up the pistol with shaky hands as I struggled to cock it. "She said—get off our land!"

Willis ignored me, turned his horse back toward the mob. "String him up again!"

The pistol shot out and fell from my hand. His hat flew to the ground. I stared wide-eyed and bent down to retrieve the pistol. Accident or not, it worked.

The man holding the rope let go immediately. "I'm getting out of here." He took off along with the others leaving Willis alone.

Out of the shadows cried a small voice. "You leave my brother alone!"

I squinted to see. It was Simon Jr. standing there.

"Why you little ..." Mr. Willis kicked hard, and his horse reared.

"Run, Simon!" I yelled.

The little boy took off through the fields toward the fire, Willis in hot pursuit.

I ran through the house and out the back door. Climbing into a wagon, I slapped the reins to head toward the fields.

Simon Jr. ran faster than lightning, darting through the rows of tobacco stalks.

I caught up to Willis and attempted to block him. "Stop!" I called out. "He's just a boy!"

"Get out of my way!" Mr. Willis ran the horse around the wagon.

He almost caught Simon Jr. in the blazing field, but a barrel came out of nowhere, knocking him to the ground. His horse bolted. Willis stumbled to his feet and looked around. He spied Simon Jr. across the field and pulled out a pistol.

"Stop!" I screamed again. "Leave him alone!"

Willis ran ahead, straight for Simon Jr. He took a shot, but the boy darted just in time for it to miss. As he reached the end of a row blocked by fire, he turned to find Willis pointing his gun directly at him.

"I've got you now!" Willis sneered. He cocked the lever and pulled the trigger. Before the bullet reached its target, someone jumped through the flames, shielding the boy.

Willis aimed at Simon Jr. again and another shot rang out. The gun fell to the ground as Willis arched his back. "Aw!" he screamed. His legs buckled, and he fell to the ground face down.

My eyes scanned the row behind Mr. Willis and found Elizabeth, her musket pointed straight at him. I ran to Simon Jr., but he ran past me to Maggie. A loud moan drew my attention back to the stranger, and I ran to check on him. As I drew closer, I recognized him. "Simon?" I fell to my knees and held his face in my hands. "Simon? What are you doing here?"

Simon took a deep breath, swallowed hard. "I...I had to see for myself."

"See what?"

His voice faded to a whisper. "My boy."

"But ... how did you know?"

Simon pleaded with his last few breaths. "You take him to Philadelphia...raise him to be free... free." His eyes, fixed on me, clouded as his head fell back against the soil.

The man I had loved for so long now lay dead in a burning field. As flames drew closer, I tried to drag his body until help arrived. The other slaves picked up

Simon's body and carried him. I followed. Maggie joined me, and we both sobbed for the loss of her son. Simon Jr. walked beside us, staring at me.

I pulled Maggie aside and held tight to her arm. "How much did you tell him?"

"Nothing, Miss Constance. I swear, I didn't tell him a thing."

I released her, but my eyes searched hers. "Then, how did Simon know?"

Maggie rubbed the place I'd held. "He said a freed slave told him about Simon Jr. He came back with Captain James to see for himself. He must have figured things out on his own."

It only made sense that Simon recognized, right away the same features I did. Stepping closer, I touched her arm again, but gently this time. "I'm sorry, Maggie. Surely you know I loved him too."

She lowered her chin, turned, and followed her son's body to the barn.

Three quarters of our crops burned to the ground that night. I walked back to the house sweaty and exhausted, covered in ash. Father stood on the back porch, barking out orders for the day.

"There's nothing more we can do now. The fields need to cool first. Everyone go and rest. We can start replanting tomorrow." He slapped his hat against his thigh and turned toward the back door.

I sat down in a rocking chair, contemplating the night's events. Simon, his death, and how he knew about Simon Jr. He saved our son's life. In silence, I grieved, daring not to show despair over a black man, free or not. My temples pounded as tears pooled.

"It's all right to cry," said a familiar voice. My head jerked up, and I pushed forward to stand. His gentle eyes beckoned me. He held his hat in one hand, rubbing it with his index finger. His comforting words drew me like a lighthouse guiding a ship in a storm. "I hear crying's good for you," Matthew McClain said.

I surrendered to my emotions, ran to him, and buried my face in his chest. My shoulders quivered as his arms enfolded me, and I leaned into him. He held me for a long time, until my shaking calmed, and my breathing steadied. I wiped my swollen eyes and a runny nose; turned away, fearing he misunderstood my vulnerability. Matthew removed the red bandanna from around his neck and handed it to me.

"Thank you," I said. I remembered the signal on the wagon, and the soon-found freedom it represented. If this farmstead did not exist, how else might slaves escape this apartheid? How would Simon Jr. go free? I realized he was the reason Simon came back, and why he risked everything. He wanted to take his son with him to Philadelphia. He wanted our son to grow up a free man in a free state.

"Are you going to be all right?" Matthew asked.

"Yes, I'm fine." I glanced up and saw the ash on his face and clothes. "When did you arrive?"

"I came as soon as I heard. By the time I reached

the bend in the road, the sky was so dark with smoke I could hardly see enough to ride."

Placing my hand in his, I said, "Thank you for coming." My arm tingled as his fingers entangled mine.

"I want you to know I'll always be here for you and your family, Constance."

"I know."

He squeezed my hand. "I'll come back tomorrow to help with replanting."

"I'll tell Father."

He turned to leave, but I didn't want him to go and found myself walking after him. I wanted to stay in his arms, to feel his skin against mine and tell him all my secrets. He mounted his horse just as Simon Jr. rounded the corner of the house.

"Miss Constance, Mama be wantin' to know what to do about the dead man in the barn."

"Do you mean the man who saved your life?"

"Yes ma'am. I don't know why he done that, but I sure is grateful to him."

I motioned for him to come to me and cupped his shoulders. "He did it because he knew you were someone special."

He scratched his head. "Special?"

"Yes! God has special plans for you, Simon Jr."

"That's what Mama's always telling me, but I don't know." He shrugged.

"You will soon enough." I released my hold. "Tell

your mother we will bury Simon next to his son's grave site tomorrow."

"Yes ma'am." He turned to run away as a wagon approached. The foot of a dead body bounced over the edge.

The foreman called out to me. "I'm taking Willis's body into town for his widow to bury him."

I nodded and lowered my head. *Poor Mrs. Willis, no children, left a lonely widow to run the store. How will she ever manage?* However, now that I think about it, she might consider this her redeeming grace. He always placed impossible demands on her. I remember times when she could hardly walk through the store. She said the heavy lifting hurt her back, but I suspected otherwise. I imagined living with him was worse than hell itself.

-28-

The Vote

"Everyone," Anna May said. "I'm afraid I must announce the Ravenswood Historical Society vote ended up in a tie." The crowd murmured.

"Now what?" I said.

"They have to get the ghost member to vote and break the tie," said Anna May.

"Who *is* this ghost member?" Marilou asked.

"Adam Myers is the only one who knows that," Anna May continued.

"How do they know this ghost member actually exists?" Kate asked.

"I guess they just have to take Mr. Meyer's word on it," my mother shrugged." The question on my mind is what's going to happen to Uncle Eyrie now?" she asked.

"That's a good question, Luella," Marilou said. "The historical society wasn't supposed to take possession of the property until he either died or became unable to live by himself."

"I've got a bad feeling about this," I said.

Mother paced the room, arms crossed. "Well, he's not dead yet and he's still perfectly capable of caring for himself, but what can we do to stop the new property owner from kicking him out?"

"Hmm! We're just going to have to put our heads together. Who all is coming to the meeting at the library this Thursday?" asked Anna May. Almost everyone nodded. "Good. Meantime, you may want to get in touch with Uncle Eyrie to see how he's doing. We might need to get a lawyer. I know someone who could help us out. I'll try to get him to come to the meeting.

"I'll call Uncle Eyrie in the morning," Marilou said.

"All right, see you all Thursday. This meeting is adjourned."

Anna May's lawyer friend appeared at the door just as the Charleston Historical Society finished up with the regular meeting. "Allow me to introduce Mr. Clarence J. Wallace. He's an attorney. I've explained most of the situation to him. What we are most concerned about is Marilou's Uncle Eyrie and his residency rights at this point. He is eighty-eight years old, and he's lived there all his life."

Wallace raised a hand. "Nice to meet you, ladies. I have here a copy of the last will and testament of, Winifred Evelyn Proctor-Walker. It does state that her brother, Eyrie Proctor, may retain residency on the property until such time he dies or deemed unable to live alone. Therefore, should the property be sold by the historical society, the new owner may be legally obligated to comply with the same stipulations. But there's a loophole. Should the new owner have full clearance from all parties involved, then they would have the right to take possession of the property upon reasonable notice to the current tenant, which should be at least thirty days."

"Oh, no. This means that Uncle Eyrie could be forced out," Marilou said,

"Yes, I'm afraid so," Wallace confirmed.

Fanny sat up. "That's *terrible*." She looked at the attorney, "They need to remember they're going be old someday too."

"When will the sale be finalized?" Marilou asked.

"The board member I spoke with said that the Beck Construction Company has already drawn up the contract and presented it to the board. All they have to do is sign it," Anna May said.

"So it has to be signed by everyone on the board?" I asked.

"Yes." Anna May squinted.

"And that means the ghost member has to sign it too, right?

Mr. Wallace pointed at me. "This young lady could be onto something here. Finding this ghost board member to persuade them not to sign the contract is your best option at this point. Then Uncle Eyrie won't have to move."

"But nobody knows who this person is," Marilou said.

After a pause, Kate said, "Maybe we should call

Ghostbusters?" A few chuckles rose from the group.

I shifted my weight and leered. "You just had to say that."

Marilou held up one finger. "Or better yet, a private investigator."

"And just how are we supposed to pay for that?" my mother asked.

Marilou stood. "We just raised over twenty thousand dollars to help renovate the farmstead. If we're going to lose it, then why not use some of that money?"

Anna May shifted her attention to the attorney. "Can we do that?"

He nodded. "As long as it goes toward the preservation of the farmstead and the property is in jeopardy."

"Well, all right then. Anybody know a good private investigator?" Marilou looked around the room.

Miss Fanny raised her hand. "My great-grandson is a private investigator."

"You go, girl!" Mother said.

"Do you have his number?" Marilou asked.

"I have it right here." She fumbled through her purse and pulled out a business card. Mother passed it to Marilou.

"Great! Is everybody in favor of me contacting ...?" Marilou read the name on the card, "*Spy Guys Investigation Services*?" Everyone agreed, and the meeting adjourned.

After a few days of research, The Spy Guys investigation team met with Anna May, Marilou, Kate, and me. Mother had a rush order to finish and couldn't make it.

"Did you find out who this ghost member is?" Anna May asked.

Tyrone typed on his laptop until a picture appeared. He flipped the screen around and pointed. "This is the original deed with the ghost member's signature. It looks like George W. Proctor is our ghost."

"George W. Proctor? Who's he?" Marilou asked.

Tyrone pulled up the most recent signature on the new deed. "Wait a minute, here's something you should see." He stepped aside so everyone could see both signatures side by side.

Kate stared down. "They don't even look the same."

"Not even close," I said.

"Exactly," Tyrone said. "We have reason to believe that the most current signature is fake."

"Forgery?" Anna May asked.

Tyrone nodded.

Anna May continued, "Well, he's definitely crossed the line now."

Marilou said, "But what about Uncle Eyrie? When do they want him to move out?"

Tyrone turned the laptop back around. He typed

on the keyboard, and seconds later had the answer. "Courthouse records show they sent him a certified letter last month. According to the date, Uncle Eyrie has to be out by the end of this month. That's this weekend."

"What?" Marilou gasped.

"The poor man is 88 years old for goodness sake," Mother protested.

"That can't possibly be right," Marilou said.

"I'm sure this is an accurate record. Evidently, Uncle Eyrie doesn't read his mail," Tyrone said.

"Where on earth do they expect this poor man to go?" Kate asked.

Cecil finally spoke up. "Apparently these guys don't care."

"Well, we've got to get Uncle Eyrie out of there or the construction company's going to show up and start bulldozing the place," Mother said.

"Surely they would inspect the place first," Marilou said.

"I wouldn't depend on that, Cecil said. "These guys get paid by the job and their main motto is get 'er done."

"When exactly will they be doing this?" I asked.

Tyrone looked at the calendar. "Saturday, first thing in the morning around eight o'clock."

Marilou gasped. "That means we only have one day left to get Uncle Eyrie out of there."

Anna May, cell phone to ear, said, "I'm calling

Clarence Wallace. There's got to be a way to delay this action somehow."

"If you find out anything, please call me," Marilou said. "Nicole, tell Luella I'll call her with an update later. I might have to go out to the farmstead tomorrow and start packing things up."

"If we can get out of doing the crafts festival this weekend, we'll go with you," I said.

"Thanks," Marilou said. "And thank you, Tyrone and Cecil. You do good work."

Tyrone closed his laptop. "Thanks, Ms. Walker. Let us know if you need us for anything else."

"Please be sure and thank all the ladies in the historical society, too," Cecil said.

"I sure will," said Marilou.

While making dinner that night, I filled my mother in on Uncle Eyrie having to move out by Saturday.

"I can't believe Judge Beck is doing this," she said, tossing the salad.

Grammy snapped green beans at the table. "I can. A lynch mob threw us off the farm our family homesteaded for three generations. They said no blacks could own land they worked on as slaves. I remember seeing them put the noose around my uncle's neck just before Mama grabbed me up and ran. I was only about four or five years old then."

Just as Dad entered the kitchen, I noticed a tear

roll down her cheek.

"Who's got to move out?" He grabbed a piece of crispy crust off the fried chicken. Mother slapped his hand.

I was glad to see Grammy snicker at them and come back into the present.

"Uncle Eyrie, the old man living at the farmstead," Mother said. "Judge Beck is forcing him to move, so he can tear down everything and build fancy new houses along the river."

"I thought that farmstead was partly ours," Dad said.

Mother gave him a quick update. "Well, technically speaking, the farmstead actually belongs to Judge Beck, now. Grandma Winnie left it to the historical society there in Ravenswood. According to her will, Uncle Eyrie was to stay there until he either died or could no longer live by himself. The historical society planned to renovate it and turn it into a museum. But then Judge Beck offered them a lot of money to build a brand new museum closer to town, and all the board members voted to sell the farmstead to the Beck Construction Company."

"Hmm! Seems that man gets everything he wants," Dad said. "So where's Uncle Eyrie going to live now?"

"We don't know. He's got to be out by Saturday. Marilou is going out tomorrow to help pack up his things. I'd like to go with her."

"What about the crafts fair?"

"Grammy said she can do it by herself."

"I want to go to the farmstead," I said, setting the table.

"You have school tomorrow." Mom reminded me.

"There's nothing going on. I don't even have homework."

Although my father and I hadn't spoken since I told him about my pregnancy, he shared his opinion. "Well, normally I would object, but since this is kind of an emergency. I think it's not a bad idea. I've got to go down to the unemployment office tomorrow. Otherwise, I'd go with you."

"Really?" I said.

"Sure," he said, fidgeting with some coins in his pocket. "Umm, I also want to...I want to say I'm sorry for how I reacted the other night, Nicole."

"It's okay." I shrugged, pretending not to care.

He shook his head. "No. I shouldn't have said the things I did. It was just wrong and I shouldn't have gotten drunk either. I'm sorry. I've started going to meetings again and I'm working the steps and..." He cleared his throat and swallowed hard. "Well, if you want to keep the baby, then we'll make the best of it."

I blinked hard. Tears escaped to my cheek. "Thank you, Daddy." I hugged him.

He held me tight. "I love you, baby."

"I love you too, and I'm sorry." I sniffed. "I never meant to put our family in danger." Relief enveloped me all at once. My dad's support meant everything to me, but I was still unsure of what to do about the baby.

Mother dabbed her eyes and turned back around to stir the gravy.

"A baby is a blessing from God," Grammy said. "Don't matter how they get here. It's all for a reason. All things work together for good."

Mother removed the gravy from the burner. The phone rang. "I'll get it in the living room." A minute later, she came back into the kitchen. "That was Marilou. She's going to pick us up at eight thirty in the morning. Please go tell your brother and sister it's time for dinner."

"Yes, ma'am," I said.

After supper, I stayed in the kitchen to talk things out with my parents.

"If you do have the baby, then I think it's only fair that Johnny's parents help with medical expenses," Dad said.

Mom patted my arm. "It was actually smart of you to get married before you got pregnant. That will give you the legal leverage for child support in the future."

Dad rubbed his chin. "But once Judge Beck finds out about the marriage and that you're pregnant..." He sighed. "Well, I'm just plain scared for your safety and ours. If things get bad enough, we may have to move."

Mother stopped drying a dish, placed her hand on her hip. "I'm not going to let that man, or anyone else run us out of our home. We've worked too hard for it."

Dad set the dish on the shelf. "I just don't want anyone to get hurt. I mean, it's going to get bad enough once Nicole starts showing. People are going to start asking questions and making assumptions about who the daddy is."

"I know," Mother said, putting a hand up to stop him. "We'll just have to take a wait-and-see approach. Take things as they come, one day at a time."

I sat at the kitchen table, listening.

Mother wiped her forehead. "Whew, I'm so glad all the drama of this day is over now." A short pause passed between us. "Nicole told me about Jasmine and Simon Miller, our descendants. What amazingly resilient people they were."

"Well, you do come from good stock." Dad leaned in for a kiss.

She pushed on his chest to stop him just short of reaching his goal. "You make it sound like I'm a breed of cattle."

"Darlin', that's only because you mooooove me so," he said.

I giggled along with them. It was good to see them laugh. I learned a lot just watching them over the years. Their marriage wasn't always easy. In fact, it was messy, hard, and just plain difficult at times.

Spouses may not always like each other, but my parents always seemed to find the love again and make it work, which was totally cool to me. I only wished Johnny were still here to share it with me. The thought of raising our child without him cut deep. I retreated to my bedroom to cry away my fears.

The next morning, Mom and I packed a picnic lunch for the trip to the farmstead. Marilou arrived and we loaded the car.

Trying to convince Uncle Eyrie to move out was more of a challenge than any of us anticipated. The more we tried, the more agitated and outspoken he got. The cell phone rang. In an attempt to get away from the noise, Marilou stepped into the kitchen. She returned a moment later. "The lawyer says he can buy us a little more time for Uncle Eyrie. He thinks he can get another month, at least."

"That's a relief," I said.

"He does not want to budge right now," Mother said.

"Uncle Eyrie, you don't have to move right away, but you do need to think about it." Marilou spoke louder. She motioned for Mother and me to come toward the door.

"All right, Uncle Eyrie. Sorry—we didn't mean to upset you," Mother said.

"Bye, Uncle Eyrie." I waved from the front porch.

"Yeah, yeah, goodbye," he said. "You're not moving me anywhere. This is my house and I'm not leaving."

"Uncle Eyrie, don't worry about a thing. I'll check back with you later," Marilou said. "Have a good day."

Uncle Eyrie slammed the door in her face. "Nobody's going to move me out my house."

Mother and I waited in the car until she returned. We drove past a wooded area near the house. I noticed something lingering—a distorted shadow—but figured it was a deer.

-29-

Simon's Legacy

Next day, the sheriff came. He spoke with Father in private, which made me wonder. Father's face was sullen as he emerged from the study. His usual gleaming eyes now framed with flattened brows, crow's feet, and dark bags. "Constance?" His glance caught mine. "Run and fetch your sister, please."

I hurried to where I knew Elizabeth hunted. A gunshot sounded, and I called out to her. "Elizabeth!" Moments later, leaves rustled and branches snapped. I looked around, spied her hat bouncing above some bushes. "Elizabeth!"

"I'm coming. Bringing supper." Her shadowy figure, shrouded in mist, drew closer. A rabbit hung by her side.

"The sheriff is here."

"Why?"

"I don't know, but Papa had a grave face." We walked the path to the house, where the sheriff and Father met us on the porch.

"Constance. Elizabeth." The sheriff nodded, tipping his hat. "We need to discuss what happened on the night of the fire and how Mr. Willis got shot."

Fear gripped me, and my heart quickened. The sheriff asked several questions about the mob. Who fired the first shot? Who actually shot Mr. Willis, and why in the back?

"Sir, my sister did not murder Mr. Willis," I said. "I was there. I saw everything that happened. Mr. Willis was chasing one of our slave boys, and he was going to shoot him. As it was, he ended up killing another slave." I didn't mention that Simon was a freed slave at the time.

"Well, there's no law that says you can't kill another man's slave. But you do have to compensate him for the cost and loss of labor." He glanced at Elizabeth. "But there *is* a law against shooting a man in the back, when it isn't in self-defense. I'm afraid you will have to come with me until a judge can decide your fate, Miss Elizabeth." He took hold of her free hand. The rabbit dropped with a thunk. He pulled her other hand back, tying them together.

"She didn't do anything wrong!" I cried out. "Father, don't let him do this!"

"Constance, calm down!" He said, turning to the sheriff. "Is this really necessary? Can't Elizabeth stay here until a trial is arranged?"

"I'm afraid not. I'm obligated under law to detain her as a suspect. She'll have to be locked up."

"But I was protecting our property! I did what any other settler in these parts does," Elizabeth said.

"I've got eyewitnesses that say otherwise," the sheriff said.

"What eye witnesses?" she demanded.

"Are you sure this isn't just because she's a woman?" I said. "If she were a man, you'd probably not even consider it."

"Begging your pardon, Miss Constance, but if she were a man she'd be dead by now."

Mother arrived. "Elizabeth?" she said as the sheriff helped her daughter onto a horse and mounted his own. "Where are you taking her?"

"She'll be locked up at my office in town," the sheriff said. "Not to worry, Miss Susanna. We'll take care of her for you." He steered his horse toward the road, and the horse Elizabeth rode followed. She looked back at us one last time.

"It's going to be all right, Mother. Don't worry. I love you all."

I visited my sister every day for two weeks. Mother and I made sure to provide good home cooked meals—buttered biscuits, baked squash, a few slices of ham, and a blueberry pie, obviously too much food for one person. I found that offering meals to the sheriff and his deputy won my sister favor. Bribe or not, it worked. In such a rural settlement, no judge wanted to make the long trip just to hold a one-day trial. With no real evidence or witnesses—save those who rode with Mr. Willis in his posse that night—the sheriff deemed Elizabeth innocent and let her go.

My thoughts went to Mrs. Willis. It was awkward going to the store, but when I opened the door, she wasn't there. A man I didn't recognize stood behind the counter.

"Top of the morning to you, lass," he said with a strong Gaelic dialect.

"I have a standing order to pick up," I said, removing my gloves.

"And what be your name, Miss?

"Proctor."

"Aye, yes, here it is," he said, pulling it from under the counter.

"Thank you."

"Shall I put it on account as usual?"

"Yes, please. Will Mrs. Willis be returning soon?"

"Aye, another week or so," he said.

Or so? Mrs. Willis never left the settlement, not even to tend to her sick mother last spring.

"And who might you be?" I asked.

"I'm her brother-in-law," he said.

"Oh!" I took a quick breath and froze. *Does he know it was my sister who shot Mr. Willis?* "I'm sorry for your loss." He looked as though he drew no conclusion from my comment and handed me the package.

"It wasn't my loss, Miss—"

"Constance," I said.

"Miss Constance," he nodded. "I'm Joseph

O'Reilly. The Missus should be back from her honeymoon soon?"

"Mrs. Willis remarried?"

"Aye, indeed she did! Just last week, to me brother. She knew him from childhood."

"And who did she marry?" I inquired further.

"The widower, Robert O'Reilly. You've heard of him, have you?"

"Uh, yes. Well, that was a bit sudden."

"Aye, it was," he said, "But with the both of them widowed, they saw no need to wait."

"I wish her well, then," I said with a smile. "Give them both my congratulations!"

"Aye, I will." he nodded. "And a good day to you, Miss Constance."

I turned and walked out, still pondering how Mrs. Willis, or rather Mrs. O'Reilly now, married so quickly after losing her husband to such a sudden death. *Perhaps my instincts were right about him, after all.*

Matthew McClain helped replant the crops, which pleased Father to no end. Mother was sure to invite him for supper every night. We sat on the porch and talked, sometimes for hours. Finally, the time came for me to return home with Sidney.

"How can you leave this place?" Matthew asked.

"I have to get back to the shop. I have orders waiting to be filled."

"Let them wait," he said, reaching for my hand.

"What about you? Don't you need to get back to your ranching?"

"Yes, I do." He glanced down for a moment and then slowly lifted his eyes. "I don't want to leave you."

I hesitated to respond, but couldn't hold back my desire. "I don't want to leave you either."

He leaned in to kiss me so gently and tenderly, I nearly forgot to breathe. Our lips parted, and he whispered, "Marry me?"

I wanted to say yes, but was this really the right thing to do? Coming back to the settlement had never been my plan. I loved living in the city. I wanted my children to grow up there. A rancher's wife was not something I imagined for myself. I pulled back, crossed my arms, and moved away. "I can't answer you now." I felt his body close to my back. His hands rested on my shoulders.

"I'll wait as long it takes," he said.

I wanted to lean back against him, feel his breath on my neck, but no. I couldn't let this happen, not now. *I know Sydney wants a father, but is he the right one? What about Simon Jr.? I need to honor his father's dying wish, secure our son's future. I can't do that here.* I turned to face him. "That might be a long time."

"Whatever it takes," he said.

"Really?"

He nodded.

"There's something I have to do first."

"What is it?"

"I can't tell you."

"Why?"

"Please, just trust me."

"Well, how long will it take?"

"I'm not sure. I've got to figure it out."

"I'll wait for an answer," he said, leaning in to kiss me again. He held me close as I embraced him, relishing the warmth of his love.

The coach ride was long and rough, but offered me plenty of time to think. We arrived home and jumped right back into life's routine. A few days later, the idea of how to bring Simon Jr. to the Northern colony came to me. I took the ferry to Philadelphia and walked the cobblestone streets to the print shop. The bell rang as I opened the door. Luckily, Benjamin Franklin was still there.

"Constance! How nice to see you again," he stepped around the counter to greet me, took my hand, and kissed it. "How are your Father and family?"

"Everyone is well, and Father is fully recovered now. I'll let him know you inquired of him."

"Please do. I hope to see him at the next conference."

"I'm sure he'll be there," I said, and then nodded.

"Well, what brings you here today?" he asked.

"I have a favor to ask of you."

"What is it, dear?" He peered over his spectacles.

"There is a young boy at the settlement who needs learning yet, but he has an inquisitive intelligence I think you'll find of interest."

"Oh? I am interested already. Who is this boy?"

"We call him Simon Jr., coincidentally," I said with a wry smile.

"Oh! I was truly sorry to hear of Simon's death. He was such a good worker, noble of character."

"He always spoke highly of you and your family as well," I nodded.

Mr. Franklin rubbed his chin. "I'm in need of an apprentice. How old is this lad?"

"But a boy, nine years-old, and he's sharp as a blade," I said, hoping the age was not a problem.

"He is a little young lad, and not learned, you say? Well then, I shall have to teach him to read."

"Yes, but as I said, he has an inquisitive intelligence, which will serve your purpose well."

"You said he's at the settlement. How will you get him here?"

"I can arrange for him to come along with Father as his page boy."

"Excellent!" Franklin pushed up on his toes.

"There is one thing you should know," I said, stepping closer.

"What is that?"

"Simon Jr. is a slave. He was found in the fields. Simon's mother raised him as her son, hence the name."

"That shouldn't be a problem as long as your father provides the emancipation papers. He can live with me. The housemaids and the Missus will see to his needs."

"You are certain they'll accept him into the household?"

"Of course!"

"All right, then." I smiled. "Thank you so much, Mr. Franklin." I held out one gloved hand.

"I look forward to meeting this young man soon." He bowed, took my hand, and kissed it again.

Once home, I set out to write Father in regards to the matter. Sidney played in the garden. She came inside and handed me a small bouquet. "Thank you," I said, taking a sniff. "They smell lovely."

"I have something else for you," she said. "Nanny took me to town today. We got some mail." She pulled a letter from her apron pocket and handed it to me. It's from Master McClain."

"I see that. Why don't you check on how supper is coming along?"

"But I want to know what the letter says," she said, holding her skirt out and swaying.

"I'll tell you later. Now run along." I gestured, shooing her away.

"Yes, ma'am." She pouted and left the room.

I turned the letter over, slipped my finger under

the M stamped seal, breaking it open. My mouth curved upward as I read. I folded and returned the letter to the envelope. My heart fluttered, remembering how it felt to be in his arms. My fingers gently brushed the quill strokes, and I pined to see him again.

Several weeks later, Father arrived, Simon Jr. in tow and formally dressed. Mother's fine handiwork shined through again.

Sidney ran to greet Father. "Grandpapa!" He picked her up and held her tightly."

"Hello, Simon Jr.," I said.

He bowed and kissed my hand. "Good day, my lady."

"Oh, my, aren't you a fine gentleman." I smiled at him and glanced at Father. "How was the trip?"

"Full of questions, this one," he said. "He didn't stop talking the entire way here, except for the few minutes he slept." He pulled out a handkerchief and wiped his forehead.

I bent down. "Well, I'm sure Mr. Franklin will be more than happy to answer all of your questions."

"Yes, ma'am," he said, tipping his hat. I couldn't help but smile.

Father hugged me. "I've missed you and so has someone else."

"Tell Mother and Elizabeth I miss them too," I said, pretending not to know whom he meant.

He looked at me with those endearing eyes. "Have you got an answer for the poor soul, yet? He comes to the farmstead every day, not one passes without him inquiring about you."

I peered at him. "I do have an answer."

"And?"

"And I wrote him a letter." I pulled a sealed envelope out of my pocket, handing it to him. "Would you please deliver this to Master McClain?"

He took the letter from me. Sadness in his voice, his gaze slowly rose to meet mine. "I was hoping for a more positive response."

I looked away, and then started to giggle. I covered my mouth to muffle the laugh. "Father, I said, 'yes.' "

He stepped back. "You're coming home?"

"Yes! I'm coming home."

He grabbed my waist and turned me in midair. "What wonderful news!"

Remarried and pregnant, I climbed the hill to the gravesites of Jasmine's baby and Simon. My palm rested on little Benjamin Franklin Miller's plot as I whispered, "Blood sisters forever." Wiping my cheek, I continued my sentiment. "I wish we could have brought your mother back home." I placed a small bouquet of jasmine flowers on Simon's grave, remembering the love we once shared.

"Oh, Simon, if you could see our boy now, you'd

be so proud of him. He's so smart and full of courage, but most of all ... he's free."

-30-

Special Moments

At home, I tried to nap, but guilt bombarded my thoughts. The trouble my actions had caused my family, Uncle Eyrie being forced from his home. I picked up a picture of Johnny on the nightstand and held it to my chest. My heart ached for him as my chin quivered. "Oh God, if we hadn't run off and got married, he might still be alive," I said under my breath. "I wish I could run away and make everything okay again." *But where would I go? How would I take care of the baby and myself?*

Grammy knocked on the door. "Nicole, I have something for you."

I quickly wiped away my tears and took a deep breath before answering. "Just a sec." I grabbed a tissue and dabbed my face. "Okay."

Grammy entered the room carrying a large bag. "I made this for the baby." She sat next to me and pulled out a quilt.

I help her unfold it. "Oh, Grammy, this is so nice. Thank you." I leaned over to give her a hug and started to cry again.

"What's the matter? I thought you liked Noah's

Ark."

"I love it. It's beautiful," I said between sobs.

"Then what's wrong?" Grammy said.

"I just feel bad for making things so hard on everyone. I mean, Johnny would still be alive, if we hadn't run off and got married. And Uncle Eyrie wouldn't have to move."

"What's Uncle Eyrie got to do with this?" Grammy asked.

"What if Judge Beck found out about my connection to the farmstead? I just think everyone would be better off, if I ran away."

"Oh, child, come on now—you don't be talking like that." Grammy held my shoulders. "This is your home. You don't need to be running away." I calmed down and wiped my tears. After a contemplative moment, Grammy shared some age-old folk wisdom. "You remember the story of Noah's Ark in the Bible?"

"Yes, I love that story," I said, smiling. "We sang that song every summer at church camp." Grammy began to sing, and I sang along with her.

"Well, Noah, he built him, he built him an arky, arky. Noah, he built him..." We sang through the chorus and named my favorite animals. "Elephants and kangaroozies, roozies, children of the Lord." We giggled.

Grammy held my hand. "The Bible says nothing can separate us from the love of God. Nothing we do will keep Him from loving us."

I held the quilt to my chest. "I know I was wrong for dating Johnny and then marrying him in secret. Do you think God will forgive me?"

"Of course He will. And your family forgives you too."

I laid my head on her shoulder. "Grammy, do you think God let me get pregnant because I sinned against Him?"

She pulled my chin up. "Lookie here. No, sweetheart. I think God blessed you with this baby. He knew what was going to happen, and He wanted to leave a part of Johnny with us."

I couldn't control my tears. "I'm scared, Grammy. I don't know how to have a baby, or how to raise one."

"None of us do. They don't come with instructions." Grammy reached for my hand. "You're going to face a lot of difficult times raising a child on your own. Just remember—when those storms of life come, nothing can separate you from the love of God. Keep trusting the Lord. He's your safe haven."

"I will, Grammy." I leaned in for a hug.

Grammy held me close a moment longer. "All right now. You get some rest." She pushed herself up and walked to the door.

"Grammy?"

She turned. "What, darlin'?"

"I love you."

"I love you too, baby." She blew me a kiss and closed the door.

I covered my shoulders with the quilt. A slight tickling sensation alerted me. I rubbed my tummy and realized something. *This isn't some sort of thing. It's a little miracle inside me. This is a baby, a part of Johnny and me. Not a curse, more like a gift. How could I just get rid of it?* I wondered if it was a girl or a boy. *If it's a boy, I want to name him after Johnny.*

I flipped through a baby magazine, pondering how much money I would need for all the baby things. Clasping the ring hanging around my neck, I tried to figure how much a pawnshop might give me. An ache of remorse swelled up in my heart. *I don't want to give up Johnny's ring, but I have to find a doctor soon. I'm too scared to ask his parents for help.*

I continued to stroke my belly. *I wish your daddy were here.* I looked at the framed photo on the nightstand of Johnny and me, the night of the Moonlight Dance. My mind raced back to that night we married and the love we shared. In the stillness of the moment, I dozed off, imagining Johnny lying next to me. I felt his warm caress, his hand touching my belly, his gentle kiss, and his whisper.

"I'm here, Nicole. Our baby's going to be just fine."

I found myself speaking as if he were right there. "But what about your parents?"

"They won't like it. Maybe my mom will come around in time, but don't count on my dad for anything."

"I'm afraid, Johnny."

"I know, but you can do this, babe. Your parents are great. And I'll be here, watching over you and the baby."

I imagined him snuggling close and fell into a peaceful sleep. When I awoke, I could sense Johnny's lingering presence. The realization he was gone saddened me again. Noticing the time, I realized Kate would be home from school by now and decided to call her and make plans for a weekend sleepover.

Monday, a cold front settled the landscape. I stared at my pooching tummy in the mirror. I'd tried several times to squeeze into my favorite pair of jeans, but my expanding waistline made it impossible. I rummaged through the closet for anything with an elastic waist. Finally, I found some fleece pants and a matching sweatshirt. *How in the world can I possibly make fleece look fashionable? Thank God, only one week until school is out for the holidays*, I thought.

I planned to home school after that. Mother and Grammy decided they could take care of the baby until I finished school. No one even considered the idea of adoption. *I mean, if I'm going to all the trouble to have this baby, then why give it up?* I'd done some research and learned a biracial baby had little to no chance of adoption anyway.

Mother spooned warm oatmeal into bowls, while I buttered my toast. Shelby and Jackson finished breakfast in no time flat. It was Dad's turn to walk them to the bus. They quickly departed, leaving us alone.

Mother poured herself a second cup of coffee. "Nicole, you really need to tell the Becks about the baby soon."

"I know, but I just don't know how." She blew on a spoonful of oatmeal.

"You won't be able to hide it much longer."

"Tell me about it. I couldn't get into my jeans this morning, but how am I supposed to tell them? I mean, what am I supposed to say?" I held my hand up to my ear in a mock phone call. "Hi, I'm Nicole Durham. Oh, excuse me, I mean, Nicole Beck. That's right. Johnny and I eloped during the Moonlight Dance, and now I'm pregnant. Surprise! By the way, do you mind helping out with the medical expenses?"

Mother set her mug down. "Well, that about sums it up, but you really do need to see a doctor either way."

"I know. Don't think I haven't been thinking about this. I'm just really scared of what Judge Beck's going to do once he finds out."

Mother spoke directly. "Well, he is Johnny's father and he needs to know. Believe me, I'm just as concerned about the outcome."

"Mama? Are you mad at Johnny for getting me pregnant?"

She looked down at her coffee. "I'm more upset

that you never talked to me about anything, and you lied to me. You didn't even think things through. Nicole, your entire future is on hold now." Her voice cracked. "You had so many things you wanted to do with your life." She swallowed hard.

I noticed her hair now a little grayer on top. My heart sank as I realized how my actions had affected her and the whole family. "I'm sorry I lied to you. I can still go to college. It's just going to take me a while longer to graduate."

She wiped a cheek.

"I really loved Johnny, Mama."

"I know you did, baby." She sniffed, patting my hand. "For all you know about love anyway." A moment of silence mingled between us. "All right," she said, exhaling. "I'll try to get in touch with Mrs. Beck, see if I can arrange a meeting. She's probably the best one to tell first."

"Will you come with me?"

She sat back, hesitated, but then said, "Well how else are you going to get there? Unless you want Kate to take you."

I took her hand. "No, I need you there."

She looked down at her cup again. "All right." A car horn sounded. "That's Kate, you better get going," she said, rising from the table.

I got up to retrieve my backpack, walked to the door, and looked back. "Thanks, Mama."

She pointed toward the counter. "Don't forget

your homework." I grabbed my math workbook, stuffed it into my backpack. "Have a good day at school. I love you."

Stepping out the door, I looked back. "I love you too." As the car backed down the driveway, I watched her grow smaller and blinked my guilt away.

-31-

Meeting Mrs. Beck

The library. Two o'clock. Anna May led us to a small conference room. My fingers twirled the wedding ring, hanging on a gold chain. *Suicide might be a better option at this moment,* I thought. A few minutes later the distinct brisk tapping of high heels grew louder and closer. My heart quickened. "Do you think she'll remember me?" I said, glancing at my mother.

Before she could answer, a woman wearing a full-length mink coat entered. Mother motioned for me to stand. "Hello Mrs. Beck. My name is Luella Durham. Folks just call me Luella. And this is my daughter, Nicole." She put her hand out, but Mrs. Beck ignored her.

"Hello, Nicole, nice to see you again," she said, eyes shifting between us.

Ice, I thought.

Anna May closed the door, leaving us alone.

"My assistant indicated this was very important. What is this all about?"

We sat. Mother looked at me. "Do you want to tell her, or shall I?"

I nodded. "Um, Mrs. Beck, Johnny kept seeing me

after you and Mr. Beck told him not to."

Mrs. Beck sat motionless. "Oh?"

I fidgeted and rubbed my thighs. "We fell in love and well...we decided to get married."

"What?" Mrs. Beck shook her head. "No, not my Johnny."

I unfolded the marriage certificate. "We went across state-lines to Ashland, Kentucky.

Mrs. Beck leaned over the certificate. Her eyes lifted halfway. "Where did you get that ring?

I grasped the ring dangling from my neck. "Johnny gave it to me."

"That was my mother's ring," she said, pointing.

"He told me his grandmother gave it to him." Nervously, I slid the ring back and forth.

"But Johnny would never have given you that ring without me knowing about it. Especially not to a ..." She sat back. "Oh! I know what you're after here. Money no doubt, but you're not getting a dime with this phony story." She crossed her arms and glared at me. "Need I remind you who Johnny's father is?"

Mother spoke in my defense. "Nicole is pregnant with your son's child."

Mrs. Beck laughed aloud. "Oh, this is rich. And *so* like you people."

Mother lowered her tone. "What people?"

"Oh, I think you know exactly what people."

"Are you calling my daughter a liar?"

Mrs. Beck rose to her feet, raised her voice.

"That, along with the fact your daughter is a teenage whore should sum it up, don't you think?"

Dumbfounded, my mother could only shake her head.

Mrs. Beck lifted her chin and tossed a glance toward my belly. "And I'm sure everyone else will know the truth in what ... five, six months from now?" She stood tall in high heels. "Did you actually think I would fall for something like this? My son, dating a girl like you? Having a biracial child? Obviously, you manipulated that ring out of him and you're going to give it back!" She reached for the ring.

I pulled back.

Mother caught Mrs. Beck by the arm.

Mrs. Beck took a step back, lifting her other hand to her trembling lips. "You are so cruel to do this to a family who has just lost our only son." She fumbled in her purse, retrieved a tissue.

Mother glared, trembling. "You're not the only one who lost a child that day."

I stepped forward and cried, "I loved him!"

Both women, stunned, looked at me.

"And I miss him too." I swallowed hard. "This baby means more to me than anything. It's the only thing I have left of Johnny." I cleared my throat. "*We* have left of Johnny."

Mrs. Beck leaned against the chair and sat back down. Silent. Finally, she pulled herself up and walked to the door. Before leaving, she turned back. "You'll be hearing from my lawyer." Her mink brushed against the door as she whisked out of the room.

I fell back in my seat and exhaled. "I knew this was a bad idea. Now what are we going to do?"

A moment later, Anna May appeared at the door. "Oh, dear, the look on your faces says it all."

Mother rubbed her head. "Do you have the number for that lawyer?"

Clarence J. Wallace, attorney at law, leaned forward. "Here are your options, Nicole. You can authorize a DNA test to be done after the baby is born to confirm that Johnny is the father. Once this is established, you can pursue a paternity suit to recover medical expenses and child support from the Beck family. But, you need to understand that in doing so, you will also be opening the door to their own rights to your child. They could fight you and try to take the baby should they consider you an unfit mother at any time in the future. However, from what you've told me about them, I don't think they want a biracial child in their family. And they certainly don't want other people knowing about it."

"That's for sure," I said. "If anybody's unfit, it's going to be them."

Wallace went on. "Well, the main thing you have to prove is that you're capable of caring for the child. From what I understand, you still live at home with your family. Is this true?"

"Yes. Mama and Grammy are going to help take care of the baby while I finish high school and go to college."

"But your father is out of a job right now—is that right?"

Mother interrupted, "He gets unemployment, and he's doing freelance work."

"I see. Luella, do you work outside the home?"

"I own an alterations shop downtown, and I make hand-sewn quilts with my mother to sell at crafts fairs," she explained. "It's not real consistent income, but it helps. Grammy gets her Social Security check, and she has Medicare. The problem is, the rest of the family has no insurance right now. Nicole needs to see a doctor, and we just can't afford to pay for that out of pocket. Doctors don't want to take you when you don't have insurance."

Mr. Wallace said, "She may qualify for free prenatal care. I'll look into that and call you."

"We don't expect any government handouts. I won't go on food stamps or anything like that. I'd sell my house and live in a trailer down by the river before that happens."

Mr. Wallace nodded. "I understand. There is a health clinic in town for the uninsured. It isn't free, but they do have significantly lower rates." He jotted the information on a post-it note and handed it to her. "You might want to give them a call."

"Thank you for taking our case, Mr. Wallace,"

Mother said, and stood.

I pushed myself forward to stand. “Mrs. Beck mentioned we’d be hearing from her lawyer. Does that mean she’s going to sue us?”

“Don’t worry, Nicole. I deal with people like her all the time. If you get a letter or hear from her, don’t do anything before contacting me first.” He gave me a reassuring wink.

-32-

Winter Escape

The weekend after Thanksgiving, Kate and I, along with our mothers, drove to the farmstead. A few historical society members met us there. Two men in a cherry picker hung a large wreath over the barn door. Other folks put lights and garlands on the front porch. Inside, a fresh-cut fir waited decorating and boxes filled the sofa. My mother and Marilou set out homemade cookies, while Kate and I unwrapped ornaments.

Uncle Eyrie, who by then had forgotten all about the moving-out incident, scanned the table. "Did you bring some more good food for me?"

Mother proceeded to unload a picnic basket. "We sure did. Here's some fried chicken, dirty rice, turnip greens with bacon, and a sweet potato pie."

"I've never had sweet potato pie before."

Marilou moved the trays aside to make room. "Must be those Deep South roots of hers coming out."

Uncle Eyrie raised his chin and sniffed. "It sure smells good. Can we eat now?"

My mother smiled and said, "Sure enough."

I set the table, while Kate retrieved some glasses.

We ate lunch and joked, careful to avoid saying anything about moving. Kate and I retreated to the living room to decorate the tree, while my mother and Marilou put away the remaining food.

Uncle Eyrie sat in his recliner. "You sure are doing a fine job on the tree, girls."

Kate grinned. "Hope so."

I bent over to pick up an ornament and yawned. "I could use a nap right about now."

Rocking in his recliner, Uncle Eyrie turned his head toward me. "Looks like someone's expecting soon."

His comment took me aback, since I didn't think my baby bump was that obvious yet. "Uh?" I rubbed my stomach, trying to decide what to say, if anything. Realizing everyone else in that room already knew anyway, I wanted to be honest. "Oh, I guess so."

"When are you due?"

"Um, this summer."

The old man leaned back. "I remember the pitter-patter of little feet running all around this house when I was little. My mother raised eleven of us."

"Eleven?" Kate said.

"Whoa," I said. "I could not imagine having that many kids."

"Yep," Uncle Eyrie said. "Right here in this house, all in the same room upstairs."

Kate untangled an ornament hook. "I remember Grandma Winnie talking about that."

Marilou walked in with some silver icicles. "Thank God by the time I came along, they had enough sense to go to a hospital."

My mother carried in another box of ornaments. "Your Grammy was born at home. That's just the way they did things back then. There was no insurance. The doctors used to come to the house, but only if something went wrong. People paid them with a chicken or a pig. During that time, midwives delivered most of the babies."

I hung another ornament on the tree and asked, "What's a midwife?"

Mother sat on the couch. "They were kind of like nurses back then. They didn't have to go to school though. Just learned how to birth babies naturally by watching others."

Kate tossed a few icicles over a branch. "Don't they still have those?"

Marilou crawled under the tree to plug in the lights. "I've heard there are some still around."

Curious, I had to ask, "Do they still deliver babies at home?"

Mother cocked her head. "Just what are you thinking?"

"Mama, if they can deliver the baby at home, then we won't have to worry about insurance."

Mother shook a finger at me. "No, no, girl. You're too young and considered high risk. Don't be thinking you're going to deliver this baby at home."

"But why not?"

Uncle Eyrie cleared his throat and interrupted. "I'm sorry. I didn't mean to cause a fuss."

Marilou pushed herself up off the floor and patted his shoulder. "No, Uncle Eyrie. Don't worry about them. It's normal for mothers and daughters to fight about things."

Uncle Eyrie chuckled.

Unfortunately, his gentle demeanor did not stop my mother from raising her voice to me. "I don't want to hear another word about giving birth at home. We can go to the emergency room if we have to, but you're not having your baby at home."

"Yes, ma'am." I pursed my lips.

Marilou stood, both hands on her hips. "Hey now, the tree's looking pretty good. Looks like we're done here." She leaned over the couch to look out the window. "The historical society folks are done. Looks good." She nudged my mother's arm. "Time to slice the pie."

My mother and Kate followed her to the kitchen.

I sat close to the fire, resting my feet on a footstool and pulled an afghan over my shoulders. A logbook, found in the attic during a prior trip, sat on a table next to me. Pulling it onto my lap, I flipped slowly through the pages. An entry dated before the Civil War caught my attention.

Ship's Log, May 24, 1825: Earlier this week, an

unfortunate incident occurred on the pier just before the break of dawn. One of the slave masters caught up to a runaway at the dock. He shot at the escapee, but missed. Master William yelled out for him to stop firing at once, but the slave master turned and pointed his musket toward Master William, calling him a slave lover. The fog enshrouded the steamboat, obscuring my view. I heard gunshot and something splashed into water, but I could only hear mumbled voices. Upon my return, I learned that Miss Elizabeth had used her father's handgun to shoot the slave master in order to save her father's life. The other slaves buried the body to protect her and Master William. Should the truth be known, no telling what the other settlers in the area might have done. Few of them held to the same convictions as Master William and others in the Proctor family.

I closed the logbook to contemplate the hardship and sacrifices my ancestors had endured for the sake of others. I looked at the picture of Captain Proctor again, now set on the mantel. A small figurine of a baby in a manger caught my attention. I remembered Marilou saying she had packed a nativity set and marked it for the farmstead. *How did this piece get separated from it?* I glanced over at the foyer and noted the nativity scene already arranged in perfect order.

Kate entered the room, forking her pie to her

mouth. She lowered herself next to me. "What are you reading?"

I leaned back. "A logbook. Captain Proctor really sacrificed a lot helping people to gain freedom."

"Really?" Kate chuckled. "So how is it he ended up having so many kids, then? I mean, if he was gone so much, when did they find the time?"

Marilou smirked. "You'd be surprised at just how little time it really takes."

Mother swallowed a piece of pie. "Yep. Nicole is living proof of that."

They all laughed.

"Mama," I said, glaring.

Marilou leaned over the sofa to look out the window again. "We really need to get going. The weather's turning bad, and I want to get home before dark."

Everyone gathered their coats and started for the door.

Uncle Eyrie managed to get out of his recliner. "Thanks again for such a great meal." He took Marilou's arm and walked with her to the front door, where she hugged him goodbye.

Mother kissed him on the cheek and said, "The leftovers and the rest of the pie are in the fridge."

"Oh, thank you," he said with a Cheshire cat smile.

Kate patted his shoulder. "Bye, Uncle Eyrie."

I returned the baby Jesus figurine to its rightful

place in the Nativity scene and headed for the door. "Goodbye."

He pointed a crooked finger at me. "You take care of that baby now."

"I will." Squeezing his hand, I wanted to stay there forever and soak in his kindness. The love I felt helped ease my guilt, offering peace, and reminding me of a Christmas past. How I wished I could go back in time, when my father danced with me standing on his feet. *But I'm not that little girl anymore. Those days are long gone.*

Uncle Eyrie stood at the door and waved goodbye. "Thanks for everything."

As the car moved along the driveway, I spotted something. When He surveyed the woods, a small herd of white-tailed deer appeared through the barren trees. They stood like statues. I nudged Kate. "Look," I said.

My mother pointed. Marilou slowed the car. A moment later, the buck leaped away and the other deer followed.

Driving forward again, a larger, shadowy figure alerted me. Before I could say anything, it disappeared.

By mid-February, the unemployment dwindled, but my dad contracted some freelance work, which helped. My pregnancy was now public knowledge, prompting me to keep a low profile. All of my friends at school abandoned me, mostly out of fear by association. Speculation and gossip soared through every social circle around town. Getting the mail every day became daunting between all the hate letters and packages. Some were sympathetic, offering help, but it all just made me depressed. After a while, I didn't bother to open anymore. Mother either marked them return to sender or trashed them.

Thankfully, the local media didn't touch the story, mainly because of Judge Beck's influence and power. The fact that he happened to be a main shareholder of the newspaper and local media stations didn't hurt either. Everyone in my immediate family came to terms about my pregnancy, and life resumed as normal as possible considering the circumstances.

Mother and Grammy went with me to visit a crisis pregnancy center. Several girls were already bragging about receiving government assistance.

One girl looked at me and said, "Girl, why don't you just go down and get your check? It's free money." Boy was she ever sorry she said that.

Both Grammy and Mother looked at each other in horror. Grammy didn't skip a beat or hardly take a breath. "Young lady, you listen here now."

The girl snapped back, "What's you got to say, old woman?"

"Don't you sass mouth me." Grammy stared her down.

Miss Hilda, the house parent stepped forward.

"Stand down, Michelle." The girl backed away.

"Now, I want all y'all to listen to me." Grammy paced the floor like a drill sergeant. "Taking government handouts when you are able bodied and capable of caring for yourself is nothing short of self-imposed slavery. My ancestors and yours worked too hard to get away from all that. Is this what you want to pass on to your own children? I know your family life is nothing to brag about, but neither was mine. You can't keep letting the devil have so much power over you. It's time to take back your own life and live it with honor and decency. Don't drag your babies down that same rat hole you grew up in." Grammy went on for at least an hour.

Mother whispered to Miss Hilda. "Once she gets started, there ain't no stopping her."

Miss Hilda replied. "Sure don't need a preacher with her around."

By the time Grammy finished, every girl in the house was crying, ready to repent, get saved and get baptized. I was a little embarrassed, but at the same time, glad I had such strong women to support me.

Back home, Grammy escaped to the living room. I could hear the whoosh of the recliner opening as the TV blasted her favorite show. A sweet aroma of freshly baked cookies filled the kitchen, where Shelby and I mixed a batch at the counter. I handed her a spoonful, scooped another for me, savoring the yummy goo.

Sugar barked at the back door. I let her out.

Mother chatted on the speakerphone while scrubbing a pot, the dishwasher still in disrepair.

Marilou's voice came through loud and clear. "You know, Grandma Winnie's house is paid off. All we have to do is keep up the taxes on it. You're welcome to live there, if things get really bad."

Sugar kept barking.

Mother looked over her shoulder at me, motioning to let in the dog. "Thank you, Marilou, but you've already done so much. Besides, what about Uncle Eyrie? I don't think Sam would want to move into your mother's house knowing Uncle Eyrie might not have a place to stay."

I put off letting Sugar in until I could get the first dozen cookies in the oven. When she yelped, I turned quickly to see a fireball crash through the window and land on the floor. Shelby and I screamed. Another crash came from the living room. Mother ran to the hallway, Shelby close behind her, leaving Marilou hanging on the line.

"What's happening?" she called.

"The house is on fire. Call 911!" I yelled and ran into the hallway.

Jackson came running out of his room. "Mama?"

Mother picked him up, Shelby and I followed her to the living room.

The drapes flamed and smoke started to fill the house. I helped Grammy out of the recliner, and grabbed Shelby's arm. "Stay close." Mother led the way through the kitchen, steering clear the fireball. When she opened the back door, a wisp of cool winter air blew my hair back.

Several men in white-hooded robes stood in the snow waving torches and screaming, "Burn in hell, Blackie."

"Oh, dear God in heaven. Help us, Lord Jesus!" Mother shut the door. She turned to face me. "Come on." We followed her to the master bedroom.

Grammy ran to the bathroom, rolled and soaked a towel. I helped her stuff the cloth edge into the door crack.

"Luella!" I heard Dad screaming. "Luella! Nicole!"

Mother called out, "We're back here!"

Jackson and Shelby cried out at the same time. "Daddy! Daddy!"

"Dad we're in your bedroom," I yelled. He hit the door so hard a loud thunk vibrated through and made me jump. I heard him slide down to the floor.

Grammy yelled, "We've got to save Sam!"

I pulled the door ajar, smoke rolled over me, making me cough.

Grammy reached down to pull the dampened towel away from the bottom, while mother tugged at my dad's limp body. She managed to pull him inside the room.

I pushed the door shut again, and Shelby helped Grammy replace the towel.

Everyone coughed and gasped for air.

Mother hovered over my dad's body and patted his chest. "Sam?" she cried, slapping his face. "Sam, wake up!"

My heart sank as I saw no movement. Then a sudden cough signaled his consciousness. I let out a sigh of relief and helped him to his feet.

Grammy struggled to open a window, now fogged with heavy breath, and Dad stepped forward to help. One hard pull and it slid open.

The white-hooded men pointed torches toward the window, shouting, "Burn, baby burn!"

Shelby and Jackson screamed and started to cry.

Dad yelled out, "Don't do this! We never did anything to you! Let us out! Please!"

Sirens blared and grew closer as the group scampered away into the darkness. Some removed their robes, stuffing them into backpacks, but I couldn't see their faces.

Dad helped each of us climb out of the first floor window before getting himself out.

I stood in the street, coughing, and watched the flames engulf our home.

A firefighter pulled a hose across the lawn and held it steady, while a blast of water sprayed over the roof.

Sugar limped across the yard to me and whimpered. I scooped her up. "What happened, girl? How'd you hurt your leg?" I handed her to one of the paramedics, who placed a dog mask over her snout and set her leg in a temporary splint.

Marilou and Kate arrived to find the rest of the family huddled together next to the fire truck receiving oxygen.

A paramedic pulled me aside to treat me for smoke inhalation. He covered my nose and mouth with a plastic mask. I watched as the police asked the neighbors what happened, but one by one they shook their heads, indicating they saw nothing, heard nothing. *Cowards.*

Marilou and Kate walked toward me.

"What happened?" Marilou asked.

I spoke through the mask. "KKK—they tried to kill us!"

"Are you all right?"

I nodded.

"Okay," she said, patting my arm. "I'm going to see about your mother."

Kate clasped my hand. "Oh, God! How horrible."

I removed the mask. "It wasl."

"Are you sure it was the KKK?"

"Yeah—men in white hoods were outside the house." I coughed and rasped. "They threw fireballs through the windows."

"What a nightmare!" Kate said.

I shivered. "I've never been so scared in my life."

Across the street, Marilou screamed into her cellphone.

"What! I'll be right there!" She stuffed her phone in her purse and rummaged for her keys.

Kate stepped closer. "What's going on?"

"Somebody just set a cross on fire in our front yard."

I stood and steadied myself, with Sugar in my arms. "I'm coming with you."

Kate looked back at me. "Are you sure?"

"I'm fine." I handed Sugar to Grammy while following Kate to the car.

We arrived at her house where a flaming six-foot cross burned on the front lawn. A fire truck arrived and extinguished the flames quickly.

"Thank God the house is okay," Marilou said.

The police took a report from a neighbor, the same one who called. He stayed elusive, I assumed to protect himself.

Moments later, my entire family joined us inside the house.

"Marilou, I'm thinking it's not a good idea to stay here tonight," Dad said.

She handed him a cup of coffee. "Then where do you suggest we go, Sam?"

We all looked at each other and knew.

Kate and I took off for her bedroom to get some clothes. We returned a few minutes later, backpacks filled.

Dad paced the floor, craning his neck, checking every shadow. Grammy, Shelby, and Jackson huddled on the sofa, asleep. Sugar curled next to them. Dad turned and said, "You two go check on your mothers and see what's holding things up. We've got to get going."

I entered the bedroom first to find Marilou pulling things out of the closet and making a suggestion.

"We can stop by a thrift shop later and see about getting everyone some more clothes."

"That's a good idea," Mother said, folding and placing clothes into a suitcase.

"We still have Grandma Winnie's house. You can always move in there until your house is rebuilt." Marilou continued.

I interrupted. "Is there anything we can do to help?"

Kate stepped forward. "Yeah, Sam really wants to get on the road."

"I think we're almost done," Marilou said. "Kate, grab that duffel bag and stuff this pile of clothes in it."

Dad appeared at the bedroom door. "Are we ready?" His eyes darted between us. "Nicole, Kate, go warm up the cars." He tossed me his keys and then shot a glance at Marilou, who handed Kate her keys. "I'm going to wake up Grammy and the kids."

Sometime in the middle of the night, our small caravan drove the two-lane country road to the only safe place we knew.

-33-

Encounters of A Ghostly Kind

We arrived at the farmstead sometime past midnight. Marilou did not want to wake up Uncle Eyrie. She found the spare key hidden near the porch swing. Kate and I followed, after she let herself in, while the others waited in the car. There was only one night light on in the hallway. I closed the door behind me. The floor creaked as Marilou walked carefully toward Uncle Eyrie's bedroom.

"Good thing the old man's hard of hearing," I whispered. The faint scent of cigar smoke floated past my nose. I gasped when something poked my back between the shoulders.

"Hold it right there!" a gruff voice called out from behind me.

I put my hands up. "Don't shoot, please!"

Marilou shouted, "What's the matter?"

"Who are you people?" he graveled.

Marilou stood next to Kate in the shadows of the hallway. "I'm Marilou Walker, the daughter of

Winifred Proctor, and this is my daughter, Kate, and her friend, Nicole."

"You're Winnie's girl?"

"Yes, sir," Marilou said, shaken. "Now will you please lower that shotgun?"

The sharp pressure left my back, and a light came on in the foyer. "Good grief, woman, what brings you here this time of night?"

I turned around to face the stranger as Marilou answered him. "The KKK is after us, and we need a safe place to stay."

My eyes adjusted to the light as a weathered old man came into focus, dressed poorly, looking as though he'd slept in his clothes for weeks.

He shifted the cigar in his mouth. "Figures, they've been giving us trouble for years."

Marilou watched as he moved toward the fireplace. "Who are you?"

He lifted the rifle to mount it over the mantle. "I'm George W."

"George W?"

"Eyrie's twin brother? Didn't Winnie tell you about me?"

She studied his face. "Not that I recall, and not exactly identical twins either."

"That doesn't surprise me. I was always the black sheep of the family."

Mother knocked on the door and waved through the window.

Marilou put her hand up to gesture for her to wait. "Uh! I have a few more people with me out in the car. Is it all right to let them come inside?"

"Oh, sure. Why don't you just invite the whole county?"

The others filed in one at a time. Mom carried Jackson, clumps of snow dropping from her boots and coat. She sat close to Kate on the couch. Shelby settled on the armrest. Grammy held Sugar and sat in Uncle Eyrie's recliner. Daddy, carrying two suitcases, stayed near the door, while Marilou remained standing and introduced everyone.

"Everybody, this is George W, who apparently is Uncle Eyrie's twin brother, which no one ever bothered to tell me about." Marilou pointed to each person as she went along. "This is Sam and Luella Durham and their three children, Jackson, Shelby, and Nicole. Grammy is Luella's mother, and this is Kate, my daughter."

George W glared at Sugar. "Who's this?"

Grammy answered, "Oh, this is Sugar, the family dog."

He mumbled something and bent over to start a fire. "I can see why you'd have trouble with the KKK. What'd they do?"

Daddy spoke first. "They burned down our house, while we were still inside."

"Lucky you got out alive," he said, adjusting his cigar. "Sorry to hear about your misfortune."

Kate said, "They burned a cross in *our* front yard."

"Yep, that's the classic warning. You were right for leaving. Let things cool down a bit." He looked at my daddy. "What'd you do to make them so mad?"

"Well ...," Daddy hesitated.

I interrupted him. "It was me."

George W lowered his eyes to my gaping coat. "Oh, got knocked up with somebody's baby."

"Not just somebody. Johnny Beck," Mama said.

He chewed his cigar and stoked the fire. "I heard about what happened to him. You got yourself in a heap of trouble over that one."

I rubbed my eyes, pretending to be sleepy, and blinked away my emotions. "Is there anybody who hasn't heard about it?"

Marilou quickly changed the subject. "Where's Uncle Eyrie?"

"He's asleep in the back room. The nurse is tending to him."

"Nurse? Has he been ill?"

George W stopped stoking for a minute and raised up to look at her. "Oh, I guess nobody told you." His face grew long and sullen. "He came down with the flu last month and just never seemed to get over it. Now he's taken a turn for the worse. They don't expect him to live much longer."

"I'm so sorry to hear that," Marilou said. "We all love Uncle Eyrie."

"It happens," he shrugged, and then proceeded

to be more hospitable. "There's four bedrooms upstairs, but it's cold. We never heat the entire house. There are space heaters though and extra blankets in the dresser drawers. You're welcome to stay as long as you need to—or at least until Uncle Eyrie passes. That construction company can hardly wait to tear this place down."

"I know. We've tried our best to hold them off as long as possible," Mama said.

Daddy walked to the foyer. "I'll take these bags upstairs and get those space heaters going."

George W started down the hallway toward another bedroom.

"Well then, I'm going back to bed. You all just make yourselves at home. Be sure and put out the fire before you go upstairs for the night. I'll see you in the morning."

"All right, thanks," Marilou said.

He disappeared down the hallway. His shadow lingered like a ghost behind him and then disappeared as he closed the bedroom door.

Mom stood, lay Jackson down, and removed her coat. "Now there's a seedy character," she said under her breath.

"I know," Marilou said. "I had no idea Uncle Eyrie had a twin brother. Hope he's not just some bum who needs a place to stay." She helped Shelby remove her coat and carried them to the mudroom, along with the snow boots.

Daddy returned, rubbing his hands together. "The space heaters are working."

Kate heated some water in a kettle, while I found mugs for hot chocolate. Marilou emptied the cooler, handing perishables to my mom, who arranged them in the refrigerator. We lingered near the fireplace, sipping our hot cocoa and chatting. Then Kate and I washed the mugs and put them away.

"Come on, let's get you kids to bed," Mom said. She carried Jackson up the stairs. The rest of us followed, while Daddy put out the fire.

The next morning came icy and clear. My parents decided to hide the cars in the barn. They rose early, just as everyone roused, to take care of that task. Grammy stood at the sink, supervising. Even though I knew how to make eggs, she obviously still felt the need to give her input, which made me nervous.

"Lower the heat under them grits. Use the iron skillet for the bacon. Keep the drippings for the eggs."

Kate flipped a pancake, missed the pan, and left a mess. Grammy handed her a washcloth and said, "Clean that up." She glanced over at Shelby and Jackson. "You two set the table." She handed them each a stack of dishes. "Just take two at a time. I don't want you dropping them."

Sugar licked pancake remnants off the floor as Marilou entered the kitchen and said, "Well, it looks like things are under control here. I'm going to look in on Uncle Eyrie."

"She got the easy part," I murmured to Kate.

George W entered the mudroom through the back door, carrying logs. He stomped his boots, knocking snow clumps free. After stacking the wood, he stretched his back and inhaled the inviting aromas. "Home cookin' just like Mama used to make," he said, grinning.

Grammy carried a pot of coffee to the table, and smiled. "Why don't you have a seat?"

The heavy iron skillet required both hands as I tilted it, while Grammy scrapped the eggs out onto a large platter. Through the back door window, I could see my parents trudging the deep snow from the barn as I carried the platter to the table.

George W pulled out a red bandanna to wipe his forehead and took a seat. Grammy scooped eggs, placed four bacon strips atop, and set pancakes and a bowl of grits next to them.

"Coffee?" She asked.

"Yes, ma'am." He chewed a strip of bacon. "Thank you." He picked up the mug and took a sip. "Hmm, that's good."

"You're welcome. Everybody come on in here and get some breakfast," Grammy said, and led us in a prayer of thanksgiving.

The back door opened and closed with a vacuumed *shush*. The cold draft chilled me. After removing their coats and boots, my parent's entered the room and found a seat.

My mother rubbed her arms. "Good morning everybody. This looks good."

George W glanced around with a crooked grin. "This table hasn't been filled with this many people in years."

Marilou stirred her coffee and asked, "So George W, how is it I've never heard about you all these years? I mean, where have you been all this time?

"I've been around. Just kept to myself, is all. Minded my own business mostly."

"But I didn't even know Uncle Eyrie had a twin brother."

"Twins do run in the family," he said, and sipped his coffee, darted a glance my way, and winked.

I stopped chewing, looked down at my round belly, and shook my head. *No way*.

"Last night you said you were the black sheep in the family. Why is that?" asked Marilou.

"I always went my own way. Daddy wanted us boys to stay on and take care of the farm, but times were changing. I wanted to see more of the world. So, one day when I was about twelve or thirteen, I just took off. I rode the trains everywhere and anywhere they would take me."

"But how did you take care of yourself?" Shelby asked.

"I took up with the hobos, and thanks to a few kind strangers, I was able to get along. Times were different back then, not like today. Occasionally, I would find my way back home. It was always fun for a little while, and everyone seemed glad to see me. But then Daddy would start up again, and I'd just leave."

Kate reached for another piece of bacon. "Where are you living now?"

"Once he died, and everyone moved away, I was able to move back. I built a cabin not too far from here."

My daddy set down his coffee. "Well, thanks for letting us stay. Sorry we got here so late last night."

"Ah, don't worry about it." He looked at Jackson and Shelby. "You kids want to go on a sleigh ride today?"

Jackson perked up. "Yeah, Daddy, can we?"

Shelby wore a longing look, which always held my father captive, and made me feel jealous for the same attention he used to give me. "Please, Daddy?" she pleaded.

George W offered a more persuasive argument. "We have sleds in the barn."

Daddy looked down at his plate and took his time to answer. "We have to be careful. Nobody knows we're here, and I think we should keep it that way."

"Don't worry," he said. "If there's one thing I'm good at, it's keeping out of sight. I don't like people knowing my business either."

The others cleaned up while I rested upstairs. I snuggled in a big, comfy quilt and an oversized recliner. The picture window offered me a majestic overlook of a snow-covered pasture. I watched Shelby and Jackson on sleds, zigzagging in the snow, leaving deep grooves. I wished I were a young girl again, enjoying my father's undivided attention, not a care in the world.

Marilou entered the room, cell phone to ear. "I can't seem to get good reception around here."

"Who are you calling?"

"Just doing a little investigation work of my own," she said, while pulling out a business card. The tone of each number pierced the air.

I was curious and listened to her responses.

"Tyrone, this is Marilou Walker." She paused, and then continued. "I need you to look at that new deed to confirm the name on the signature line again."

She positioned herself on the recliner arm, and I waited for the answer, her fingers tapping her leg.

"Are you sure?" she asked. "Can you send me a picture of both signatures to my cell phone? Thanks. Bye, now." When the picture came through, she held the phone out for me to see. "I think we just found our ghost."

-34-

Uncle Eyrie Goes

Kate called from downstairs. “Mom? Nicole? The nurse needs something.” We descended the stairs and headed to Uncle Eyrie’s bedroom.

The nurse stood at the door. “I’ve called Dr. Boswell to come out here as soon as possible.”

I stepped up behind Marilou and asked, “What’s wrong?”

“He’s starting to go,” she said.

Kate and I met Dr. Boswell at the door and led him to the bedroom. We waited in the living room.

My mother wiped her cheeks as she entered the room where we awaited our turn.

I sat up in my seat. “Can we see him now?”

“It’s fine. Go on in,” she said.

As we entered the room, Uncle Eyrie looked frail. Dr. Boswell stood on the other side of the bed, monitoring his vitals.

Uncle Eyrie spoke weakly. “Hi, you two.”

“Hi,” Kate said, taking his hand.

He blinked several times, trying to focus and lightly squeezed Kate’s hand.

I stepped in as close as I could. “Uncle Eyrie? It’s

me, Nicole."

He released Kate's hand and reached over to lay his palm flat on my tummy.

I placed my hand over his, pressing gently.

He struggled to take a shallow breath. "Thanks for bringing new life into this house."

It was the first time anyone had thanked me for having a baby. I felt special, like I had actually done something right for a change. "You're welcome Uncle Eyrie," I tried to hold back my tears, but one escaped down my cheek.

Kate wiped her eyes as Uncle Eyrie took her hand again. "Keep up with the history."

"Okay," she said, tight lipped.

A few minutes later, George W entered the room, carrying his hat. Following him, the Pastor Clark, a long-time friend, arrived.

"Eyrie," he said, taking his hand. "We've had long talks about how knowing Jesus is really about the relationship you have with Him, not the religion you choose to follow. It's about the love Christ had for us first and if we choose to accept His love or reject it." The old man gave him a weak thumb up sign. Pastor Clark nodded. "I was there the day you asked Christ into your heart, and I've seen first-hand the difference He's made in your life. I know you know Jesus, and you're going to see him soon." He paused, swallowed hard. "Say hello for me?" Eyrie smiled. "You'll be missed. See you on the other side, my friend." The pastor prayed, said his final goodbye, and left.

Dr. Boswell held Uncle Eyrie's hand and said, "Goodbye, old friend. God bless you." Uncle Eyrie could hardly speak. He just closed and opened his eyes to acknowledge the doctor.

Kate and I followed the doctor to the living room, leaving the twin brothers alone.

Less than an hour later, George W joined us. "Well, he's gone."

My father placed a hand on his shoulder and said, "I'm sorry."

George W sat in his brother's recliner and stared into the flames of the freshly stoked fireplace, while the nurse cleared out medical equipment.

"We'll send the coroner out later to take his body," she said.

My father helped her carry everything out to the car.

Marilou and Mother had barely enough time to prepare things for the funeral. They found some clothes for everyone at a consignment shop in town. Some of the women at Uncle Eyrie's church heard about my pregnancy and gathered some baby things. They delivered the donated items the day before the funeral.

George W stayed behind at the farmstead. He said he would remember Uncle Eyrie in his own way. I saw him out the window as we drove away. He stood near the dock, skimming stones across the icy cold river. I imagined the loss of his twin brother was difficult.

There was standing room only at the church. Marilou stood, looking around the crowd.

"It looks like every person in town showed up."

"At least everyone looks presentable," Mother said. "It's obvious Uncle Eyrie was a well-loved man."

I felt tired, but determined to be at the funeral. I wanted to honor the memory of this beloved man, who left a lasting impression on so many, myself included.

The presiding pastor read a Scripture. "For I am persuaded that neither death, nor life, nor angels, nor principalities, nor powers, nor things present, nor things to come, nor height, nor depth, nor any other creature, shall be able to separate us from the love of God, which is in Christ Jesus our Lord."

As I listened, I remembered Grammy saying a similar thing. *Nothing can separate us from the love of God*. To be honest, I still had concerns about where I stood with Him.

After the graveside ceremony, several church members busied themselves, organizing a potluck dinner in the fellowship hall. I looked around the room, but didn't recognize anyone, not even the folks sitting at the same table.

I turned to Marilou, and asked, "Who are those people?"

"They are aunts, uncles, and cousins of the Proctor clan. There's just a few left now."

"But you'd think out of eleven brothers and sisters there'd be a lot more."

"They all moved away and didn't bother to keep in touch," Marilou said. "My mother was the only one interested in hosting a family reunion every now and then, but only a few attended."

As the guests started to leave, I squirmed in my chair.

"What's wrong," Mother asked.

"I just can't seem to get comfortable, and my feet are starting to swell again."

"You need to lie down and rest. I'll get the keys to the car and run you home. I can come back for the others later."

Marilou interrupted, "Oh, I'll take her home, Luella. You stay here."

"Are you sure you don't mind? Don't you need to stay until the guests are gone?"

"No, I don't know hardly anyone here, and I've already spoken to the few I do know. Besides, everyone's starting to leave now, and I need to check my messages at the office."

"All right then. I've got to look for Shelby and Jackson anyway. We should be along shortly. Thanks."

Kate stood. "I'll go warm up the car." She grabbed her purse and whisked past me.

"We'll meet you out front," Marilou called out to

her. On the way to the car, she confessed, "I really didn't want to be stuck watching Shelby and Jackson while your mother drove you home. Don't get me wrong, they're good kids. I'm just past that stage of child rearing and don't really have the patience for it anymore."

Upon our arrival, she braked to a stop, I saw a black Suburban parked near the trees.

"Who's here?" Kate asked.

Marilou made a quick call, and then followed us to the front porch. "I just called the police. You two go on inside."

Sugar barked when I opened the door. Kate unlatched her crate, allowing her to roam freely. Her leg was better, and the splint removed. I unbuttoned my coat and climbed the stairs just as Kate called out.

"Where are you going with that rifle?"

I turned around to see Marilou walking out the front door.

"Just stay here," she said.

Kate headed for the back door, and my curiosity got the best of me. I grabbed my coat and trudged through the snow toward the dock, where I spotted Marilou standing at the top step. To avoid her seeing me, I stooped, hiding behind some trees lining the embankment. I peeked through the dead brush and recognized the two men below. Their voices resonated, and I could hear every word. Kate crawled over to me.

On the dock, Judge Beck stopped at the bottom step, while George W turned to face him.

"Can't you wait for us to bury our dead before tearing down everything we've ever known and loved?"

Judge Beck smirked. "Well, well, George W. Fancy meeting you here. Sorry about Eyrie."

"No, you're not!" he growled.

Beck stepped onto the dock. "Why I'm surprised. You sold this property to me without raising any objections whatsoever."

George W didn't take his eyes off of his enemy. "How could I, when I wasn't even here?"

"Well, I guess that sort of thing is to be expected. Who's going to know anyway, if you're a ghost?"

Pointing his finger at Judge Beck, George W said, "You forged my signature on that contract. I'm going to sue you. I'll make sure you never set foot on this land again."

"I didn't sign anything," Beck said.

"Well, then you put somebody up to it."

"You can't prove anything." Beck pulled out a handgun. "Like I said, who's going to know? After all, you're just a ghost, remember?"

Kate gasped, "He's got a gun."

I shushed her.

A stern voice shouted from the top of the steps. "Hold it right there, Beck!" My eyes darted to the top step, where Marilou held the rifle pointed at him.

Judge Beck turned toward her voice. George W leapt to tackle him. The two men struggled, hitting each other in the face and gut, arms flailing, legs kicking. The gun slid to the side, out of reach. Beck punched his opponent in the jaw, knocking him into a boat. Marilou reached the dock, heading for the gun, but Judge Beck beat her to it.

Kate grabbed my hand. "Let's go!"

"Where?" I whispered as she helped pull me to my feet. I held my sides and stayed low to remain hidden. We continued down the path, stopping at every bush to keep watch and hear everything happening below us.

Judge Beck held the gun with both hands, pointing it at Marilou as she backed up the steps again. "Little lady, I suggest you put that rifle down and walk away. This isn't between us." Puffs of smoke billowed from his mouth as he panted.

"It most certainly is between us!" Marilou yelled back. This is my family's farmstead, and I'm not about to let you steal it out from under us."

"Now, wait a minute. I bought this land legally. All the board members signed it over to me."

George W rose to his feet, still inside the boat. "Don't believe him! He's a liar!"

Marilou held the rifle steady. "We hired a private investigation team. They found the original deed and compared the signature to the new deed. They were completely different, which means you forged the most recent one."

"How do you know that was me who forged those papers?"

"So you're admitting it?" she asked.

Judge Beck shook his head. "No, there was a witness to those signatures. Now, just put the gun down. I don't want to hurt you."

George W managed to climb onto the dock. He picked up an oar and positioned himself for a hit. Judge Beck turned quickly and fired, sending his opponent toppling backward into the boat.

Kate and I ran toward the steps. I slowed when the baby kicked, reminding me not to overdo it.

Marilou screamed, "George!" She lowered the rifle and hurried down the steps.

Judge Beck whirled around and pointed the gun at her again.

Holding up the rifle, her eyes met with his.

Another shot rang out.

-35-

Mad Man

Kate and I arrived at the steps to find Judge Beck waver, stumbling face down on the dock.

"George, are you all right?" Marilou asked, climbing into the boat.

"Yep, just grazed is all," he said as he tried to sit up. "Ahhh!" He winced, falling back.

"Mom!" Kate screamed, heading toward the boat. She stopped once she reached Judge Beck's body and walked carefully around him. I walked around Judge Beck with caution as well, eyeing him for any movement. Holding out my arms, I offered George W support as he stepped onto the dock.

"Oh, no!" Marilou said. "I shot Judge Beck!" She screamed, pushing back her hair. "I shot Judge Beck!" she screamed again, while stepping around his body, which still lay face down. "What have I done?"

George W held his shoulder and shouted back, "Calm down, woman! You didn't kill him!"

"What do you mean? You saw what happened. I pulled the trigger and shot the man point blank."

Kate said, "But it was self-defense, Mom. Nicole and I saw the whole thing."

"You didn't kill him," George W growled, applying pressure to his bloodied shoulder. "That rifle only has buckshot in it. All you did was knock the breath out of him and maybe gave him a bad rash." Seeing the handgun, George W limped over to retrieve it. He checked the clip, no shots left. "He's still alive," he said, hobbling up the steps, his left leg now sprained from the fall. "Crazy old fool," he said under his breath.

Kate called emergency services on her cell, while Marilou studied Judge Beck. She tapped her foot against his leg, arm, looking for any movement or sign of life.

I removed my glove and said, "Maybe we should check for a pulse." I bent down. Suddenly, he gasped for air and raised his head. "Oh!" I screamed and jumped back, holding my belly.

"Judge Beck, are you all right?" Marilou asked. "I'm so sorry."

He managed to stand, blood red in the face.

"Come on!" Kate screamed, motioning for us to follow.

We ran to the house. I grasped the sides of my belly for support, but cramps gripped at my lower abdomen, and pain surged throughout my body. We ran past George W on the path. I looked back and saw Judge Beck push him away. The look on his face made me shudder. A sharp cramp struck me hard. "Ahh! Kate, help."

Kate ran back and pulled me along the path. I walked as fast as I could to the front porch, but Judge Beck was closing in on us.

To my surprise, the demolition crew was ready and waiting at the house. I entered the living room and knelt on the sofa to look out the window. Judge Beck ran to the demolition ball crane, reached inside, and turned the key. As the engine revved, the driver, startled to see the judge in such a rage, dropped a half-eaten sandwich.

Marilou stepped out onto the porch screaming and waving her hands, "Stop! No!

Kate stood beside her and yelled. "Stop! Someone's inside!" The equipment was so loud it blocked out their voices.

The construction manager held up a megaphone. "Ladies, you're going to have to move. This building is coming down." The crane moved into position.

Marilou remained on the porch, still screaming. A big burly man stepped onto the porch and hoisted her up over his shoulder. The rest of the crew laughed as she beat her fists on his back, kicking and screaming. "Let me down!" He carried her to a safe spot near a tree and forced her to stay there.

Judge Beck looked like he was going to blow a gasket as his face reddened and he gritted his teeth. He pushed the construction manager aside and pulled the driver out of the cab to climb aboard.

I stepped out onto the porch, Kate following close

behind. Like a deer in the headlights, I stood there, riveted at the sight of a huge wreaking ball. The drama happening in the cab snapped me back to reality. Judge Beck hit the button, drawing back the ball.

The construction manager pulled at Beck's arm, and yelling, "Stop! Are you crazy? There are people in there!"

Beck knocked him out, leered at me, and shifted into gear.

Kate ran off the porch, and yelled, "Come on!"

Just as Beck readied to release the ball, he was pulled from the cab. A booted foot to the neck pinned him to the ground.

"Who's the crazy old fool now?" George W yelled.

Kate grabbed my arm and yanked me back inside the house. We ran through the living room into the kitchen.

Marilou opened the back door and yelled. "Get to the basement!"

Kate pulled the trap door open and disappeared down into the dark hole. I followed her cautiously; the pain and cramps now subsided. Marilou found a flashlight, clicked it on, and led the way.

Running my hand down the rough basement wall, I found the lever and wrapped my fingers around the cold metal. When I pulled it, a cracking sound opened the hidden tunnel.

Once we all got through, Marilou said, "I'm closing the door so he can't follow us." Everything went pitch black. The flashlight beam provided limited visibility.

I patted the cold dirt wall from one support post to the next as tree roots and embedded rocks scratched my fingers. A musty odor filled the air, making me cough.

Suddenly, the walls vibrated, and dirt dusted our hair, shoulders, and clothes. A rumbling above moved ahead. I leaned against a post until the shaking stopped, but then a cave-in opened a huge hole a few feet ahead. Sunlight streamed in, and I squinted to focus. Marilou dropped the flashlight, knocking the batteries free. A diesel motor idled, loudly. I stared at the opening as the figure of a large man caught himself against the tunnel wall, his stocky and deliberate stance fully recognizable.

"It's Judge Beck! Run! Back to the basement!" I yelled to the others. We scrambled back into the darkness, Judge Beck in close pursuit.

I looked back to see him stumble over a tree root and twist his ankle, which slowed his pace considerably. I grasped Kate's jacket, panting heavily, while trying to keep up the frantic pace. The sound of stomping boots, getting closer, gave me heart palpitations.

"Hurry!" I cried out.

"We're here!" Marilou said. "Help me find the lever."

We knelt at the stone wall, feeling our way along.

My finger brushed the bristled fur of an unknown creature. “Ahhh!”

“What is it?” Marilou yelled out.

“I don’t know. Something creepy.”

“Are you all right?” Kate asked.

“Yeah,” I said, shaking it off. “Keep looking.”

We continued our search, but then the atmosphere changed. We stopped patting and stilled, while taking shallower breaths to listen. The heavy booted stomps behind us had stopped. Another moment of haunting quiet, then a cracking sound, and the stone wall opened slightly. A sliver of light slipped through, and I breathed.

“Who found the lever?” Marilou asked.

“Not me,” I said.

“I didn’t either,” Kate said.

The secret passage opened completely, and a flashlight brightened the doorway. A shadowy figure stood before us, and a gruff voice called out.

“Well, get in here. What are you standing around for?”

Relieved it was George W, we moved toward the lighted entrance. Marilou stepped through, then Kate, but when I stepped forward, a hand grabbed my neck and pulled me back into the darkness.

I screamed. A hand across my mouth cut off my voice. The dirty, salty smell made me want to gag. A sharp kick from deep within pushed against the wall of my abdomen as if to defend me. I held my belly tight and tried to take a deep breath, to calm the babe inside me, helping it feel safe.

George W ran through the entrance into the tunnel and held up the flashlight.

I struggled and whimpered with Judge Beck's arm cuffed around my neck. His other hand held a gun to my temple.

"Stay back or I'll shoot her!" he yelled.

Marilou and Kate looked through the passage door.

"No, don't hurt her!" Kate screamed.

"Judge Beck, please think about what you're doing," said Marilou.

"I have thought about it!" he yelled back. "Over and over again, in every waking moment, day and night. I can't even sleep without dreaming about it. It's like a never ending nightmare."

I sobbed, "Please don't hurt my baby. It's all I have left of Johnny."

Judge Beck tightened his grip. "He's dead because of you. This baby will only remind me of what I'll never have again. I'm not about to let your tainted blood ruin my pure bred lineage."

George W stepped back a little and softened his voice a bit. "I guess you have a right to be angry, but taking another life won't ease the pain none. You've got to let this go now, James. Let Nicole go."

"No!" Judge Beck seethed. "Not till she pays for what's she's done."

"Let me pay for it." My father stepped through the passage door into the light. He pushed his hands up in surrender.

Judge Beck pulled me back, leaning against the dirt wall. His eyes shifted between the two men.

"Please don't kill my little girl," Daddy pleaded. "I can't imagine the pain you must be going through, but please don't put another family through the same thing. It's not going to help anyone."

"You stay out of this!" Judge Beck yelled.

Mother poked her head through the passage doorway. "Don't hurt my baby!" she screamed.

Marilou pulled her back inside the basement. "Shhh!"

"He's got my baby!" Mother cried. Through misty eyes, I could see Marilou trying to console her.

George W tried to reason further. "You're only going to cause a lot more pain for a lot more people."

"He's right," my father said. "This isn't going to help anyone."

"Shut up!" Judge Beck yelled. "Both of you just shut up!"

"What are you going to do? Kill all of us?" George W asked.

Judge Beck adjusted his hold again. "No—just her." I grasped his arm tight and shook with fear beyond my control as tears streamed down my face.

"Don't hurt her!" my father said, looking directly into Judge Beck's eyes. "Take me instead."

"How 'bout I take both of you," he said. "Now all the rest of you get out!" He pointed the gun at George W and moved closer, forcing him to step back through the passage door. "Toss the flashlight over and close the door!"

"No, I won't let you do this!" he protested.

Beck pointed the gun at my head again. "Close the door now!"

George W hesitated, and then glanced at my father, who nodded at him to comply. He tossed over the flashlight and pulled the lever.

The door began to close, and I gasped for breath again. I watched my mother's face disappear. She reached out. "My baby," she said as the door shut. I reached for her with whimpering sobs.

Beck pointed the gun at my father. "Now pick up the flashlight and start walking." When we passed the cave-in, he loosened his grip and dragged me behind him as we crept like spiders along the tunnel walls. The cramps started again, and I fell down to my knees.

"Ahh!"

"Come on," he said and pulled my arm to force me to my feet. I gasped for air, cried, and held my belly tight.

"I see a ladder just ahead," my father said.

"When we get there, hand me the flashlight. I'll hold it while you climb up," Beck instructed.

My father reached the ladder and held out the flashlight. Judge Beck switched the gun to his other hand, pointing it at my head. He grabbed the flashlight with his free hand. I rubbed my wrist, relieved to be free from his gripping hold. The contractions stopped.

Beck waved the gun, and said, "Go on up." My father just stared at him. "Go on!" Beck demanded.

My father started to turn, but hesitated. "You're not going to hurt her, are you?" he asked.

"He was my only son," Judge Beck said, as the gun trembled in his hand.

My father stepped forward, "I can understand. Let me help you through this." He swallowed hard and looked at me.

"I love you, Daddy," I cried, fearing I might not ever see him again.

"I love you too, sweetheart," he said, holding out one hand toward me. I reached for it.

Beck screamed, "Shut up!" He forced my father back and pointed the gun at his face. "Go, right now!" he ordered through clenched teeth.

My father turned away and started up the ladder, but then he stopped and jumped down. "No! I can't let you do this! Let her go and take me instead!"

Beck pointed the gun directly at him. "You must have a death wish."

"Freeze!" a voice yelled out from the darkness.

Judge Beck's hand trembled as he held the gun, unsteady. He slowly lowered his arm.

"Drop the gun or I'll shoot."

Judge Beck blinked and opened his hand, allowing the gun to fall.

Another cop retrieved it and yelled. "All clear."

I ran into my father's arms. He held me tight, and we both cried.

The hatch opened and several members of the SWAT team descended. They handcuffed Beck, read him his rights, and maneuvered him up the ladder.

Mother followed the paramedics as they slid me into the ambulance.

Marilou stuck her head in and said, "Sam's riding with George W. I'll meet you at the ER."

Pain hit me again. "Ow!" I grabbed my stomach. "It's too soon." I flinched again. "Ah!"

"Breathe." Mother pursed her lips with short puffing sounds.

"Ask and it will be given to you; seek and you will find; knock and the door will be opened to you." —Jesus Christ, Matthew 7:7 (NIV)

-36-

New Life

Barely conscious, an antiseptic smell turned my stomach. I blinked, swallowed, and licked my lips until the sick feeling subsided. Muffled voices floated about the room.

Mom's distinct voice—something about wanting coffee—reminded me of home.

Dad's deep tone resonated in my ears. "Sure, I'll be right back," he said.

My eyes opened just enough to see his back slip through the door. Another shadowy figure entered the room right after him, probably the nurse. She wrestled a plastic bag and inserted a needle into my IV. I shivered, and tiny bumps filled my arm. She pushed some buttons and left.

Sudden warmth brushed my skin, a blanket now covered my shoulders. "There now, just go on back to sleep." I recognized the gentle touch brushing aside my bangs. Sweet comfort engulfed my thoughts as memories began to surface...

Cameras clicked and flashed as I walked the runway...my best friend, Kate, in the dress I designed for her...at the library discovering the secrets of the star sampler...holding onto Johnny at the Moonlight Dance...kissing Johnny...loving Johnny.

The squeak of a door brought me out of my stupor, and my most recent memory came rushing back. My baby...Judge Beck grabbing me...cold metal to my temple...my father silhouetted against the darkness—gunshot!

"Daddy!" I screamed.

Hot liquid splashed onto the sheet, soaking my leg. "Ow!" It burned. I flinched, recognizing the smell of coffee.

"Nicole, wake up!" he said.

"Daddy!" I cried.

My mother placed a cold wet cloth on the burned area. The soothing coolness helped shock me awake.

I took a deep breath, rubbed my eyes, and blinked to focus on my father. "I thought Judge Beck killed you."

"No such luck. You're stuck with me, kiddo." Setting down the coffee, he moved to the other side, leaned over, and held me close. "That man's locked up safe and sound. He won't be hurting us anymore."

Grabbing his middle, I held tight, resting my head on his chest. He rubbed my arm and kissed my forehead. I snuggled closer to bask in my father's love, soaking it up like a withered crop drinks in the rain after a long drought. "You're stuck with me, too."

My leg throbbed where the coffee had splashed. I heard water running and soon a cool cloth offered instant relief. More memories flooded my thoughts, and panic set in as I continued to cling to my father.

I pushed back and held my tummy. "My baby!"

"The baby's fine," Mother said, rubbing my arm. "They gave you some medicine to stop the premature labor. The doctor said you'd probably have post traumatic syndrome for a while."

"What's that?"

"Bad dreams, mainly. But they should bother you less and less as time goes on," she assured me.

I lay back down. "Daddy?"

"Yes," he said, using a paper towel, wiping the coffee stain on his pants.

"When we were in the tunnel, and Judge Beck was going to kill me, why didn't he just go ahead and shoot me?"

"I think he was dealing with so much pain inside he didn't know what to do."

A pause lingered. "Thanks," I said, quietly.

"For what?"

"For loving me so much that you'd die for me."

"You're worth it, pumpkin," he said.

He hasn't called me that since I was a little girl. A precious memory came to mind: my father swinging me in his arms, a beautiful day, and a sunflower filled meadow. "I love you, Daddy," I said, my eyelids struggling to stay open.

He kissed my forehead. "I love you, too. Now get some rest," he said, pulling up the blanket. "You and the baby have been through enough today."

My eyes barely opened when Marilou entered the room.

"George W's being as cantankerous as ever," she said, turning to my father. "Old fart's never even had an EKG before. How's Nicole?"

"She's having nightmares," my father said. "Why don't you stay here and keep Luella company, while I check on the old fart?"

"Sounds fair to me," Marilou said. "See you later."

George W and I got our discharge orders and returned home to the farmstead.

The next day, Marilou arranged for the farmstead deed to revert to the historical society. The members voted to allow us, the Durham family, to live at the farmstead until we could rebuild our home.

On July the fourth, Shelby and Jackson said they were looking forward to seeing the fireworks display during a celebration at the farmstead. By late June, doctor's orders restricted me to limited movement and bed rest. I watched the fireworks from the upstairs picture window. The space now held cozy chairs and a small sofa. Mother and Grammy found an old quilting frame in the attic and moved it down to the new living space. They used it to sew a new quilt as I reclined and read a style magazine.

"Ow!" The magazine fell to the floor as I grabbed my side.

"What's wrong?" Mother asked.

"This pressure started last night, but I thought it was just gas."

Grammy perked up. "Baby's on its way."

"This could be a false alarm," Mother said. "It's a little early yet."

"But the doctor said he could be off as much as two weeks," I reminded her. "This might be it."

Mother put away her needle. "Dr. Boswell's here for the celebration. I'll have Kate ask him to check on you."

I nodded. "Okay."

A few minutes later, Dr. Boswell entered the room. "Let's move to the bedroom so I can take a look."

A couple of hours later, a baby's cry echoed throughout the house.

Grammy ran to the stair banister. "It's a boy!" she announced. "Nicole has a baby boy!"

I could hear George W's gruff voice all the way down the hallway offering congratulations. "How about that?" he said. "One man leaves this world and another one comes in to carry on. Congratulations!"

"Thanks," Father said. "Talk about an express

delivery." Both men laughed.

Suddenly, another pain hit me. "Ahh!"

Dr. Boswell said, "It looks like we have another one coming."

Minutes later, Grammy ran to the hall and cried, "It's a girl!"

"Ha! Ha! Don't look so surprised," George W called out. "I told you twins run in the family."

"Them babies is healthy as horses," Grammy said, entering the bedroom and plopping into a chair. "Whew, I'm exhausted. I didn't get my nap this afternoon."

Dr. Boswell said, "Biracial twins are rare, but they do happen. Your little girl looks healthy otherwise. She just has darker skin than the boy."

"Okay," I said, still panting and wondering how the rest of the family might react.

Dr. Boswell washed and toweled his hands dry. He stepped into the hallway, leaving the door ajar. "You can visit now if you'd like," I heard him say.

My father set Jackson down at the door. Mother grabbed the knob and pushed him back. "Not yet, honey. We have to clean them up first."

"All right, we'll come back in a few minutes." He waved at me. I gave him a wry grin as he shook the doctor's hand. "Thank you, Dr. Boswell, for staying. If you hadn't been here, I don't know what we'd have done."

"My pleasure. It was nice bringing new lives into

this world instead of having to see them go." He left.

Her back against the door, my mother took a deep breath. "Wow. This was the last thing I expected."

The look on her face worried me. "You and me both," I said.

"One black and one white?" She shook her head. "This is going to take some getting used to."

Marilou helped clean the babies. She laid the boy next to me.

Grammy carried the girl and placed her on my other side.

I looked over each one carefully, counting fingers and toes.

"Are they all there?" Mother said. "I did the same thing when you were born."

"I can't believe I did this. How did they both fit inside me?"

Marilou sat in a chair near the bed. "Looks like you got your home birth after all."

"All things work together for the good," Grammy said.

Mother added her own twist. "No matter how many surprises we get along the way."

I swaddled my baby boy. "I know what to name you."

"What?" Kate asked, sitting on the bed.

"Johnny Beck, Jr.," I said.

"Cool! We can call him JB," said Kate.

"But I think I would like to name him after Uncle Eyrie too. I think I'll make it his middle name. But then, there's Sam, Daddy's name and other family names, John and William..." I paused to think, and Grammy handed me an extra baby blanket. "I think his name should be John Samuel Eyrie Simon William Beck."

After hearing all the names, Grammy did a double take and glanced at Mother. "Think she got 'em all in there?"

Mother folded her arms. "Uh, hum."

I handed my baby boy to Kate and picked up my baby girl. "Let's see ... what should we name you? You look like a Jasmine to me. Jasmine, Elizabeth, Pearlie..." I glanced up at Kate and continued, "Kate, Winifred Beck. Ha-ha! Pearlie Kate sounds like pearly gate." I laughed.

"Thanks," Kate said. "I think."

Mother stood next to the dresser and picked up two documents. "Dr. Boswell left these birth certificates here for us to fill out." She paused. "Are you sure you want to use the last name of Beck?"

"Maybe you should consider giving them your maiden name instead," Marilou added. "That's what I did with Kate, so she wouldn't feel apart from the rest of the family."

I turned to my mother. "I'm a Beck, Mama, and so are my babies."

"All right, darlin'. Whatever you want," she said.

Everyone decided to take a break, leaving my

babies and me alone.

"JB, Jr. you look just like your daddy." I touched my baby girl's nose. "And you, my little princess. I'm sorry you'll never know your father. I miss him." I sniffed, wiped my face. "I love you both so much." I shifted and felt a slight poke in my side. Reaching back, I folded my fingers around a small object and pulled it out. "What? How did you get here?" I turned the nativity figurine. It was the baby Jesus. "Okay," I shook my head. "Grandma Winnie must be trying to tell me something." I spied a box labeled Christmas stuff in the corner and rolled my eyes. *Shelby was playing with it on the bed.*

The baby squirmed; I adjusted the blanket as a tiny hand folded around my finger. "Hi," I said, amazed at his strength. "You know I'd do anything for you, don't you?" JB cooed.

I studied the figurine again, remembering when I asked Jesus into my heart. How I believed so purely, simply trusting Him, like a child. *If only life could be that easy now.* The dresser mirror reflected a cross, a reminder of what He did for everyone—for me. "Sacrificial love," I whispered. I thought about my father asking Judge Beck to take his life instead of mine, and the Scripture Grammy always quoted. *Nothing can separate us from the love of God.* A realization came to me. *So this is how God feels about us, His children.* I felt a tickling sensation deep inside. "Whoa!" *Is this you, Lord?*

Overwhelmed, eyes closed, my lips formed a silent prayer. I held the figurine tight, lowered my head, and cried. God's peace enveloped me, wooing me like a long lost love. His presence so sweet, so real, I couldn't deny it. Right then and there, I surrendered my heart to Him all over again, just as I did when I was a child. I was sorry for doing things my way and not seeking Him first. I wasn't sure if He'd forgive me after all I'd done, but then I remembered Scriptures in Romans I'd memorized as a child. *While we were yet sinners, Christ died for us...everyone who calls on the name of the Lord shall be saved.*

"I'm calling Lord. Please forgive me." The burden of guilt lifted. I felt...new...like a butterfly shedding its cocoon and taking flight. My emotions settled. I opened my eyes to check my babies—still sleeping.

"Jesus," I whispered. "Stay." A sweet sensation filled the atmosphere all around me. I recalled Pastor Clark's last words to Uncle Eyrie. "Knowing Jesus is about the relationship you have with Him, not the religion you choose to follow." Pondering those words, I sensed a strong desire to learn more about God and His Son, Jesus. Praying more and reading my Bible came to mind as I drifted into a peaceful slumber.

-37-

Solving the Case

Someone once told me—in order to get to heaven, you have to go through a lot of hell first—and that was certainly true in this case. The summer went by in a flurry of court appearances. Beck was found guilty on seven counts of attempted murder: me, my two unborn babies, Kate and Marilou, George W and my father. As expected, he pleaded temporary insanity. Since he never actually killed anyone, I feared he might get off with a light sentence. However, Ronald Ripley worked with the Spy Guys; getting the forensics, the lawyers needed in order to prove forgery. Once Beck served time in the state penitentiary, he then had a hefty probation period, psychological therapy, and evaluations to follow.

Kate and I ordered lattes, found a table, and waited.

Ronald Ripley entered the local coffee shop, toting a laptop. "Hey," he said, logging into his computer. "I'm glad we could meet on such short notice."

"Hi, Ronald," I said.

Kate just nodded.

"I found several things Judge Beck signed the week of the demolition. Turns out, he uses the same pen for everything, which he possessed during his arrest. And although, the forged signature doesn't look like his, I determined it was the same pen and person who signed."

Kate sat forward. "How?"

"By using a combination of writing analysis and chemical compounds." He flipped the laptop screen toward us. "See how this signature doesn't look anything like the authenticated one on the left? But after applying my chemical compound ..." He touched the screen to change the images. "You can see how the strokes align. The writing analyst determined the penmanship was in fact the same person."

Kate crossed her arms. "I'm still not seeing how a few strokes from the same pen could prove he forged anything."

"Me neither." I confessed. "Anybody could have used the same pen."

Ronald tapped on the keyboard a minute. "The pen is a five-hundred and twenty-five dollar custom, handmade exclusive by Christopher Higdon, who caters to the rich and famous." He flipped the screen to show us. We leaned forward. "Judge Beck's pen is a limited edition, constructed of recycled box elder, carved by the ambrosia beetle through a process using dyed wood and hand-mixed resins. The ink used came from his own specially formulated private reserve, kept under lock and key, only accessible by him. We found the same ink and resin components in all his signatures, including the forged one."

"Way to go, Sherlock," I said, clapping.

Kate smiled. "I'm impressed."

Ronald set his laptop aside and looked at Kate. "Sorry about the dress." Sheepishly, he asked, "Friends?"

"Okay." Kate said. "But limit the calls."

He nodded. "Agreed."

"And texts." She sipped her latte.

I sat back, crossing my arms. "Would you two just kiss and make up already?"

Kate glared. "We are *not* dating."

I rolled my eyes. "Whatever."

George W never showed his face in court. Instead, he gave a deposition.

From the upstairs window, I watched as reporters swarmed the farmstead and found him near the dock. He jumped into the boat, using the oar to push away. His gruff voice so loud even I could hear him yelling.

"I don't do public hearings! I don't do public anything!"

I figured he rowed down river, found a secluded place, and fished the rest of the day.

Gathering the mail, I fingered the letters while strolling back to our newly rebuilt home. One envelope got my attention right away. The return address read Offices of W. W. Swartz, Attorney at Law. Tearing open the flap, I read as I walked into the house.

"Well, it looks like Mrs. Beck decided to settle the paternity suit," I said, entering the kitchen where my parents sat, drinking coffee.

"That's good news, right?" Dad asked.

Mom wiggled her fingers. "Let me see it, honey."

I sat close, handing her the letter.

She and Dad studied it. "Hmm, very generous," she mumbled.

Dad pointed. "She's setting up a trust fund for the twins and including college tuition for you?"

"Yeah," I said. "Guess she wants to make sure I get a good job so I can take care of her grandchildren."

"Obviously, grand*daddy* didn't have much say about all this," Dad surmised.

"I imagine incarceration knocked the judge right out of him," Mom said. "Mrs. Beck just wants to put all this behind her now."

"More like, get rid of us," I said. "Did you read the conditions?" I moved my finger down.

Mother read the fine print. "Oh."

"Hush money," Dad said.

"Yeah. This says I can't talk about the case to anyone. I can't tell anyone who the real father is except for medical, school, or other legal identification purposes only. I can't tell anyone or influence my children to tell anyone that we are in any way associated with the Beck family. How am I supposed to comply with that?"

Mother said, "You should talk things over with your lawyer and consider other options."

Dad checked his watch. "I better get to work, got a story to write." The *Charleston Gazette* offered him his old job back, but he still did freelance jobs on the side.

"Have a good day," Mom said, giving him a kiss.

He searched the counter for his mini recorder and tucked it into his pocket. "I just got an idea for my new book."

"Aren't the first chapters due next month?" Mom asked.

"Yep, and my advance should arrive any day now."

"Hallelujah," Mom said. "We've got bills to pay." Although the fire destroyed our house, the insurance did not cover all the rebuild, the additional room needed for the babies.

Dad hugged me. "Kiss the babies for me. Love you, pumpkin."

"Love you, too." Before he reached the door, I called, "Dad!" He turned. "Thanks," I said.

He nodded, gave me a thumb up, and winked.

-38-

A Wedding to Remember

At the bridal shop, Kate and I goofed around, trying on veils, while my mother and Marilou browsed the invitations. Not far away, I posed, viewing myself in a three-way mirror.

"How about this one?" Mother said.

Marilou scooted closer to see. "Oh, that's so elegant."

Mother moved her finger over the invitation. "We could simply put...You are cordially invited to celebrate a reenacted wedding honoring Simon and Jasmine Miller, our family patriarch and matriarch, by Sam and Luella Durham as they renew their vows. Put the date here, place and time here, dinner and dance immediately following."

I leaned over her shoulder. "Don't forget to include that it's on the same day as the Pioneer Days Festival."

Marilou agreed. "Oh, Luella, she's right. People might get confused if you don't include the specifics."

My mother waved a hand. "All right, just let me figure out how to word it."

Fall came with bright vivid leaves dancing on the ground. The second annual Pioneer Days Festival commenced at the farmstead. Orange pumpkins lined the walkway to the porch. I stepped through the front door, my four-month old boy snuggled comfortably on my hip. Little JB, Jr. poked his head out from a hooded jacket as his bright blue eyes surveyed. His lighter tone contrasted little Jasmine's darker complexion. She slept contentedly in the playpen, my mother watching, dutifully.

"Sit here," Mother said, taking the baby. "How's my little JB doing?"

He cooed and smiled at her.

"Oh, did you see that? He smiled at me."

"He's *been* smiling," I laughed. "Is this the first time you've noticed?"

Goofy-faced, she sat JB in her lap. "Hehehehe, you're so cute. Yes, you are!"

The baby giggled.

Anna May lifted the microphone, feedback shrilled. I covered my ears.

"Ladies and gentlemen, we have a true pioneer among us today. Please give a warm welcome to Miss Fanny Miller ... otherwise known fondly as Miss Fanny from Savanny."

A covered wagon carried the ninety-year old Miss Fanny, who waved and smiled. The hat she wore slipped, concealing her face. She pushed the rim back, smiled, and continued to wave. Further research showed Miss Fanny also had family ties as the great granddaughter of Pearlie Anne Miller.

A special memorial dedication, honoring Winifred Evelyn Proctor-Walker, followed. Flowers encircled a plaque and several other indigenous plants filled the landscape.

"Have you ever seen jasmine bloom this late?" Luella asked.

"I don't recall," said Marilou, taking a whiff. "But it smells wonderful."

Music and fanfare summoned everyone for a welcome speech, a poem, and a choral performance. The historical society members including George W gathered as Mayor Somner approached the podium.

"I am proud to make this announcement. The Proctor farmstead is now officially a national historical landmark. A complete renovation is scheduled to begin next year." The crowd cheered and applauded.

Marilou made one last announcement. "We hope to see everyone at the wedding this evening—right before sunset. Meet us out back at the gazebo."

Ivy and roses laced a white-latticed archway canopying the garden entrance. Sweet-scented white Jasmine greeted guests at the gazebo. Mike Coolsby made himself useful, acting the usher.

In the upstairs bedroom, Marilou handed Mother a string of pearls. "Grandma Winnie would want you to wear these."

"Oh, they're beautiful." She grabbed a tissue.

"Thank you," she said.

"Mom," I said, entering the room. "You look stunning."

Kate shadowed me, closing the door behind her. "Wow!"

"I feel like a bride all over again," Mother giggled. "This is so exciting. Isn't this dress flawless? I can't believe you found it in the attic, and it's still in such good condition."

Marilou studied the train. "Grammy did a great job restoring it. Didn't miss a stitch or a pearl. And it fits you perfectly."

"I know. Isn't that amazing?" Mother said.

A knock alerted everyone. "Five minutes," a voice called out.

"Be right there," Marilou said. "Girls, are you ready?"

"Yes," I said.

Kate pulled the door open. "Let's go."

A string quartet played colonial era wedding music as my father, Sam, and his best man, George W, tiered the gazebo steps. Marilou walked the aisle first, Kate and I followed. Shelby threw rose petals, while Jackson carried my parent's rings.

Upfront, Grammy, a freshly groomed, Sugar, and Miss Fanny sat together. My babies slept soundly in the stroller beside her. The preacher faced the audience, lifting both hands. The crowd stood as the music swelled. My mother appeared, walking gracefully toward the gazebo. My father could not take his eyes off her. Joining him, she took his hand.

The preacher began. "In 1774, a man and a woman entered into covenant before God. Though slaves, Simon and Jasmine Miller believed freedom promised a better way of life. Simon claimed his dream, and Jasmine followed. Their covenant served as a bridge for all generations. Before his death, Simon discovered he had a son, who would in fact follow his father's dream. Today, we witness the culmination of this freedom as their descendants, Samuel and Luella Durham, renew their vows to honor their ancestors and reseal the covenant. Thus, continuing the legacy."

Following the ceremony, the disc jockey arrived for the reception. I called out, "Let's get this party started y'all." The music cranked and a strong beat urged people onto the dance floor.

I laughed, seeing Jackson weave the line to the chicken wings. He almost snatched one, but Grammy pulled him onto the dance floor.

Mother, holding a microphone, grabbed Marilou. "Come on girl, let's sing it together. "We are family. I got all my sisters with me..."

Kate carried a present behind her back, while I led her to the table where Ronald Ripley sat.

"Hey Ronald, I have something for you," she said, handing him a wrapped box, a big bow on top.

"For me? What for?" he said, grinning.

"It's a thank-you gift for your help in proving the

forgery," Kate said.

"And for taking us to the Moonlight Dance," I added. "Even though it did turn out to be a disaster."

"Oh, it was nothing, really. But thanks." Ronald picked the bow off, tore open the paper, and lifted the top. "Wonder what it is?" he teased, moving the tissue aside. "Ah ha ha," he laughed, pulling out a Teddy bear wearing a lab coat and glasses. "Thanks. I think I'll call him Einstein."

I kissed Ronald on one cheek, while Kate kissed the other. Ronald smiled so wide, his glasses tilted, just as my father snapped a picture.

"Thanks Ronald," I said.

Kate echoed. "Yeah, thanks. We appreciate all your help."

A slower song started, and Mike Coolsby sauntered over. "May I have this dance?" He led her to the floor, and I watched as they swayed together like reeds in the wind.

Realizing my sudden aloneness and not wanting Ronald to get any ideas, I made a quick escape.

My father came up behind me, poked my sides. "Boo!" he teased.

"Dad," I giggled. "Mom and Grammy went to relieve the babysitters."

I took his arm, and we entered the gazebo. Sitting on a bench, I slipped off my shoes. The pink and purple hues of sunset spanned the horizon as the sun slipped under a distant ridge. "God's promises are true," I said. I snuggled my father's shoulder, wrapping my arm around his. A smile crossed my face when I heard Lionel Richie singing *Ballerina Girl*.

"Do you remember dancing with me to this song when I was little?"

He nodded, rose to his feet, held out his hand and bowed. "May I have this dance?"

I stood and joined him.

"Wait," I said, pushing his shoulders. I looked down at my bare feet, and stepped on top of his shoes. "Too heavy?"

"Light as a feather," he said. He teetered a short dance, and then spun me around.

"Whoa!" I almost fell, but caught myself. When he stopped, I threw my arms around his neck and said, "I love you, Daddy."

He wrapped my waist. "I love you too, pumpkin."

Someone screamed. "Nicole!"

Pulling back, I said, "Who's that?"

"I don't know, but we better go check it out."

"Nicole!"

I reached the table where a group of women surrounded the screamer. "I'm here," I said as the crowd parted. "Kate?" I asked. "What happened?"

"Look at my hair!" she said, crying, while holding an entangled gooey wad.

"How did ..."

"I don't know, he just did," she whined.

A ticking time bomb started in my head as I

caught my breath and yelled. "Jackson!"

"Calm down," Mother said. "I'll take care of this."

Grammy pulled Jackson by the ear. "I got him," she said. "Give me that chicken wing," She snatched it away. "Look here, what you did."

Jackson grimaced, barbecue sauce smearing his face and fingers. "I'm sorry."

Grammy dragged him to the house. "I'll make sure you're good and sorry."

Mother followed. "Young man, you've gone and done it now."

Daddy cleared the crowd. "It's all right everybody. Crisis averted. Let's go back to dancing."

The DJ started a country set and played *Stuck like Glue* by Sugarland.

Kate glared at the DJ. "Really?"

Mike Coolsby scooted his chair closer, singing along. "Wha-oh, wha-oh, stuck-a-like glue, you and me baby we're stuck-a-like glue."

"Mike!" Kate growled.

"What? I think it's kind of cute. Rather stylish, if you ask me."

She raised a brow. "I'm not asking."

"Stop fidgeting," I said. "I'm trying to keep it from spreading."

"Last time this happened I smelled like peanut butter for a week." Kate huffed. "Do you have any idea how much money I spent to get my hair looking halfway normal again?"

"Daddy?" I called.
"What, honey?"
"Write her a check."

-39-

Jasmine in Bloom

Early March, we visited the farmstead. Snow graced the grounds.

"Where's Simon buried?" I asked.

"Why don't you ask George W?" Mother said, "I bet he'll know."

Sure enough, he led us to the site. Our boots crunched the snow, leaving indented footprints.

"Why didn't we think of this earlier?" Marilou asked.

"Yeah," Kate said. "We should have done this way before now."

Mother replied, "Guess we were too busy with everything else."

George W stopped. "Here it is."

"Which one is Simon's?" I asked, puffing.

"One of the groundskeepers removed the gravestones. I guess so he could mow easier. But I remember. Simon's grave is over here."

We followed him to a large tree, its branches stripped bare. "There." He pointed a gloved finger. Snow-dusted rock borders outlined each plot. "Here's the baby who died. And this plot's Simon's mother,

Maggie, and here's his other son, Simon Jr., who she raised. Here's Simon Jr.'s wife, Pearlie. All their kids and families go on up the hill. They had a bunch of 'em too, but that's another story. Jasmine's parents, Tessa and James, are over here." He pointed to a more ornate iron fenced area, rusted and unkept. "The Proctor family plots are over yonder. At least *their* stones are still in place."

"This isn't right," I said. "We have to fix these grave sites."

We decided to replace the tombstones, landscape both areas, and include a pathway to the house. Near Simon's grave, we placed a memorial plaque honoring Jasmine. Mother contacted Anna May to add the gravesites as historical tour features.

Winter passed, and summer cracked open the ground. The newly renovated memorial gardens needed grooming. We waited until after dinner, taking advantage of the cooler evening breezes near the river's edge. Shelby and Jackson readied for bed, and Mother volunteered to watch the twins for me. I handed her the baby monitor.

"Got the babies in bed," I said, slipping my fingers into gloves. Grammy toted a basket, filled with garden tools, citronella burners, and bug spray. I followed her, carrying a flood lamp and an extra-long extension cord to provide light once night fell.

Violet illuminated the sky at dusk, the nearby

ridge silhouetted in sunset. Grammy pruned, while I pulled weeds. An earthworm squirmed as bare roots appeared. Owls, toads, crickets, and cicadas throbbed in rhythmic symphony. My skin glistened in the steamy, one hundred percent humidity. Taking in the sweetest aroma, I lifted my head, scanning for the source.

"Mm ... what *is* that smell?"

Looking up, Grammy smiled. "Jasmine's in bloom."

-40-

Confluence

Tu-Endie-Wei State Park in Point Pleasant, West Virginia offered one of the most beautiful overlooks I had ever seen. I studied a map. Reviewing Underground Railroad routes, I ran my finger along the Kanawha River, while Kate ran hers the opposite direction along the Ohio River, eventually bumping into mine. I chose a huge oak tree to shade the stroller. Kate helped spread the Noah's Ark blanket, and we sandwiched both babies between us. The smell of fresh cut grass set me at ease. At the tree base, a dandelion stood in graceful form. I plucked the stem and with one breath sent tiny spores parachuting in midair. Laying back, my senses lulled to the sound of leaves rustling in swaying branches and cooing doves. "If this old tree could talk," I said. "It was probably here when Jasmine and Simon were alive."

Kate brushed away a fly. "It's kind of like a portal to the past. Have you ever thought about what it might be like to actually talk with them?"

My mind recalled the story Grandma Winnie had shared. "I think it would be interesting to see

Constance and her twins."

"Yeah, but I'd bring them back to this time so they wouldn't have to be separated."

"And they could all stay together as a family." Feeling remorseful, I said, "I'd bring Johnny, and we'd live at the farmstead to raise our children."

JB got fussy. I rummaged through the baby bag and found a bottle. A few gulps later, he was satisfied. "I guess you could say this is where our two rivers meet."

"Through our family bloodlines," Kate said.

"Yes, but also through life and circumstances forcing us together."

"Like you and Mrs. Beck?"

I snickered. "And our mamas." We laughed. Little Jasmine grew restless. I decided a walk might help.

At the overlook, Kate slid a quarter into the slot and looked through the telescope. I stood next to her, taking in the panoramic view. A taller shadow covered the guardrail, catching my sight. I looked back, recognizing a familiar face. Tapping Kate's shoulder, she glanced at me. I pointed. Her eyes followed.

She turned and crossed her arms. "Well, howdy, stranger."

Mike Coolsby stood, hands in pocket. "Sorry, I haven't been around. I had to work."

"Well, you could've called." Kate scowled.

Despite the grimacing look, Mike attempted to appease her. "Your hair looks good."

"Hi, Mike." I interrupted, trying to deflate the tension. "Thank God that's over."

"Hi," he said.

I decided to leave them alone. "I'm just going to take the babies for a ride. Be back in a little while." I slung the baby bag over my shoulder and pushed the stroller along the scenic view path.

Kate and Mike walked in the other direction. Rounding the corner, I spied them. Sunlight shimmered on the water, silhouetting their profiles as they kissed.

I turned away, missing Johnny. The ring felt cold as I slid it back and forth on the gold necklace. *How can I live without him? I don't know if I can do this on my own.* I wiped my cheeks.

Tucking the Noah's Ark blanket around my babies, I thought about Grammy, her kind, unselfish ways, her words of wisdom. Even without Johnny in my life, I could still picture a future: birthday parties, pony rides, piñatas under the big oak tree, white Christmases, tons of presents, and family picnics down by the river. I thought about the place I now called home, a place where family and friends, black and white, gathered as kindred spirits, a place filled with love, hope, and dreams. A free world, where JB and Jasmine could play, read, write, and learn whatever they desired. Be whoever they dreamed to be. *Is this really possible even in my world today?*

Looking through the telescope, two boats moved

toward the bridge connecting West Virginia to Ohio, crisscrossing midway. I thought about how the decoded star sampler showed two rivers, symbolizing the bloodlines uniting, black and white. I thought about how Judge Beck blamed me for Johnny's death, and how he refused to accept anyone who was different. It all seemed so foolish.

But how could *I* stop racism or bring about change? What could *I* do? I looked at my twins. "My children," I said softly. "Maybe I already *have* done something."

A glimpse of red caught my attention. Searching around JB, I pulled out a handkerchief and tied it to the handle. The red bandanna fluttered in the wind as I pushed the stroller along the path.

The End

Epilogue

Doing personal genealogical research led me, the author, to discover a book titled "Washington's Woods, A history of Ravenswood and Jackson County, W. Va.," written by Dean W. Moore. I decided a visit was in order, so I took a road trip to Point Pleasant and Ravenswood to confirm my suspicions. My father always said we had a connection of some sort to George Washington, though he never knew how. Years later, I found my father's birth certificate, which revealed his full name, George Washington Proctor. I realized it wasn't unusual for folks to name their children after famous people and really didn't think much of it. However, our particular branch of the Proctor family tree, from the South Carolina area, have several generations of Georges listed.

On my way to Point Pleasant, I stopped for gas and asked God to give me confirmation to make sure this was indeed the direction I should be going. I didn't want to waste my time by going down rabbit holes. The book lay open in my lap while I prayed, and the wind picked up a bit, sending pages flying. When I finished praying and looked at the book, my eyes caught a glimpse of my maiden name on a survey commissioned by, of all people, George Washington himself. Looking along the Ohio River, the name Proctor came into view. It was a chill bump moment to say the least, and a definite answer to prayer. I proceeded onward to discover the last living relative in a branch of my family tree I never knew existed. Sue Proctor Miller was more than happy to learn more about her own family tree and shared my enthusiasm for genealogy. In subsequent visits, I viewed her old photos and an original map of the Virginia territory our ancestors helped to settle, listened to stories, and exchanged newspaper clippings. Sue has long since passed away, but I wish to thank her for inviting me into her home and sharing her family history with this distant cousin.

During my last visit to Point Pleasant, I stopped to view the confluence where the Ohio River meets the Kanawha River. The title and inspiration for this book came to me at that time. It took several years of research while raising three active boys, then a few more years to learn how to write a novel—a constant challenge and learning experience—and finally here it is in print form for your reading enjoyment. Living in Memphis the past twelve years has also taught me much about human frailties, politics and prejudices, all of which I've used to develop strong characters and a compelling story.

This is a work of fiction. To the best of my knowledge, the Proctor family was not involved with helping slaves during either the Revolutionary War or the Civil War. However, diary entries indicate empathy for the slaves and their plight, as well as a definite loyalty from the family servants who chose to stay after emancipation was offered to them. Other than that, who's to say they didn't help in some way or another?

Before the turn of the 18th century, it was customary for everyone to own slaves, including many Quakers who had compromised their religious and moral views. It took many years of traveling and preaching throughout the colonies by John Woolman and many others, laboring intensely to reestablish foundational truths and moral understandings in order to resolve the inhumane treatment of slaves among their Quaker brethren and communities. Progress was eventually made to raise freedmen's relief funds and establish scores of freedmen schools.

The Quakers did move into the Washington's Woods, aka Ravenswood area and influenced abolitionism but not until sometime later during the nineteenth century. All quotes are exact with only slight modifications made to excerpts taken from John Woolman's journal in order to maintain readability. All characters bearing famous historical or local names are fictionalized but kept within true historical content.

A copy of the original survey commissioned by George Washington is included for reader reference. Thank you for purchasing *Where Two Rivers Meet*. I pray you are blessed with knowledge you didn't know before reading this book, and I hope you are encouraged to research your own family history. After all, as Grandma Winnie put it, "History can be quite fascinating."

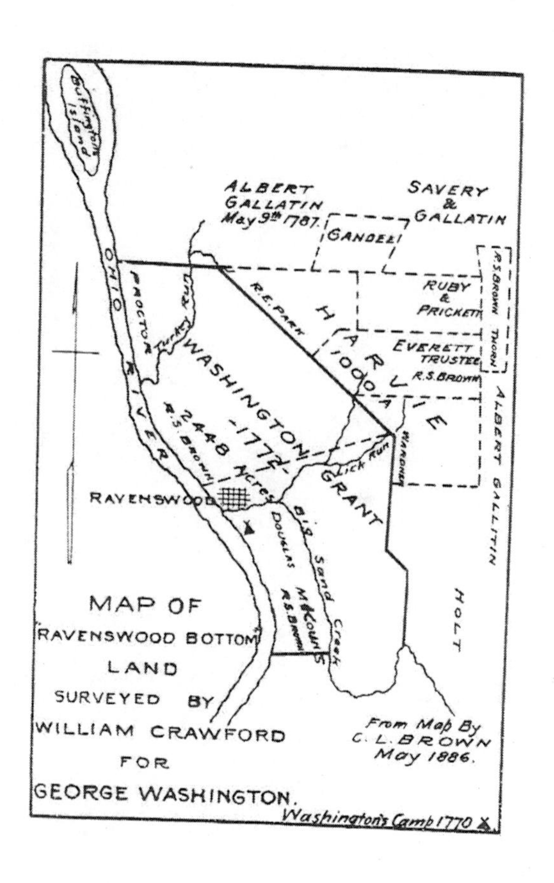
Buffington's Island
ALBERT GALLATIN May 9th 1787.
SAVERY & GALLATIN
GANDEE
R.S. BROWN
RUBY & PRICKETT
THORN
OHIO
PROCTOR
Turkey Run
R.E. PARK
HARVIE
10000 A
EVERETT TRUSTEE
R.S. BROWN
WASHINGTON
-1772-
2448 Acres
R.S. BROWN
RIVER
ALBERT GALLITIN
Lick Run
WARDNER
GRANT
RAVENSWOOD
Douglas
Big Sand Creek
McCown
R.S. Brown
HOLT
MAP OF "RAVENSWOOD BOTTOM" LAND SURVEYED BY WILLIAM CRAWFORD FOR GEORGE WASHINGTON.
From Map By C. L. BROWN May 1886.
Washington's Camp 1770